THE WAY UP

The Duchess of Duke Street
Book One

Mollie Hardwick

THE WAY UP

Published by Sapere Books.

24 Trafalgar Road, Ilkley, LS29 8HH

saperebooks.com

ISBN: 978-0-85495-347-9

CHAPTER ONE

She came out a pace or two from the narrow arched porch of the two-storeyed, brick-built terraced house and looked skywards, assessing the weather. The light of the early spring morning was diffused, bright. The cloud mass was solid, though high. She thought it seemed like a tent had been put up over London, to keep any rain off for the day. She smiled at the pleasing fancy and turned back to reach for the doorknob.

'Ta-ra!' she called into the recesses of the little house.

Without waiting to listen for any response she shut the door firmly behind her and sailed off down the short street, heels clicking, long skirt swishing about her ankles, chin held high, bright eyes alert to notice any little change in the familiar surroundings of the pretty Essex village just south of Epping Forest, protected by flat open land from the clawing reach of the metropolis.

It was across the broadest of these virgin stretches of grass and low scrub — Wanstead Flats — that the young woman walked after leaving the village behind. She was embarking upon a day's voyage of exploration, a sortie from behind those green defences which would take her info the heart of the bustling, noisy, grimy, smoky, snobby agglomeration of poverty and luxury, splendour and squalor that bore the name London.

Louisa Leyton was not, however, the sort of person to be deterred, or frightened, or even overawed by this combination of almost wholly alien elements. At twenty-one years of age, she had the moral confidence of having graduated to womanhood. She was healthy and vigorous, almost without experience of lassitude or boredom, and well seasoned in the business of looking after herself. Although she was presently living with her parents, she had been out and about in the world of domestic service since the age of twelve. She had discovered early that while hard work could not be less than hard, it could be made less onerous through efficiency and good organisation. If brass were there to be polished, she would polish it as though it were her own, delighting in the result. Fellow servants, watching her, had scoffed, and gone on taking short cuts and making do with the least they could get away with. Louisa had shrugged her shoulders and continued to give of her best, for her own satisfaction as much as for her employers' She was confident that she would not be doing such work for ever. So, meanwhile, what was worth doing was worth doing well; and if something was not worth doing, she was not afraid to say so. Even in the year 1900, there was enough of a servant shortage to enable so capable a one to risk being given the sack.

And she was beautiful. Louisa's beauty was not of the lush, exotic kind. Her eyes did not smoulder; they were bright blue and huge, and they twinkled. Her lips were not invitingly full; they were simply in perfect proportion to the oval, clear-complexioned face. Her dark-brown hair shone. Her figure was trim and slender, again exactly suited to her five feet five inches of height.

The description does not, perhaps, add up to an impression of a beauty. Indeed, Louisa Leyton was not a Beauty with a capital B. But she was beautiful; and as she walked on that morning into the busy Stratford High Street and made for the Swan Inn, many men glanced at her and then gazed, openly or furtively. She swept by imperviously, having long since become unselfconscious about her looks. Ambition, with the capital A, was the sole preoccupation of Louisa's mind.

The Swan was the starting point of the Bow and Stratford service of the London General Omnibus Company Limited. Every ten minutes, from 8 a.m. until 10.40 p.m., there departed one of the green-painted horse-omnibuses, which, for sixpence, would carry one as far as Regent Circus, the heart of the West End of London and (there were those in distant countries who nostalgically averred) of the very British Empire itself.

As she came in sight of the Swan, Louisa hurried her progress a little, for an omnibus stood ready to depart. The burly driver, walrus-moustached and top-hatted in the old fashion, already had his rug strapped about his knees and the four leather strands of the reins in his left hand, while with the right he was lifting the long whip from its socket. The conductor, a much younger man wearing a curly-brimmed bowler and a dusty suit and overcoat, occupied the iron platform at the rear, at the foot of the curving metal stairs. He was reaching for the bell-pull. While she was still some twenty yards away Louisa heard the sharp *ping-ping* as he jerked it twice.

'Hey!' she yelled, clutching up her skirt and breaking into a sprint. A little cheer went up from a group of loafers propping up the pub wall as she threw herself at the slowly moving vehicle, grasped the stair-rail, and heaved herself aboard, giving a fine display of ankle in the process. Louisa's ankles were well worth seeing, as the young conductor noted, leaning back against the rail and watching her all the way up the stairs.

It never so much as occurred to her that he was looking. It was the pink of sudden effort, not embarrassment, which coloured her cheeks as she emerged on to the open top of the swaying omnibus. Most women, especially unaccompanied ones, preferred to travel in the glassed-in downstairs compartment, leaving the outside to the men, with their uninhibited talk and their tobacco. Not so Louisa Leyton. She loved the top of a 'bus, that tallest of horse-drawn vehicles, with its bird's-eye viewpoint of all that was going on in the street below and beyond the windows of the offices and homes it passed.

It was mid-morning when she left Stratford and the top of the 'bus was completely empty. The choice amongst the banks of seats was hers. Steadying herself with both hands, she lurched forward along the ticket-littered gangway and took her favourite vantage point, just behind the driver, from where she could see forwards as well as to the side. The old man sensed her arrival and glanced round briefly. He grinned and winked. Louisa returned a friendly grimace and settled herself to enjoy the journey.

A ride into central London was no new experience for her, but if she had had to do it every day she would have been unlikely to have found it boring. People fascinated her: people of all kinds. And the route from Stratford to Regent Circus offered a more cosmopolitan cross-section of them than any other stretch of a few miles in the world could have done. It took her through the very heart of the East End, along Bow Road, the Mile End Road, the Commercial Road, Whitechapel, Aldgate. Their pavements teemed with folk. Idling groups of men leaned against public house walls, smoking and spitting. Respectable working-class housewives and artisans hurried past them about more purposeful pursuits, carrying baskets, bundles, tools, laden sacks, passing in and out of shops whose signboards bore not only such names as SMITH, NELSON, HOARE, MIDDLETON, but LEVINSKI, TAUB,

JAKOBSON, ALVAREZ, WYSZOGRODZKI and others as exotically complicated, which Louisa tried silently to pronounce, and found she couldn't.

And there were types of people to match such names wherever she looked in this district of the densest immigrant population. She tried to put a nationality to the appearance of a portly man with snow-white hair and intensely sad features who stood on the kerb awaiting the chance to cross the road. Was he German, Polish, Russian…? From what far-off homeland had he come to this teeming, overcrowded neighbourhood, where poverty, filth and crime — if not so rife as Louisa understood them to have been not many years earlier — were still rampant? Had he come here willingly, a shrewd man with some capital, tempted by reports of an easy living to be made by taking advantage of the vulnerable poor? Was he some sort of exile, parted from a wife and family — or even one of the anarchists who, rumour had it, had been sent to this part of London to prepare for the revolution, or whatever it was to be?

The omnibus rattled on and the man was lost to her sight and as soon forgotten. She saw black faces, sallow faces, fat red faces whose owners stumbled and swayed as they progressed; skeletal faces of women with thin, lank hair, who sat motionless on boxes and bundles against garbage-stained walls, so deeply asleep that they might have been dead. And she noticed gaudily dressed and painted young women — children almost, some of them seemed — parading arm in arm, chaffing groups of passing men who were clearly foreign sailors from the docks. Louisa knew that between the stall-lined Commercial Road, along which the omnibus was carrying her, and the Thames on their left, lay the notorious Ratcliff Highway, rechristened St George's Street and to some extent cleaned up, but still known to sailormen all over the world for its low public houses, its places of unspeakable entertainment, its opium dens, its polyglot and, to a considerable extent, criminal population.

And just over on the right sprawled the dangerous, narrow warren of Whitechapel where, in her own lifetime, Jack the Ripper had wrought the butchery of which she had read with such fascinated horror in her father's newspaper when no one had been present to snatch it from her.

The 'bus stopped frequently and fellow passengers came and went. Louisa was scarcely aware of them, absorbed by the pageant below her. Now the shellfish stalls, and the cheap bright-cloth merchants, and the darting children, and the street musicians, and the scavenging dogs, had been left behind and they were entering a more orderly, more sombre and, to her, less interesting district of narrower streets, tall buildings which seemed to lower down upon the neatly dressed men who scurried about the pavements carrying little brown suitcases and wearing preoccupied expressions. This was the City, where she knew life was earnest and grim too, although in a different way from the East End; and criminal, also, in some of its doings, though not in the Jack-the-Ripper sense.

Leadenhall Street, and Cornhill, then out into the congestion of the junction where stood the imposing Royal Exchange, the Mansion House and the Bank of England, and where the Duke of Wellington sat high on his stone horse which did not have to contend with the other horses of all sizes and conditions, drawing vehicles of every conceivable kind, as they converged from six major thoroughfares and sought to cross on the way each wished to go.

'Get back to the bloody bogs!' Louisa heard her driver bellow at a startled-looking little man driving a hooded country cart with the name MURPHY painted on its canvas. The advice was supplemented by cruder suggestions from other drivers, obviously more accustomed to London than this interloper. His horse had stopped with fright in the very middle of this broad junction and was impeding the progress of several dozen vehicles, some of which had become locked against one another in trying to squeeze round. Louisa watched with amusement as a huge bearded City policeman strode fearlessly into the mêlée, calmly took the petrified animal's head and proceeded to lead the country wagon across into Poultry, ignoring with dignity the ironic cheers of the other drivers, supported in some instances by their outside passengers.

They were able to move on again, past the begrimed majesty of St Paul's, down the steep slope of Ludgate Hill, with the driver's feet bearing hard on the brake. There was a further hold-up at Ludgate Circus, where a motor omnibus had broken down, to the derision of the crews of passing horse trams; but Louisa's veteran driver espied a brief opening, jerked his reins, and took them clattering through, with barely an inch to spare between imprisoned vehicles on either side.

'Well done, driver!' a well-dressed gentleman called out from a seat across the gangway from Louisa. Without turning, the old man raised his whip in acknowledgment. Louisa smiled agreement across at the gentleman, startling him into raising his top hat. Without looking at him again she was aware of his gaze upon her as they passed between the crowded pavements and the newspaper offices of Fleet Street, but by the time they had traversed the Strand and stopped at Charing Cross, and she chanced to look his way again, he had gone.

The journey was almost at an end. They negotiated Trafalgar Square, Waterloo Place, with its striking memorial to the

Guards' dead in the Crimea, and up the short stretch of Lower Regent Street to their destination, Regent Circus, already becoming more widely referred to as Piccadilly Circus.

Clutching her skirts, Louisa went carefully down the steps, to the further gratification of the young conductor, who had stationed himself in readiness at his oft-proven best vantage point. She saw his eyes on her legs and stuck out her tongue. 'Mucky ha'porth!' she told him.

He grinned and made as if to pinch her bottom, but she evaded him with a deft swing of her hips and jumped down to the pavement.

'Ta-ra, ducks,' he called. 'See you on the way 'ome.'

'Like hellers,' Louisa answered, and went off down into the ladies' conveniences. Having done what she had been increasingly longing to do ever since they had been somewhere in the neighbourhood of St Paul's, she washed her hands and face and examined herself in a mirror, thankful to note that the white parts of her attire were still white. It was not one of London's grimier days, which was fortunate in view of the nature of her visit to it.

When she had climbed the steps again and regained the surface, she stood doubtfully, looking this way and that, staring up at the Eros statue as if hoping it might call down some advice as to the next move she should make. Instead, a female voice at her elbow asked, softly and ingratiatingly, 'Are you lost, my dear? Stranger in London, are you?'

She turned to find a plump middle-aged lady, well dressed and wearing jewels, smiling at her. The expression was pleasant, but Louisa didn't fail to observe a certain watchfulness in the eyes, which were not smiling in a way to correspond with the lips.

'No thanks,' she answered politely but firmly. 'I'm just wondering which way to take.'

'Oh? Where for, my dear?'

'Charles Street, Mayfair.'

'Mayfair!' the woman exclaimed. 'Oh, that's the other side of town almost. You weren't thinking of walking?'

'I don't mind,' Louisa said. The fact that she had walked several miles to catch her 'bus earlier that morning did not deter her, even though she was wearing her best boots, which were new and still rather stiff.

'I tell you what,' the lady said, leaning a little closer. 'Come and take a cup of tea with me at the ABC just across Piccadilly, and I'll draw you a little map of the way. You'd never find it otherwise.'

'No you won't, Annie,' another voice intervened: a man's, gruff and authoritative. The lady's smile vanished instantly and Louisa looked up to see a tall, grizzle-haired policeman towering over them both. 'You know her, miss?' he asked her, jerking his head at the other.

'No, officer.'

'Thought not.' He turned to the older woman, who was bridling angrily. 'I've warned you once this month, Annie Cork,' he told her, 'and I'm warning you now for the second and last time. If I catch you accosting any more young women I shall take you straight in. I've had my eye on you the last half-hour, so don't think I shan't know where to watch for you if you try it anywhere else on my beat. Now, buzz off back to Seven Dials and your own kind.'

He stared implacably at the woman, almost as if taunting her to insult him and give him the excuse to arrest her. She tossed her head, sneered in Louisa's direction, and flounced away.

'What's all that?' Louisa asked, mystified.

'An old pro. Keeps a couple of places now up Seven Dials way. On the lookout for new talent for her customers. Strangers in London are meat and drink to the likes of her. But,' he added more grimly, 'she's not finding any on my patch if I can help it. Not her, or any others of her kind. Now, miss, where was it you wanted to be?'

'Charles Street, Mayfair. Is it the other side of town?'

He grinned, showing tobacco-stained teeth. 'No. Look, you could go up Regent Street here and cut across Berkeley Square way. You know that?'

'Not really,' Louisa admitted. None of her previous visits to London had taken her much further west than where she stood now.

'Right, then,' the policeman said. 'See there — Piccadilly? Just you walk along there and keep going ten, fifteen minutes till you get Green Park on your left. Then keep watching the turnings on the opposite side and you'll come to Half Moon Street. All right?'

'Half Moon Street. Yes.'

'Go up there and bear left and across into Queen Street. Go up that, and Charles Street runs right across the end, left and right. You can't miss it.'

'Half Moon Street and Queen Street,' Louisa repeated. 'Ta very much.'

'Whole way won't take you more than about twenty minutes,' He winked. 'Not a sprightly young lass like you. But don't go speaking to strange women — or men.'

She rewarded him with her warmest smile, and Louisa's smile really was reward for any man. The policeman touched the brim of his helmet in salute and stood, watching admiringly the sway of her behind as she trotted off in the direction he had indicated.

The walk down Piccadilly proved as interesting to her, in its very different way, as the 'bus trip had done. The pavements were again crowded, as was the broad thoroughfare. But now the people she passed between were almost all well dressed, some exceptionally so; and amongst the omnibuses and trams and cabs moved trim, highly polished private carriages, with glossy horses and liveried drivers, and sometimes a footman standing on a little platform at the rear. Behind the windows Louisa glimpsed elegantly attired men and beautifully dressed and coiffured ladies. They were of all ages and combinations. The common factor they had was that they were rich, assured and obviously aloof from the surroundings through which they were being borne in privileged isolation.

As she walked, she was astonished to recognise so many famous buildings which until now had been mere names to her: Fortnum & Mason's grocery store; Burlington House, behind whose courtyard the Royal Academy lay, and next door to which she found herself with surprise at the triple-arched entrance to the Burlington Arcade. This glittering cavern of jewellers', hosiers' and other fashionable clothiers' shops would have drawn her in, had she not caught the sternly critical eye of the uniformed beadle standing watchfully at the entrance, and funked the temptation to join the throng of exquisitely clad strollers within.

She passed on, looking up that other thoroughfare of high fashion, Old Bond Street, also on her right, and immediately afterwards, on her left, down St James's Street, with the red-bricked, battlemented royal palace at the foot. A little further on the right ran the forbidding walls, adorned with superbly wrought iron, of Devonshire House, a disappointing building itself from Louisa's viewpoint, although she paused to admire the beautiful iron gates which, she had read, had been brought only recently from the Duke of Devonshire's house at Chiswick.

And there on the left, as the policeman had instructed, began Green Park, fringed by trees which overhung its tall railings, which in turn were fringed by a long line of hansom cabs awaiting hire. The gleam of water caught her eye beyond the grassy stretches, and flights of white birds wheeled and settled. Louisa's spirits, already exhilarated by so many interesting sights, lifted further at the country-like prospect.

But now she must begin looking out for Half Moon Street. Stratton Street, Bolton Street, Clarges Street… Could she have missed it? No, here it was — the next turning. Thankfully, she took it. At its end she found herself in what seemed almost to be a replica of some old-fashioned village, with a cobbled square and small, spruce houses with sash windows and bow-windowed shops. But there was nothing old-fashioned-looking about the many young women who sauntered here or leaned against doorways and corners; unless, Louisa thought, with another of her happy fancies, it was their profession that was old-fashioned. She read a sign, SHEPHERD MARKET, and recalled having heard of it in some scurrilous connection.

She passed through it, incurring a variety of curious and hostile glances from the women, and found Queen Street and, at its end, Charles Street at last. And now she paused, and from her little handbag brought out the letter bearing the precise address she was seeking. Looking left and right, she located the branch of the street in which the house number would be. She read the letter for the last time, checked again the address and the name, then put the paper back into her bag.

For the first and only time her heart gave a little flutter of apprehension. She took a deep breath and swallowed. *Come on, girl,* she admonished herself silently. *Here we are. Let's get on with it.*

And, bracing her shoulders back and sticking her chin an inch higher into the air, she strode meaningfully towards Lord Henry Norton's town house.

CHAPTER TWO

The woman who greeted Louisa, in a plain but comfortable room far beyond the front door of the Georgian house, could have been no bigger than herself, so far as actual feet and inches went. But her middle age, her long firm-jawed face and her black attire made even the sprightly young woman feel very much the raw junior, offering herself up for scrutiny. The instinct irritated her and she consciously fought back at it.

'I am Mrs Catchpole, Lord Henry Norton's housekeeper,' this quietly formidable dame was saying. 'And this —' she indicated a heavily built, mournful-eyed man of about her own age, dressed in black morning coat and striped trousers — 'this is Monsieur Alex, his lordship's *chef de cuisine.*'

Louisa hesitated whether to offer her hand to either, but since neither made any move to offer theirs she refrained. The heavy man did not so much as nod. He regarded her sadly, as if anticipating her bringing some further burden of sorrow for him to bear.

'Please sit down,' Mrs Catchpole said. It was more order than invitation. Louisa sat on the hard chair indicated, keeping her back straight and her chin up, a pose which, assiduously studied some years before, had now become habitual to her.

Mrs Catchpole picked up a letter from the table in front of her. Louisa could recognise it despite the distance between them. 'We have here your letter applying for the position of assistant cook in Lord Henry Norton's household,' the housekeeper went on. 'Tell me, Miss Leyton — do you *enjoy* cooking?'

'Oh, yes, ma'am,' Louisa could reply honestly.

She heard a rumble as the man cleared his throat, preparatory to speaking. His accent was, she presumed, French. 'Miss Leyton … *why* do you want to come here?'

'I'd like to come and work, and learn things — from a proper French cook like you, sir.'

She saw his eyebrows rise at the word 'cook' and realised too late that she should have said 'chef'. He looked even more sorrowful.

Mrs Catchpole said, 'Your references are good. But it appears you haven't worked before in an establishment such as this one.'

'No, ma'am.' Louisa put all her ambition into her further words. 'But I've always wanted to. Ever so much. For years and years. Ever since Mu — my mother took me away from school and put me into service.'

'Oh? And how long ago was that?'

'Nearly ten years, ma'am. When I was twelve. I'd learned a bit of cooking at the board school, you see. They gave you classes when you was older. But I've had to do everything — kitchen maid, scullery maid, tweeny … until the last year or two, that is, when I've been cooking.'

The chef asked, 'What standard of cooking have you reached?'

She turned to face him and answered frankly. 'Not too bad. I mean, nothing really fancy or special. That's why I want to come here and learn.'

It seemed to do nothing to reassure him. He fell silent again.

Mrs Catchpole went on, 'We aim to achieve a very high standard of service in this house. We maintain a large staff, and there are strict rules.' She watched keenly for Louisa's reaction. 'We do not allow followers.'

'No, ma'am.'

'You yourself ... are not in any way attached?'

'No, ma'am,' Louisa answered, with a firmness which clearly surprised her interrogator. 'Nor do I intend to be.'

'I see. One half day off a week is allowed and every other Sunday. Church attendance is expected. Are you Church of England?'

Louisa hesitated fractionally, then reminded herself that she had been a few times in her life to the beautiful Georgian parish church of St Mary's at Wanstead. 'Yes, ma'am,' she answered.

If Mrs Catchpole noticed the hesitation, she let it go without comment. 'You would have to provide all your own uniform. You would have twenty-six pounds a year and a bedroom to yourself. Do you wish to be considered for the position?'

Louisa's heart leaped. 'Yes, please, ma'am.' There was no hesitation at all this time.

'Very well,' Mrs Catchpole said with finality. She rang a little handbell and the young footman who had opened the door to Louisa and escorted her to the housekeeper's room returned for her. 'Then if you have no questions,' the housekeeper said, 'you will report with your belongings on Monday morning.' She glanced at the letter again. 'You have a long way to travel, so not later than ten o'clock will be in order on this occasion.'

'I'll try to get the first 'bus, at eight,' Louisa babbled in her excitement. 'Only there's a lot of men crowds it out, usually I won't be late, ma'am. Thank you, ma'am. Sir.'

She could feel the cook's hooded eyes on her as she marched smartly away in the footman's wake. No! Not cook. *Chef de cuisine.* As was her habit with anything she knew she must learn, or sensed would be useful to her sometime, Louisa Leyton imprinted the title firmly into her mind. Like everyone else, she admitted, she made mistakes. But it was her proud boast that she never made the same mistake twice.

'Assistant cook?' her mother echoed when Louisa got home, after a journey during which, for once, even her powers of observation had been in suspension and she had sat oblivious to everything except the day's achievement. 'Assistant cook? That's not much to write home about. You were a proper cook in your last place.'

'Oh, yeh. To a pipsqueak of a dentist in Muswell Hill. They hadn't no class. Nothing. They even had high tea.'

'We have high tea!' Mrs Leyton bridled. She was in her late forties, handsome about the eyes, with narrow cheeks and large upper teeth which showed prominently when she drew back her lips in a laugh or a sneer. A volatile, emotional woman, she was capable of doing either with little provocation.

'For pity's sake, Ma,' Louisa said, 'it's nothing to do with high tea. It's with getting on in the world.'

'Well, I just don't understand you, Louisa. Cook and now assistant cook…' Her tone softened. 'Look, you've grown up into a very nice-looking girl…'

'Think I should go up the West End, then?' Louisa enjoyed baiting her mother. 'If I'd have known, I could've taken me chance today.'

'If you talk like that I'll clip you one,' her mother threatened. 'And you know what I mean. I mean there's at least three or four respectable, hard-working young men round here would marry you like a shot, and you know it. And there's no need to snort like that. Frank Belling's been round to see your dad and me.'

'Frank Belling!' The young man was a harmless, insignificant being, apprenticed to his father's family upholstery business. 'You never told me.'

'Well, he has. He's a nice boy and not bad-looking…'

'Sort of thing you turn up under a stone. Anyway, I don't want to get married to Frank Belling or anybody else. I want to get on for myself, by working for the best people there is. Rich people. Lords and ladies, with big houses, and jewels and lovely clothes. And the best food. I want to see it all. Be part of it.'

Her mother rolled her eyes.

'You know what they say?' Louisa continued. *'Rub against gold and a bit may stick to you.'*

'Marvellous! Think you're a duchess already, I suppose. And all the time getting less than you had before.'

'That's all you worry about, isn't it?' Louisa shouted back, really stung. 'It's all you've ever worried about. Well, you'll get your money regular, same as before, so don't you worry.'

'That's not fair!' Mrs Leyton answered indignantly, but her daughter's principal wound had been opened, and it never failed to bleed copiously.

'It is fair,' she retorted. 'You may not like it, but it *is* fair. It's all you've ever worried about with me. It's why you made me into a skivvy when I was twelve and wouldn't let me stay on at school and be a teacher, like I wanted. You wanted me off your hands, and that's what you've got. Only now I'm going to do what *I* want to do — and no one's going to stop me.'

She stamped away to her little room and began sorting through her limited belongings, deciding which garments would still do and which would simply have to be replaced from her few pounds' savings.

Her insistence that the accusation she had made against her mother was a fair one was partly justified, partly not. She had been taken from school against her will at the age of twelve and sent into service, and she had been made to hand over a proportion of whatever little wages she had earned. But she did not know — and her parents intended she never should, if they could help it — that her mother's apparent avarice was, in fact, need. They were much poorer than Louisa would ever have believed.

Both Ernest Leyton and his wife came from respectable lower middle-class origins. His father had been a senior clerk in a mercantile office in the City. Hers had been a craftsman, an engraver and setter of precious stones. Both were now dead.

Louisa's parents had been married nearly twenty-seven years now, living for almost all that time in the southern part of Essex. They had two children only — Louisa and her older brother, Gerald, three years her senior. Her father's trade was self-employed clockmaker and repairer, and her recollections of childhood were of a happy atmosphere in the home and less of the pinching and scraping which seemed to have been going on now for almost as long as she could clearly remember.

Gerald had stayed at school until he was fifteen. He had gone into an insurance office, where he had stayed four years before dismaying the rest of the family by throwing up a well-prospected job because of some apparently petty dispute with his manager and joining the Army as a trooper. He was now serving in the South African war with his regiment, but seldom wrote home.

What Louisa didn't know was that her parents had been agreed that she, too, should be allowed the benefit of a full school career. She was bright and eager, and her teachers had hoped with her that their own profession would not be beyond her chances of attainment. But when she was twelve her father had sunk his savings into an automatic mechanism shown to him by a plausible German traveller who had persuaded him that, by taking on the sole British agency, he would make a small fortune. Ernest Leyton had discussed with his wife what sounded like a most favourable gamble, and she had agreed to his taking it.

The traveller had never visited Mr Leyton again, and letters to his German address were returned as undeliverable. Small supplies of the mechanism had, indeed, arrived. It was a good device and well made. Its only defect was that it was copied from someone else's recent patent, and it was not long before Ernest Leyton was being notified of this by lawyer's letter, after he had disposed of six new clocks incorporating it to a well-known firm of customers. The clocks could not be sold over the counter without infringing the patent law. They were returned to Mr Leyton, who was just able to scrape up enough money to make a full refund. The premium he had paid for the exclusive rights, though, was irrecoverable.

Without money to buy legitimate stock he could carry on business no longer, but he had no source of such money except the freehold house in which they all lived in Epping. There was nothing for it but to sell up and look for something smaller. Nothing suitable had been available in Epping, but the little house in Camden Street, Wanstead, had been brought to their notice. In size it was quite a come-down from what they had been used to. The neighbours were respectable, though, and Wanstead was no less agreeable a place in which to live than Epping. So they had moved. And Louisa, who had sadly expected to be transferred from her happy board school at Epping to an unfamiliar one at Wanstead, had been shattered to be told instead that her schooldays were over, and she must work for a living.

Her parents could have confided the reason to her, and she would have understood. But they did not do so; some false sense of shame and pride prevented Mr and Mrs Leyton from explaining what had gone wrong for them. The firm which had discovered Ernest Leyton's unintentional deception had acted harshly against him, implying that he had known perfectly well that the clock mechanism was being used without licence, and had accused him of endangering their good name. Since none of the clocks had actually been sold to the public, and full restitution had been made, they had been prepared to let the matter rest without recourse to legal proceedings, they had told him in a severe letter. But there could be no question of future dealings.

This had left the susceptible Mr Leyton feeling like a reprieved criminal. Together with the self-reproach he had adopted for letting himself be fooled so easily, as he saw it, it had broken his will to work. An embittered ruin of a once-eager craftsman, he now worked at home, taking in what repairs he could get from advertisements in the local newspaper and making only an occasional clock to order.

So Louisa's small contributions to the household expenses had been of more importance than she had ever known. Her mother had bitten her lip and kept silent on the occasions when her daughter had reproached her for taking her away from school. Her consolation was that, with such looks and vivacity, the girl would make an early marriage and would soon forget all about ever having wanted to teach.

Oddly enough, though, Louisa had never shown any romantic inclinations. She had openly scoffed at the news that this or that girl in the neighbourhood was going to be married, commenting that that was about all they were fit for anyway. For a while, Mrs Leyton had believed that this was merely adolescent braggadocio, or even secret envy. In recent years she had become less sure. She still made attempts at matchmaking, but Louisa's response was unvarying.

For her part, after getting over the initial shock, and the many little humiliations associated with a first experience of menial service, Louisa had started to grow ambition almost like growing an extra limb of a kind most people could manage without, but which proved either a blessing or a curse to those who possessed it.

Her first visits home from her place of employment had been ones of blissful release. But in time she had come to find the little house less inviting in its crampedness and with its atmosphere of gloom, emanating from her father. She had struck up some quite warm below-stairs friendships — although keeping the male servants firmly in their place — and she found herself reluctantly having to admit to feeling relief when the time came for her to end her brief visit home and go back to work.

Not that she had worked in any grand households so far. Her first employment — eight pounds a year and no washing — had been in the home of a manufacturer whose servants numbered a female cook, a serving man (scarcely grand enough to be termed a butler), a housemaid, a lady's maid, a young man of-all-work, and herself as general help and bottle-washer. It was a modest enough detached suburban house in a couple of acres of ground, but the discipline was strict: up at half past five for a 'spit and a lick' of her face from the cold water in the ewer, then downstairs to clear out the grates and riddle their contents, to salvage for re-use any fragments of coal still usable in the fires which she then proceeded to light — kitchen fire first, of course, on which she had to set tea and bacon cooking ready for the other servants coming down.

Then shoe-cleaning, linoleum-washing, black-leading, dusting, sweeping, going errands, carrying heavy loads up flights of stairs (while pretending to be invisible, should the mistress or her visitors be encountered on the way), and scores of other duties which filled the day to the full, only to be repeated the next, and the next, and the next, for as far ahead as could be seen.

But she was strong, and she was young, and she was cheerful. And, as has been said, she soon adopted a positive attitude towards her work, taking pride in doing it well. It made the most thankless task lighter if you convinced yourself that you were contributing to the efficient running of an organisation, which in turn was enabling the master to conduct his business efficiently and prosperously, which in turn… Louisa's philosophy of work amused her fellow servants, none of whom seemed to share it — except the cook.

This elderly spinster who bore the honorary title 'Mrs' before her name, which was Wilkinson, was a no-nonsense Yorkshirewoman whose plain style of cooking was superbly carried out. She had been cooking all her life, she told Louisa, who reckoned she would be in her mid-sixties, but even on the most ordinary dish Louisa never saw her work without care and concentration.

'There's steak-and-kidney, and there's steak-and-kidney,' Mrs Wilkinson declared, after being complimented on one of her pies for staff luncheon. 'Doesn't matter a scrap how much tha spends on what goes in if tha doesn't bother to think on all t'time tha's making it. I say, *think on*.'

Louisa had learned a lot from this excellent woman; not least that cookery was the most creative of all the domestic crafts, and the one least taken for granted by those for whom it was done, or capable of being done by just anybody. She resolved at that time that, if she were to remain a servant, she would become a cook, and run someone's grand kitchen the way *she* wanted it running, and no more scurrying about at everyone else's beck and call.

She was many years becoming a cook at all, though. The domestic ladder was too steep for a child to climb, and for every cook there were a dozen other kinds of lesser servant. Her first employer died suddenly when she had been at his house less than a year. The widow sold up and the staff was dispersed. Louisa went down to an agency and found another place. But it was like starting all over again, in a less agreeable household, amongst less agreeable servants and employers. So she tried elsewhere, and then elsewhere again, learning the truism that the atmosphere below stairs reflected that upstairs, and that hard masters and mistresses made for tyrannical butlers and discontented cooks, who took out their resentment on their underlings. Her own refusal to be put upon brought her into several conflicts in consequence of this. In seven years she had twelve jobs, and her references began to read less than enthusiastically.

Then she became a cook at last, because she was in one of those households which only ran to a cook, a man and a little maid. She lied her way into the post, the mistress of the house having been called away for a few days and only the master being there to interview her. Luck went her way: he ate out at his club on each of the several days before his wife returned. It gave Louisa time to get herself organised in the kitchen, read up the notes she had taken from Mrs Wilkinson all those years before, and do some experimenting on herself and the other two servants. They expressed themselves satisfied with what she gave them. Louisa, judging it against her memories of her Yorkshire mentor's products, reassured herself that she'd got the touch all right. When the household was reassembled she was able to cook for it with confidence; and when, at length, her master's firm moved him away and she had to find yet another situation, she took with her a truly glowing testimonial to her abilities as a 'good plain cook'.

There had followed the less-than-fulfilling months with the dentist's family at Muswell Hill. During this time, Louisa had given herself a good catechising one Sunday as she sat on Hampstead Heath amongst hundreds of others of her class. It was not long after her twenty-first birthday. She had spent nearly ten years in a sphere of life she hadn't wished to enter at first, but with which she had come to terms. They hadn't been wasted years. She had used them to gain knowledge and experience. All she had lost had been some of the outside pleasures which a less confined occupation might have let her enjoy, and she didn't mind about those. (She had also lost, without realising it, something of the good speaking accent she had once had. Without knowing it, she had let herself be influenced by the prevailing Cockney of most of the servants she had lived amongst.)

So, nothing had been wasted yet; but from now on, it could be.

'Come on, gel,' she said to herself, getting up impatiently and brushing grass from her bottom. 'It's time you was making a move, 'cos you've a long way to go.'

After a few days of searching the newspapers she had come across the advertisement which had led her to Charles Street, Mayfair, that later morning.

CHAPTER THREE

As she travelled in one of the crowded early buses on the Monday morning, with her small amount of luggage tied to the outside of the stair-rail by the same cocky young conductor, Louisa congratulated herself yet again on having got a toehold into a great house as helper to a real *chef de cuisine* — she no longer needed to remind herself not to think of him as a cook. She couldn't know how miserably he himself was viewing the prospect of her coming.

'Nonsense, Monsieur Alex,' Mrs Catchpole was at that moment defending the awaiting newcomer in the face of further despondent speculations. 'She seemed tidy and clean, and well mannered.'

He gave a Gallic shrug. 'But does she look like a *cook*? More like a chorus girl.'

It was Mrs Catchpole's turn to shrug. 'Her references are very satisfactory. I've spoken on the telephone with her last employer.'

'The dentist?' he asked with an edge of sarcasm.

'His wife, of course. An intelligent, educated-sounding woman. She assessed the girl's qualities very candidly.'

'But I do not want a woman. Women make cooks, not chefs.'

The housekeeper sighed and reminded him yet again. 'There were no male applicants for the post. They all want restaurant work, you know perfectly well, Monsieur Alex. We must simply do our best with her.'

He gave a great indrawn sigh, raising his shoulders high before expelling his breath in a way whose meaning needed no seeking out.

So, although she didn't know it, Louisa already had the housekeeper as her champion, which was no bad way to begin at all.

Her theory of servants reflecting masters would have seemed insubstantial — if she had even given it thought at the time — when Mrs Catchpole introduced her to her colleagues that morning. They seemed to be a mixture of the aloof, the indifferent, the friendly, and, she sensed in two instances, the downright hostile.

The kitchen of Lord Henry Norton's house was larger than any Louisa had yet been in, let alone worked in. It had all the appearance of a small factory, with benches, machines, brass wheels, pulleys, and rack upon rack of the equipment of cooking and serving. The number of servants passing to and fro astonished her.

The dislike she encountered was in the eyes and manner of the two kitchen maids. The elder, Jean, was dark and Scottish, in her late thirties, perhaps. She was neat and prim, and a contrast to the other, Ivy. A much younger blonde girl, Ivy was grubby and untidy, with a hoarse, coarse voice which seemed to fit perfectly with her appearance. Her accent was a mixture of London and the country.

A third maid, the maid of-all-work, gave Louisa a warm smile and a decent handshake. She was the youngest of all, and the smallest, still in her teens. Her pretty round face was topped with neat dark hair. She was introduced as Mary, and when she spoke it was with an engaging Welsh lilt.

Louisa sensed accurately that Jean and Ivy were jealous of her appointment as assistant cook. She would soon be giving them orders. Meanwhile, she anticipated that they would put plenty of obstacles in her way, in the hope that she would pack up and go. Well, she'd show them about that!

That they were also jealous of her looks never occurred to her.

'Looks a proper little trollop to me,' Ivy confided to Jean beyond the glass window of the scullery, not long after Louisa had been set to her first task by Monsieur Alex.

'I've no doubt that's exactly what she is,' Jean agreed loftily.

Mary, scrubbing the floor, said, 'I think she looks nice.'

'No one asked your opinion,' Jean reminded her.

'No,' Ivy said. 'And don't you speak till you're spoke to.' She and Jean peered through the glass. 'What's she doin'?'

'Making *crème caramel*,' Jean answered. 'Like he always tests them with.'

Ivy snorted. 'I bet she hasn't the first idea. I mean, look at them clothes. Button-up boots in the kitchen! I dunno why you didn't get the job, Jean. Honest, I really don't. I reckon Monsewer Alex must've gone soft in the 'ead.'

'Nothing to do with him,' Jean answered darkly. 'He's very upset about it. It was all influence, if you ask me.'

'What influence?'

'*Upstairs* influence.'

'What? You don't mean 'is lordship…?'

Jean tossed her head and went on with her work as she saw the chef enter the kitchen and go over to inspect the new girl's progress. He picked up the copper mould, containing a set yellow mass, and put it down again without a second glance.

'Who taught you to do this?' he asked in his monotone.

Louisa missed the nuance. She replied proudly, 'Oh, I just picked it up. You know, from other cooks.'

His response startled her. 'It will be *dégoutant*. Disgusting.'

She stared into the heavy features. 'Give us a chance, Monsieur Alex. Wait till it's cool.'

'My dear young lady, I don't need to wait until it is cold to say that it will be uneatable. Like leather. Too many whites of egg. Overcooked.'

Even his low tones were audible to the girls through in the scullery. They nudged one another delightedly as they heard him add, 'For the moment you will please go and help Ivy with the washing-up.'

What came next took them completely aback.

'No, I will not!' came the high, ringing response. 'I didn't come here to wash up. If you wish it, I'll go. But if I stay, I'll stay as your assistant cook, not as a scullery maid.'

The watching girls stared as Monsieur Alex stared, too. They saw him glance towards the window and see them watching. He turned sharply and walked out of his kitchen, followed, moments later, by the new girl, chin held high.

They giggled together.

'Well, I never did,' Ivy said. 'Thought she was going to hit 'im, for a minute.'

'She's a real little minx, that one,' Jean agreed. 'I don't want her coming in here, and I shall tell Monsieur Alex so.'

'Don't worry, luv. She'll be out by dinner time — on the street.'

'Aye. And that's where she should have been in the first place.'

Louisa had gone straight to her attic room, in obedience to the first instinct that had come to her. She took down her cardboard suitcase from the top of the small wardrobe, unclasped it, and started to throw things into it from her drawers. After a few minutes there came a knock at the door.

'Yes?' she demanded, not caring who it was.

The door opened and the little Welsh maid came cautiously in, carrying a cup and saucer on a tray, and a plate of biscuits.

'I thought you might like a cup of tea,' she said shyly. 'As I was making some for the others.'

Touched and deflated, Louisa said, 'That's very kind of you, Maisie.'

'Mary, miss. It's really Merri, you know, only no one knows that name here, so Mary's the easiest way.'

'Sorry, Mary,' Louisa said, taking the tray. 'You been here long?'

'Quite a long time,' the girl answered. 'At least, it seems so. It will be fourteen weeks next Monday.'

'Happy?'

'Well … no. Not very happy.'

Louisa poured her tea. 'Well, that was a silly thing to ask, anyway. How can a maid of-all-work be happy?'

'But I'm very grateful for the position,' came the eager answer. 'It's a lot better than nothing.'

'You know how to make tea, at least. Was it "nothing" before?'

'Almost worse. There were so many of us at home, we were nearly sleeping on the roof. They said in our street that every time my father sneezed my mother had another baby. Only, my father died last year. My Aunt Gwyneth brought me up to London and found me this job. So I was lucky really, wasn't I?'

Louisa smiled sympathetically, pleased to meet a fellow philosopher.

Mary continued, 'Though, there's some days, with Jean in one of her moods, and Ivy going on at me all the time, I could just run away.'

Louisa put down her cup. It rattled sharply against its saucer. 'Don't you run away, Mary. Don't you *ever* run away. Wait till they chuck you out first.'

Mary looked doubtfully at the half-packed case and asked, 'Have they given you your notice, then, miss?'

'No,' Louisa had to admit. She sighed. 'It's all my own fault if they do. I can't keep my big mouth shut, Mary. That's my trouble. Never have been able to. I need a clothes peg. I got a temper, too, and that's not much help.'

But Mary was looking at her admiringly. 'I thought it was wonderful, the way you stood up to Monsieur Alex,' she said. 'He had no right to treat you like that.'

'Turn the other cheek,' Louisa quoted. 'Fighting back doesn't get you nowhere.'

But Mary replied, 'I don't know so much. I remember one day when my Uncle Ifor had had a few drinks he came back swearing and saying he'd knock my Aunt Gwyn's block off. And she just stood up to him and gave him what for and spat in his face. And he just sat down in a chair by the fire, quiet as a little dog. And he's a big man, my Uncle Ifor. Played rugby for Neath.'

'There you are, then,' Louisa said, personally fortified by this. 'Next time Ivy gets at you, just remember your aunt.'

'Oh, I couldn't do that.' The girl smiled wistfully. 'It's not in my nature. But I'll remember you, miss. Finished?'

She took the tray, and went quietly away. Louisa sat on for a few minutes, thinking. Then she got up, unpacked the bag and put the things away. She returned the bag to the wardrobe top. She went to the washstand mirror to check her hair, put her tongue out at her reflection, and went back downstairs.

Monsieur Alex had obviously been waiting for her. He beckoned her to follow him into his little office. Her instinct was to apologise, but he forestalled her.

'Frankly, I do not understand why I should have to waste my valuable time teaching you to do something for which you have no talent. But I am told that I must do what I can with you.'

All thought of apologising left her at this. 'I'm sorry you feel like that,' she answered. 'All I want is a chance, like I was promised when I was took on.'

'*I* never promised anything,' he retorted, then lapsed into some moments' baleful silence, as if engaged in some inner conflict with himself. At length he gave one of his sighs and continued, 'Tell me, Leyton, what do you personally consider is the most important piece of equipment of a cook?'

'Well, I suppose the stove…'

'No, no, no.' He tapped his nose. 'It is this. And after smell, taste — the tongue. And then the eyes.'

'I see,' she said unconvincingly. He shook his head.

'I don't believe you see at all. You are a good-looking girl. Why don't you try to find something else to do? Why do you want to be a cook?'

She determined, once and for all, to squash these attempts to deter her. ''Cos I do. I can't say why — not exactly, but I do. I may be a lousy cook now, but I'm willing to learn. I'll work myself to the bone and won't skimp nothing, if you'll teach me. I love cooking. I do really.'

Her sincerity was evident to him, and he capitulated to it.

'Please sit down,' he said, in an altogether less dispirited tone. Then he began to pace the floor, saying, 'The first thing to learn is that cooking is not just *un métier* — a job. It is an art. The kitchen is as important as an artist's studio. To be a cook needs hard work, but it also needs talent. Nothing is worse than to be a bad cook. It is better to wash dishes than to cook badly. So first you have to wipe your mind clean. Forget everything you have learned before. Yes?'

Louisa nodded eagerly. He had put into words exactly what she already felt about cooking.

'*Bon!*' he said. 'Now, first principle, everything must be clean, exact, planned. Plain, simple food, well cooked, is always the best. But always the best materials. *Michelange* always used the best marble. And only one way is possible to be sure of the best. That is to go out to the market and choose everything yourself. Even a potato.'

He beckoned her to follow him again and led her back to the kitchen. She could see Ivy and Jean watching through the scullery window. She fancied their expressions changed when, instead of sending her to her room to pack, as they had confidently expected, he took her to the working table and indicated the objects on it.

'Here is how you must each day lay the table for me, for the *chef de cuisine*. Each item must be exactly in the correct place — salt box, pepper mill, chopping board, knives, cloths, thyme, parsley —'

He was interrupted by the arrival down the kitchen steps of a tall dark-haired man in black. Louisa recognised instantly that he must be the butler. She was surprised by his youthfulness for the high office. He could not be more than thirty-five or so.

'Good morning, Monsieur Alex,' he said.

'Good morning, Mr Trotter. May I introduce my new assistant here? Miss Leyton. Mr Trotter, the butler.'

The butler shook her hand and granted her a formal little smile. Then he and the chef went away into Monsieur Alex's office, discussing the wines to accompany that evening's dinner, leaving Louisa to wander round the kitchen, familiarising herself with its layout and equipment.

When the butler had gone back upstairs Monsieur Alex returned to her. *'Eh bien,'* he said. 'Now, for the next few weeks you are going to learn how to make pastry. I expect you think you know how to make pastry, eh?'

'No, Monsieur Alex,' she had the sense to answer. It pleased him.

'Give me your hands,' he surprised her by saying. She held them out across the table and he took each in one of his. Louisa noticed Jean crossing the kitchen with a mixing bowl. Her face was a study as she watched the chef's incredible behaviour. But his expression had nothing of emotion in it. He released her hands with a nod of satisfaction.

'You have cool hands. That is a good start. For pastry, everything must be cool.'

He turned aside for something, and Louisa took the opportunity to grin sweetly at Jean, who went on her way with a set face.

Louisa was able to pay Mary back for her kind gesture within a few days. She came into the kitchen one evening, to hear her crying from the scullery. She went through and found Mary washing up a great pile of crockery and cutlery and crying helplessly, so that the tears ran down her nose and into the washing-up water.

'What on earth's the matter?' Louisa demanded.

The Welsh girl shook her head. 'Nothing, miss.'

'I thought it was your evening off.'

'So it is,' Mary managed to answer. 'Only I broke another plate breakfast time, and Ivy said I was to stay in and do the washing-up tonight. And she's gone out in my place.'

'Has she?' Louisa remarked grimly. 'But that's not enough to cry about, love.'

The girl wiped her face with her forearm. 'It's not that, miss. It's my Auntie Gwyn. She lives in London now and she's been took poorly with the failing of the lungs. She's in hospital, and I'd promised to see her tonight.'

Louisa made up her mind. 'So you shall. I'll finish this.'

'Oh, no, miss, that's not your place. Anyway, the hospital's away the other side of the river. It'd be too late by the time I got there.

'Then you must go in a cab,' Louisa told her. She got out her little purse and produced some silver coins and held them out to Mary, who shook her head.

'I could never take that from you, miss.'

''Course you can. It's not anything valuable. It's only money.'

Mary had never in her life heard anyone speak so casually of that most important of all things — money. She took the four shillings in a soapy hand and said, 'You're … a saint, miss. You really are.'

'No, I'm not. Now, you go and get yourself tidy, and just leave all this lot to me.'

The girl hurried away to change. Louisa rolled up her sleeves and began a more orderly assault upon the washing-up. There was a lot of it, and she was still working when Monsieur Alex came into the scullery. He was wearing his coat, ready to go to his regular rendezvous at one of the servants' public houses in the neighbourhood. He frowned when he saw Louisa.

'Why are you doing this? We have two girls.'

Louisa said quickly, 'Ivy had to go out and Mary's a bit poorly. I dunno where Jean is. Anyway, I don't mind. It's here to be done.'

He shook his head. 'It is a question of dignity. You are a cook. You do not do menial tasks.'

'I'm sorry, Monsieur Alex. I won't do it again.'

He grunted and went out. Louisa smiled to herself. Only a few days earlier she had risked the sack by refusing his command to her to go and help with the washing-up. Yet, here he was telling her off for doing it voluntarily, and reminding her of her dignity as a cook, a post he had resented having to admit her to in the first place. At least, she felt, he had accepted her completely now.

The irony was rounded off soon afterwards when Jean came in and expressed her own resentment of Louisa's doing work which was not rightly hers. This was the very Jean who only the day before had refused Louisa's request to fetch a cooling tray for some cheese straws Louisa had just drawn from the oven. 'You've got two arms and two legs, same as everyone else,' had been Jean's response.

'Yes, I have. But I happen to be using all four of 'em, just at this very minute.'

'Well, too bad. Let's get one thing clear, Miss Leyton — I'm Monsieur Alex's kitchen maid, and no one else's. If you want someone to fetch and carry for you, ask one of the others.'

Louisa had managed to restrain her tongue, for once, in the interests of future relationships. She did so again in the face of Jean's complaint about the washing-up, merely remarking, 'I must say, we get through an awful lot of stuff for a bachelor household.'

Jean said in a superior tone, 'The fact that Lord Henry is unmarried doesn't mean that he lives like a hermit. There are guests almost every evening.'

'So I notice.'

'Hello, hello!' A male voice from the doorway surprised Louisa. It was not Mr Trotter, nor any of the footmen, but a tall, very well-dressed young man. She noted instantly how handsome he was, with fair hair and smiling grey-green eyes. But it was Jean he was addressing.

'How nice to see you again, my dear Jean. And how *is* the "fair maid of Perth"?'

'I'm very well, thank you, Mr Charlie,' she replied. It was obvious to Louisa that he was some connection with the family and seemed to be on very free-and-easy terms with the maid. He glanced at Louisa and smiled, but Jean made no move to introduce her.

'You may have heard I'll be staying with my uncle for a while,' he said to Jean. 'Just got here in time for dinner. Actually, I came down to say hello to Monsieur Alex and congratulate him on that delicious lemon sorbet.'

She said, 'I'll tell him when he gets back, Mr Charlie. I'm sure he'll be pleased.'

This was too much for Louisa. She withdrew her hands from the washing-up water and dried them vigorously, saying, 'Excuse me, sir. I made the sorbet. I'm Monsieur Alex's assistant, Louisa Leyton.'

He glanced from her to the washing-up and back, then smiled and came to shake her hand. 'Did you indeed?' he said. 'I'm Charles Tyrrell. So, my compliments to you, then, Miss Leyton.'

He smiled at them both and went out again.

'Of all the cheek!' Jean seethed.

'No, it wasn't. It was the truth. Anyway, who's he when he's at home?'

'"He" happens to be the Honourable Charles Tyrrell, Lord Henry's nephew, son and heir of Lord Haslemere.'

Louisa was impressed. 'Nice looker, too.'

Jean scowled at her. 'If you take my advice you won't start trying any of your tricks on Mr Charlie.'

In the event, though, it was the other way round. That night Louisa trudged thankfully upstairs for the last time, looking forward to the comfort of her little bed. She opened the door of her attic room. To her surprise the electric light was on. In the little wicker chair beside her bed sat the Honourable Charles Tyrrell. He was wearing a silk dressing gown over pyjamas. At the sight of Louisa's shocked face and open mouth he quickly put a finger to his lips.

'My dear Miss Assistant Cook,' he said in a low voice, 'I just came to congratulate you on that sorbet — properly.'

She had half closed the door, but made no move to close it completely, though she instinctively kept her voice down. 'I'll bet you have,' she said. 'And to sample some of my other wares, no doubt.'

He smiled broadly. He was very handsome indeed,

'What a percipient young lady you are,' he said. From his dressing-gown pocket he had withdrawn a long, slender box of expensive appearance. He held it out to her. 'Here is a little token of my admiration for your cooking ... and your "other wares".'

She did not take it, so he opened it and tilted it forward to reveal a jet necklace. It was attractive, but Louisa said resolutely, 'I don't want nothing from you, thank you very much, sir.'

He got up, still smiling confidently. 'I'm sure you're a sensible girl. Experienced, I don't doubt…'

'Here!' Louisa retorted indignantly. 'What do you take me for? What do you mean by that?'

He was startled into checking his advance towards her. Her voice had risen and he glanced nervously towards the half open door.

'I … I'm sorry,' he stammered. 'Please forgive me.'

It was not every day that noblemen's heirs begged the forgiveness of Louisa Leyton — especially ones so good-looking as this — but she refused to let that influence her.

'There's nothing to forgive, and there isn't going to be, neither. So push off.'

He grinned again and ventured a step towards her. She pointed to the door.

'If you so much as lay a finger on me I'll scream, and I'll go on screaming till Lord Henry himself hears me.'

'Ssh! You don't mean it.'

'You just try me.'

He hesitated, looking as though he was weighing up the risk. Then he gave a shrug of defeat and went out. Louisa went to close the door behind him, and only then saw that he had left the necklace in its box on her washstand.

She took off her cap, rubbed her tired eyes with the backs of her hands, then began unfastening her dress. The sight of her bared neck in the mirror caused her gaze to travel automatically to the necklace. She couldn't resist taking it out of the box and slipping it on. It looked charming. She pulled down the top of her dress, the better to admire the effect of the necklace in conjunction with her slender neck and the fine skin of her shoulders.

'Marvellous!' she heard his quiet voice behind her. 'You look like a princess.'

Louisa jerked her dress back up, pulled off the necklace and turned to toss it at him. 'Ooh, you are a sneaky devil, you are!' she told him.

He held up his hands. 'I'm not going to touch you. I promise. May I sit down?'

His manner was so disarming that Louisa relented enough not to object when he quietly closed the door and sat down again in the wicker chair. 'You seem to do what you like in here,' she said. 'Liberty Hall.'

'I'm disappointed in you, Louisa Leyton,' he said, almost seriously.

'And I'm disappointed in you, the Honourable Mister Charlie Tyrrell. You're all the same, aren't you? You think we're here just for your pleasure, like animals. Have you ever thought what happens when a servant gets put in the family way by one of you lot?'

This frank allusion to his unspoken purpose startled him visibly. He murmured, 'Some … some arrangement is made … as a rule.'

She shook her head. 'Arrangement my foot. Chucked out with a week's wages, and no reference, and no hope. If she gets over the baby, which a lot of 'em don't, there's only one thing left — the streets. You go out and ask any tart you like. Even money, she'll tell you she started out in service. At my last place but one there'd been a housemaid called Mona had gone with a sailor. They found her body in the river at Wapping.'

He said uncomfortably, 'I didn't really come here to be lectured on the problems of the —'

'I know what you came for. And it's ones like you that causes the problems.'

'Look,' he persisted, 'I want to talk to you. I mean, seriously.'

This surprised her. She said suspiciously, 'It's a funny time, and a funny place — and in funny clothes, if you ask me.'

He had regained the initiative and answered masterfully, 'I'm *not* asking you. You see, I'm at a … a bit of a loose end. I thought of going out to the war…'

'Good idea. Give you something to do. Take your mind off other things.'

He let the rebuke pass and went on, 'The trouble is, all the world and his wife's gone dashing off to South Africa. They don't want any more amateur soldiers, except to dance with generals' daughters. Of course, there's this new Chinese rebellion. That looks quite amusing, but Peking's a long way to go just for a lark. So the long and the short of it is that I'm thinking of setting up an establishment in London. I can always come and stay here, but there must be a moment when even a favourite nephew outstays his welcome.'

He broke off and looked at her earnestly for some moments. She wasn't aware that she was smiling sympathetically at these ingenuous confessions. When he continued, he picked his words with care.

'If I did … set myself up … I'd need someone to look after the place for me. To look after me, come to that. I was wondering if that … that someone might be you?'

Louisa was staring at him now, genuinely astonished and rather bewildered. 'Bit … quick, isn't it?' she managed to reply. 'You hardly know me.'

'Oh, I'm quick at making decisions. Miss Leyton, I'm serious. It would be a little house, somewhere secluded. A carriage at your disposal, clothes, servants…'

Some of his excitement transmitted itself to Louisa, despite herself. Suddenly, totally unexpectedly, she was being offered a position which, while not exactly in high society, would bring her into its ambit and could take her who knew where? She had no doubt about the precise nature of what he was proposing to her. It wasn't a 'respectable' situation in the conventional, suburban sense, but she knew that these things were looked at quite differently in society. She would no doubt be accepted readily by his friends, and she knew she was capable of adapting herself to the new way of life. It was a chance she had never dreamed would come her way, and brought her instantaneously in sight of the goal she had vaguely in mind for herself.

He was looking at her hopefully. She had only to say the word…

Instead, she said, 'Look, don't think I don't see a gentleman like you doesn't need that sort of place. And, of course, you'll need … need a lady to … well, you know. That is to say, I'm very honoured to be asked … but the fact is, I wouldn't be no good for you.' She saw his disappointment, and felt for him, but she had to go on. 'You'll think I'm barmy, I expect. But I know what I want to be. I want to be the best cook in England. That's *all* I want to be.'

She had only realised it herself at that same instant. Either way, it had to be all or nothing, and she had chosen in the direction her strongest instincts urged her towards. She looked at him, expecting him to persuade, to argue, even perhaps to laugh.

But he only said, very quietly, 'What a good idea.' He got up and picked up the necklace again, holding it out to her. 'Please keep it, Louisa. From one friend to another.'

'All right,' she said, and took it. 'Thanks, Mr Charlie.'

'Goodbye, Louisa,' he said, his hand on the doorknob. 'Good luck.'

He went out, quickly and quietly. He did not see Jean, in the dark corner of the landing, where she had been standing, straining to hear what was going on in Louisa's room.

Left alone, Louisa sat on the bed and looked at herself, in the mirror. She held up the necklace again and looked at its effect against her neck.

'Louisa Leyton,' she said to the reflection, 'you need your head looking at. That's what's wrong with you.'

And she proceeded to undress and go to bed. But she went to sleep knowing that whatever had made her make the decision she had, it had been the right one for her.

CHAPTER FOUR

It was not the custom for Mrs Catchpole or Monsieur Alex to take their breakfast with the rest of the servants. They were served in solitary state in their respective rooms. Louisa was in charge of all breakfast operations, although most of the actual work was done by Jean and Ivy.

When staff breakfast was over the next day, Louisa set out the kitchen table with Monsieur Alex's equipment and waited for him to appear. Instead, one of the footmen came to her and said she was wanted in Mrs Catchpole's room. It was not unusual, although most of the instructions she received came from, or by way of, Monsieur Alex.

Today she was surprised to find them both awaiting her, wearing grim faces.

'Morning, ma'am,' Louisa unsuspectingly greeted the housekeeper. The greeting was not reciprocated.

'We have a very serious matter to discuss with you, Leyton,' Mrs Catchpole said. Louisa wondered whether her doing the washing-up had been a graver breach of discipline than she had imagined; or whether she had done wrong in giving Mary the money to go to her aunt, when she had been ordered to stay in.

'I'm sorry, ma'am,' she began, but Mrs Catchpole waved her silent. 'Do you admit,' she asked, 'that there was a man in your bedroom last night?'

Louisa felt the shock of the unexpected, but after the initial confusion she managed to pull herself together. 'Oh. Yes, ma'am.'

The housekeeper seemed surprised by the ready admission. 'You know it is completely forbidden to admit a man to your room.'

'I know, ma'am. Only, it wasn't me admitted him. He admitted himself. He was sitting there, bold as brass, when I went up to bed. And I chucked him out.'

Louisa had not referred to her visitor's identity. She wondered whether they knew it. She wondered, in fact, how they knew any man had been there at all.

Mrs Catchpole's next words made all clear. 'We have heard that Mr Tyrrell was in your room by your invitation, and that you made the assignation with him when he visited the kitchen.'

It was immediately plain to Louisa who had carried the tale. She let her temper go.

'Well, you heard wrong. You've been told a pack of lies, and I can just guess by who. Creeping and crawling about … spying on people. That's what she was doing, wasn't it? Poking her nose in where it doesn't belong. And you believe her.'

The vehemence of this outburst had silenced Mrs Catchpole. She was looking perplexedly at Monsieur Alex, whose customary lugubriousness had changed under its influence to an air of keen interest.

'Jean has been with us for some years,' he reminded her.

Louisa turned on him savagely. 'So it's her word against mine, is it? All right, you can have my notice here and now. Or we'll all go up and see Mr Tyrrell and ask him the truth, shall we? Yes, and take Jean up with us.'

Both her superiors recoiled from this notion. Mrs Catchpole said quickly, 'Now, Leyton, we … we mustn't get all hot and bothered about this. As we know, even in the best establishments there are bound to be upsets from time to time. It's up to us to try to settle them in the most sensible way.'

Louisa appeared far from appeased, though. The housekeeper went on with difficulty.

'You've done very well here so far. Monsieur Alex was telling me only yesterday that he is quite happy to leave the kitchen in your hands when his lordship's away and he himself is on holiday. In view of the circumstances, then, and in the light of your own honesty, I think the best thing is for us to forget the entire thing.'

Louisa said, more calmly, 'Thank you, ma'am. I'm quite prepared to forget all about the incident ... on one condition.'

The others looked sharply at one another, but they turned back to listen to her finish.

'On condition that Jean apologises to me in front of Monsieur Alex.'

Mrs Catchpole was about to reply that this was quite unnecessary and to remind Louisa that it was not for her to dictate terms to her superiors. Monsieur Alex sensed as much, though, and nudged her under the table with his knee. She looked at him and read enough in the almost expressionless face to make her desist.

'Very well,' she told Louisa. 'I think that would be only right.'

Jean was sent for, there and then. After some hedging and protestations that she hadn't meant to accuse Louisa outright, but had merely been 'doing her duty as she thought fit', she had to capitulate. She turned to Louisa and held out her hand, saying, 'I'm sorry I made a mistake about you, Miss Leyton. I wish to apologise.'

There was no apology in her eyes; but Louisa took the hand and said, 'Do you? That's nice. Thank you, Jean.'

When the two women had gone, the housekeeper and the chef breathed a sigh of mutual relief. Clearly Louisa's wrath was a great and a terrible thing. Each of them made a mental note not to stir it up again without complete justification for taking the risk.

Lord Henry Norton, a bulky, retiring man in his late forties of whom Louisa had seen very little in the few months she had been in his employment, duly went off to Scotland in the summer, taking his nephew with him. Monsieur Alex departed to Spain to visit a sister who had married and settled there. Dust sheets were spread over the furniture in most of the upstairs rooms and the drawing-room chandelier was taken down, dismantled and sent away for re-gilding.

Usually, Mr Augustus Trotter, the butler, travelled with his master, but on this occasion he had not been required to do so. He and Mrs Catchpole remained to preside over an empty house and a much-depleted staff, with Louisa in full charge of the kitchen.

One afternoon Louisa was summoned again to Mrs Catchpole's room. This time she found Mr Trotter there. He held a piece of paper in his hand, and both of them regarded her with serious speculation as she entered. She wondered what she had done wrong this time.

'Miss Leyton,' Mrs Catchpole began, to Louisa's relief — it would have been just 'Leyton' if there had been trouble coming — 'Mr Trotter has received a telegram from his lordship. He is returning from Scotland earlier than we had expected.' The butler flourished the telegram. 'There is to be an important dinner party for ten on Thursday.'

Louisa stammered, 'But we haven't got a chef. Could we borrow Lord Haslemere's?'

Mr Trotter shook his head. 'The family have taken him to Yorkshire with them.'

Mrs Catchpole said, 'We would like *you* to cook that dinner, Miss Leyton.'

'Me?' was Louisa's reaction. 'You … you said it was important.'

'So it is. Monsieur Alex has expressed every confidence in you. You've a full kitchen staff, so there should be no problems about the number.'

Mr Trotter gave Louisa an encouraging smile. 'You might regard it as your big chance,' he said encouragingly.

Feeling rising excitement, Louisa swallowed and said, 'Well, I'll have to, then, won't I? I wouldn't like to let his lordship down.'

'Good girl. Now, come with me and we'll discuss the menu in detail.'

The butler led her off to his pantry, where they remained a full hour, with paper, pencils and Mr Trotter's invaluable pantry book, in which he had written and pasted innumerable scraps of information, garnered over his years in service.

The menu which transpired was as follows:

Chicken Broth
Sole with White Wine Sauce
Roast Grouse. Bread Sauce
Game Chips. Mixed Spices
Champagne Water Ice
Pears in Lemon Juice

'So,' he said finally, reviewing the list of wines he had needed no list to choose from, 'Madeira with the soup, Champagne, Dry Monopole '87 with the fish, Richebourg '84 with the grouse, Château Yquem '79 with the pears in lemon juice. Should do very nicely.'

Louisa said admiringly, 'How ever do you remember all of them, Mr Trotter?'

'Practice. Experience,' he announced proudly. 'I think I was almost born with a certain interest in wine. And travelling with his lordship has somewhat sharpened that interest.'

'Where've you been mostly?'

'Most years we shoot partridges with the Duc de Noailles, near Paris. Then on to Count Metternich for the boar shooting in the Eiffel. And at home, of course, it's the pheasants mainly, at Sandringham, or Chatsworth, or Welbeck.'

'"We"? D'you mean you're allowed to shoot as well?'

'Yes, indeed. I act as his lordship's loader but I'm often permitted to be one of the guns. I'm a fair shot, come to that. In my opinion that's an inherited talent, too.'

'Oh. Did your father teach you, then?'

Mr Trotter didn't answer immediately. Then he said portentously, 'It, er, is not talked about, but I think it is generally known in this household that my, er, parentage is somewhat veiled in mystery. It is fairly certain that my mother was of noble birth. As to my father…' He shrugged eloquently.

Impressed, Louisa said, 'Oh, I can see that, Mr Trotter. I ain't … haven't got much to boast about in that line, I'm afraid. Except my mother's dad helped to make some of the Crown Jewels.'

'Did he indeed!'

'With his own hands. And he was an engraver, too.'

He indicated the notes she had been taking. 'Perhaps that accounts for his granddaughter's beautiful handwriting.'

'Oh, no. I taught myself that. From one of them copybooks.'

'Well,' he said. 'I'm sure the menus are going to look splendid, then.'

'I don't know I can manage it all in French,' she said. 'I might spell some of it wrong without noticing.'

'What's the matter with English, then?' he smiled. 'Now, I must go and supervise the opening of the rooms. Good heavens, the chandelier! I've got to get it back urgently.'

He hurried out. Louisa gathered up her notes, feeling she had found a friend.

In fact, he treated her as a true equal, just before the arrival of the guests, that Thursday evening. She had ventured up to have a look at the dining room, which she had never yet seen in its full array.

She looked at it almost incredulously. The long, high room was decorated and furnished exactly as it had been in the 1750s. The walls were elegantly panelled and painted in pastel colouring, with gilt linings to the angles. The sideboards were not the heavy Victorian-made affairs she was accustomed to seeing in any room of such size, but delicately proportioned, with galleries and decorations of reeded urns with acorn finials at each end. There were no mirrors in clumsy, carved mahogany frames, but a profusion of portraits, glowing under their high varnishing, and in carved, gilded frames. Most of them were of men, in uniform or hunting costume, with reds and blues predominating the other colours.

The great many-legged table itself was crowded from end to end. A many-branched candelabrum dominated its centre, with smaller ones to right and left and silver *épergnes,* their numerous little dishes filled with pickles and savoury bits of all kinds. A floral arrangement in a silver vase stood by every place, and each setting consisted of four sets of knives and forks, four gleaming glasses of different shapes, and a starched white napkin, elaborately folded.

The footmen, in full livery and powdered white wigs, were applying the finishing touches under Mr Trotter's elegant supervision. He smiled at Louisa, who was carrying her menus in a paper cover to keep them pristine.

'Do you approve, Miss Leyton?' he asked.

'Oh, lor', yes! Yes, I do. Who's coming?' She had noticed that while most of the settings had silver-framed place cards to them, one or two had not.

'Just one or two of his lordship's more intimate friends,' he answered nonchalantly. 'By the way, I wanted to ask you something.'

'Yes?'

'How do you wish the boiled truffles to be served?'

Delighted to be treated with such deference by the senior servant, Louisa answered as casually as she could, 'Oh, just in a plain white napkin, please, Mr Trotter.'

He gave her a slight bow. 'So it shall be done, Miss Leyton.'

Supervising the presentation and serving of her first really big dinner was a test of Louisa's nerves and stamina. Fortunately, Jean and Ivy were kept at such full stretch by the sheer press of duties that there was no scope for back-biting or sullen slowness. The only fracas was between the two of them, when Ivy, carting dirty plates from the serving lift to the scullery, blundered into Jean, knocking a dish of four grouse to the floor. Louisa firmly and calmly terminated their exchange of abuse and got things back into smooth motion.

It was only when the dirty savoury dishes had come down that she was able to relax, her duty done. She felt drained.

'Didn't leave much, did they?' Jean remarked, in quite a friendly tone for her.

'Must've been hungry,' Louisa agreed, gratified to have noted that no dishes had come back down untouched. 'They say the proof of the pudding's in the eating. But I suppose Monsieur Alex would've done 'em a bit more proud.'

She was surprised to hear Jean say, 'He wouldn't have done much better.'

At that moment Mr Trotter came down the steps. He looked strained and serious.

'Miss Leyton,' he summoned Louisa. 'You're wanted in the dining room.'

'Me? Oh, lor', what's gone wrong? Look, whatever it is, I did my best. I only…'

His mouth twitched in a smile. 'They want to see whoever cooked the dinner.' He winked.

'Oh, lor'!' Louisa cried again, partially reassured but stricken with panic. She dashed though into Monsieur Alex's room, where there was a good mirror, and tidied herself up quickly. When she emerged again Mr Trotter gave her a comforting nod and, taking her arm, piloted her up the stairs, watched open-mouthed by Jean, Ivy and Mary.

Outside the dining room Mr Trotter paused and looked at her. She returned his gaze, smiling tentatively. He seemed to want to say something, but finally he pushed open the double doors, went in first, then turned and beckoned her to follow.

Five men were clustered at the far end of the table, where they had evidently regrouped themselves after the ladies had withdrawn. Cigar smoke was heavy on the air, and the light of the many candles twinkled on the ruby colour of their port glasses. Louisa recognised Lord Henry, and Charles Tyrrell, who had turned to smile at her. Two of the other men she did not know. She didn't give them more than a glance, in any case. Her gaze was riveted on the fifth member of the party. He was fat and bearded, with heavy-lidded eyes. A huge cigar protruded from his mouth. Anyone in England would have recognised him at once.

Lord Henry had nodded to his butler, who addressed this lounging figure. 'Your Royal Highness, I beg your pardon. Might I present Miss Leyton, who cooked the dinner tonight?'

Edward, Prince of Wales, withdrew the cigar from his mouth and exhaled smoke. Louisa correctly interpreted this as an invitation to advance towards him. She curtseyed.

The prince cleared his throat with a rasp and said in a surprisingly guttural voice, 'I sent for the chef to congratulate him, and I find it's you. So I must congratulate you instead. And I do congratulate you. Here is my hand on it.'

He held up a podgy white hand. Louisa took it. It was soft as silk, she thought afterwards. He held it for two or three seconds, searching her face steadily. Louisa felt too honoured to recognise the thoroughly searching nature of that scrutiny. At length he let her hand go and fished with finger and thumb in one of his tight-stretched jacket pockets. He took out a little case, from which he produced a gold coin.

'Here's something to show how much we liked our dinner,' he said. He placed the coin in her palm. 'A present sovereign, from your future sovereign.'

The other men murmured appreciation. Mr Trotter caught Louisa's eye and his hand moved slightly but significantly. With a murmur of thanks and another curtsey she left the room, the butler following to close the doors behind her. He grinned, and took her arm warmly to lead her downstairs.

'Mr Trotter!' she admonished him, when they were out of earshot of the dining room. 'Why ever didn't you tell me before?'

'Mrs Catchpole thought it might put you off your cooking.'

Louisa made a face. 'It might, at that.'

When they reached the kitchen she faced her helpers and told them whom they had been unwittingly serving. 'He said,' she lied, 'to thank you, one and all, for his lovely dinner.'

Even Ivy smiled gratefully at her. Poor little Mary was almost in tears.

A slight popping noise sounded behind her. She turned to see Mr Trotter advancing with an opened bottle of champagne and a little tray with tulip-shaped glasses.

'This'll make you all feel better,' he said, pouring deftly. He passed the glasses about and then held up his own. 'To Miss Leyton and her staff. May I add my own congratulations to those of His Royal Highness the Prince of Wales?'

They all drank. Mary giggled, spluttering. 'Ooh! It's gone straight up my nose!'

Louisa had sipped carefully. She liked the taste. Although she didn't say so, it was her first experience of champagne. She imagined she could take quite a fancy to it, given the chance.

The memory of it lingered with her as she combed her beautiful hair that night. She heard a creak and looked round at the door, half expecting, half hoping that it would open and Charlie Tyrrell would come in. But nothing happened. She got into bed. Then she got out again, took the sovereign from its resting place, and fondled it for some moments before placing it under her pillow.

She turned out the gas and soon fell asleep, to a fantasy of thoughts of Charlie Tyrrell, the sovereign, and the prince who had given it to her.

CHAPTER FIVE

Despite the formal reconciliation between Louisa and Jean, the latter did not stay much longer in Lord Henry Norton's employ. Something in her Scottish pride refused to let her forget the rebuff she had been given as a result of her own mischief-making. It was clear to her, as to everyone else, that the newcomer was making an unexpected impression on both Monsieur Alex and Mrs Catchpole with her eagerness to learn and her aptitude for doing so. Jean gave in her notice and went back to her native heath to live with, and look after, a maiden aunt, who eventually left her enough capital and income from it to become a maiden aunt herself, and persuade a niece to come and look after her in turn, in the *ad infinitum* way in which such things can progress.

Unknown to Louisa, the impression she had made had been anything but limited to the members of the household she served.

A few weeks after the triumphant royal dinner party, Mr Trotter announced a caller to his master. Lord Henry was in the library after breakfast, drinking a final cup of coffee over the *Times* leader page. His visitor was a sporty, good-looking man in his late thirties, with dark hair and green eyes. He was a major in the Grenadier Guards, but now occupied a post requiring a good deal more finesse than the mere military calling.

'Good morning, Harry,' he greeted Lord Henry with the familiarity of an old friend. 'Sorry to burst in so early.'

'Not a bit, my dear Johnnie. Matter of fact, I've been expecting you.'

'You have?'

'Oh, come on. I know what you're here for, and I apologise. I apologise.'

'What on earth for?' Major Farjeon asked, accepting Lord Henry's waved invitation to pour himself coffee and take a chair.

'My behaviour,' his host was explaining. 'Last night. I dozed off over the baccarat and HRH was offended. You've come in your official capacity to give me a wigging for it, haven't you?'

'My dear Harry, it wasn't even noticed. Except by me, and I was able to nudge you awake for your turn.'

Lord Henry said, 'Oh, thank God for that. Look here, can't you get him to play bridge? Much more civilised game. I mean, baccarat goes on so long. With bridge, at least it's usually over by midnight and some of us poor devils can get home to bed.'

Major Farjeon could sympathise all too readily. As equerry to the Prince of Wales he had to endure it all: the tedious, over-taxing meals; the prolonged gaming; the boring ritual conversations; the cold and damp of the field sports; the discreetly organised hide-and-seek after bedtime…

He nodded. 'As a matter of fact, he's playing bridge tonight. At Lady Savile's. Shall you be there?'

Lord Henry nodded without enthusiasm. 'I expect so. I've been asked. D'you know, I find his energy at the moment astonishing. He's — what? — coming up to fifty-nine. That makes me ten years younger, and I can't begin to keep pace. Anyway, if you haven't come to wig me, what is it you're after me for?'

Farjeon answered in a slightly uncomfortable fashion which escaped the older man. 'It's a domestic matter, actually. A … request for the services of your cook.'

'My cook? Oh, you mean my chef. Monsieur Alex.'

'No, Henry. Your *cook*. The young woman who cooked for you the other week when HRH dined here.'

'What? Miss, er, Leyton?'

'Yes. She is still with you, isn't she?'

'Eh? So far as I know.'

'I hope so. The prince, if you remember, was most impressed, and he'd like to borrow her. He's entertaining the Kaiser privately at Mrs Markham's next Wednesday. Now, can you spare the girl, do you think?'

Lord Henry wrinkled his brow. 'So long as she's still working here, I'm sure I'd be honoured. Some servant or other left, but I'm dashed if I can remember who. Soon find out. But, look here … do you think she's up to it? I mean, isn't she inexperienced, or something? It's quite an undertaking.'

'So was the other night,' the younger man reminded him, amused at the vagueness, which he knew was part of the inborn aristocratic mien.

'Yes, yes,' Lord Henry agreed. 'But that might have been a bit of a fluke, mightn't it? Is it fair on the girl? That's all I'm asking.'

'I'd say so. The brief impression I gained of her was that she's intelligent and rather ambitious.' Farjeon paused slightly, before adding, 'Capable of handling … the situation.'

'Oh! Is she? Oh, well, if you're happy about it…'

'I am. So I'll get on with the arrangements, may I? Assuming that she's still here, of course.'

'Ah, yes. Please do, my dear fellow. Please do.'

Major Farjeon sought out Mrs Catchpole and ascertained that Louisa was still, indeed, a member of the staff. Then he interviewed Monsieur Alex and went away, leaving the chef and the housekeeper to break the news.

'I congratulate you, Miss Leyton,' Monsieur Alex said sincerely. 'An honour for you.'

Louisa was not unaware of that fact. 'Thanks, Monsieur Alex,' she said. 'Yes, it is.'

'And what will you delight His Royal Highness with this time?'

Mrs Catchpole interrupted, 'That's all taken care of. They're sending the menu round in a day or two.'

'I'd want to do my own marketing,' Louisa said abruptly. 'I want my own vegetables.'

'There won't be anything wrong with their vegetables, Miss Leyton,' Mrs Catchpole replied, with a look at Monsieur Alex.

He said kindly to Louisa, 'When the menu arrives, I think you had better pass it to me. We shall go through it together. I shall instruct you in every detail, and you will have a grand success.'

To his considerable surprise, Louisa answered, 'Very kind, and I much appreciate it, Monsieur Alex. But I prefer to manage on my own, thank you.'

'Pardon?' was all the response he could manage.

'Well, there's no point in going, if all I'm going to do is serve it up — is there? I'm sorry, but it was me he asked for. Look, I'm sure if you'd done that dinner for him, he'd have been asking for you now. But you didn't, so...'

She looked from one to another of their incredulous expressions and went out of the housekeeper's room where the interview had taken place. They shook their heads sadly at each other. In neither of their experiences had such a phenomenon as Louisa Leyton been encountered.

When the day itself came, though, Louisa's *sang-froid* briefly deserted her.

'*All* the buttons, Mary,' she raved at the little Welsh girl, who was helping her into a simple but elegantly cut white dress. 'Don't miss any.'

'I won't, Miss Leyton. Oh, do stand still, please.'

'Well, hurry up!'

'I'm going as fast as I can. There. That's it.'

'Boots. Where's my *boots*?'

'Under the chair.'

'Give 'em here. Quick. Oh … they're too tight. Me feet must've swelled up with nerves. Push, Mary.'

'I am.'

'*Push!*'

At last she was ready, looking virginally beautiful in her white. All the other servants contrived to see her go to the carriage, bearing royal arms, which had been sent for her.

'We all wish you well,' Mrs Catchpole said, with almost a hint of affection in her tone.

'*Bonne chance,*' Monsieur Alex intoned, as gravely as ever. 'I take it as a compliment that my *protégée* has been chosen by the Prince of Wales.'

'Good luck!' said Mary and Ivy in chorus.

Mr Trotter winked and said, 'You look nice, my dear. No — I'll take your bag.'

So, with such civility and honour attending her, Louisa Leyton set off in a royal carriage to cook dinner for a prince.

All the discomposure Louisa had been experiencing left her soon after her arrival at Mrs Markham's house. The kitchen was smaller and inferior in equipment to Lord Henry Norton's. It was also less than clean. The resident cook, a fat old woman, stayed just long enough to see what Louisa looked like before making her pre-arranged departure to her room, in long-worked-up umbrage at having her position usurped for the evening by an outsider, and a chit of a girl at that. Louisa felt positively superior and proceeded to throw her authority about right and left.

'No!' she rebuked the elderly butler, Mr Pritchett, who was about to place a large floral decoration amongst the massed dishes on the dining-room sideboard. 'I'm putting this there.' She indicated a dish of pheasants, being carried by a young footman accompanying her.

The butler made way for the footman to put down his dish, then handed him the flower vase. 'Far be it from me to make any suggestions, miss,' he said, with the weight of years of office, 'but it is often the look of a room that contributes to a happy and successful dinner. Elegance might seem old-fashioned to a modern young woman, but I can assure you that His Royal Highness —'

Louisa cut him short. 'I believe in elegance, too, Mr Pritchett. Look at me. Aren't I elegant?' She smiled away his surprise. 'But I also believe in simplicity and things in their proper place. And the proper place for *that* is a lily pond.'

The old man couldn't help smiling, as he said, 'In truth, Miss Leyton, you are a most amazingly … confident creature. I can only say … I can only say…' He turned to the waiting footman. 'Oh, take the damn thing out!' When the man had gone, the butler addressed Louisa again, this time in a more ironic tone. 'Will you be requiring me for anything, Miss Leyton?'

She shook her head impatiently, her mind concentrated on the many duties before her. The old butler gave her a little bow and went out, thinking of more orderly times.

But even he had to admit, at the evening's end, that the dinner had been as successful as any he had ever witnessed. The Prince of Wales had been in his finest fettle, almost throwing himself at every dish, gobbling at it as voraciously as if he had been a starving man instead of a sated old glutton whose figure was its own description of him. But the other guests, less greedy and some of them with appetites affected by nerves in the royal presence, had also done ample justice to the meal.

At the prince's request, Mrs Markham had sent for Louisa, and once more she had curtseyed before that heavy-lidded appraisal, and had her hand held in the podginess of his. Now she was on her way back to Charles Street, in the same carriage which had fetched her, again escorted by Major Farjeon, with whom she had begun to feel considerably at ease.

'Always cook the potatoes and the beans and the asparagus yourself,' she was pontificating at him, as they creaked through the gaslit streets. 'My rule is not to leave 'em to a scullery maid or anyone else with no brains. I tell you, I take more trouble with the cabbage than most cooks do with a chicken. I take trouble with the chicken, of course, but I won't chop it up and decorate it with all sorts of stuff that's not going to be used. If it's a chicken, you want it tasting like a chicken, don't you?'

Farjeon, quietly amused, confessed that he did.

'No messing things up, that's what I believe,' she went on. 'Leave things with their natural flavour.'

'Did you, er, learn all this from your mother?'

'Her? She's not interested in cooking. You can't be, if you can't afford to buy good food. I mean, it was easy tonight. Anyone could've done it.'

'Have you a large family, Miss Leyton?'

'No. Just my father and mother, and a brother. That's all.'

'What does your father do?'

'He's a clockmaker and repairer. Only part-time, though. I dunno why. He used to have his business, but he doesn't seem interested any more.' She smiled at him in the gloom. 'But my mother's side of the family, they're engravers. My grandfather made part of the queen's coronation crown. Least, I think he did. So, you see? I've got some connection with royalty, haven't I?'

'Oh, yes,' he agreed with a grin. 'Anyway, you're a … royal cook now.' She reflected upon that in silence for some moments. Then he asked, 'What about your brother? What does he do?'

'He's a soldier. In South Africa.' Then she surprised her companion by adding suddenly, 'Wish I'd been a boy.'

'You don't really?'

'I do. Wake up every morning hoping for the miracle.'

'But why?'

'Well … cooking, for one thing. How many women are *maîtres chefs?* I've always thought boys get a better chance in life.'

'I don't agree,' Farjeon insisted. 'Think of all the beautiful women through the ages — loved and pampered and doted on…'

Her sharp laugh interrupted him. 'Cor! I wouldn't want that. It's not my way of living. You're in the fellers' power, and what happens when they go off and leave you? What's a woman to do then?'

He regarded her speculatively. He seemed about to renew the conversation, but turned his head away to look out of the window. They were passing along Park Lane and would be in Charles Street in a few minutes. Louisa decided she must ask a question which had been hovering on her lips for some time.

'Excuse me, sir…'

He turned to look at her again.

'Do I … get paid anything for this evening?'

To her relief he smiled and said, 'My goodness, I'd almost forgotten!' He felt in his breast pocket.

'Sorry for asking, only…'

'No, no. Quite right.' He had produced an envelope and handed it to her. She thanked him and put it away in her bag without opening it. But he was delving into another pocket, in his overcoat. He brought out a small box and put it into her hands.

'And this is a small token from the prince. He intended giving it to you personally, but the Kaiser detained him, so he entrusted the pleasant task to me. He sends it with his thanks to you for a most successful and enjoyable dinner.'

Louisa had not opened the box. He looked enquiringly at her.

'Another sovereign?' she speculated.

'Look and see.'

She did, and gasped aloud to find a small gold pendant on a slender chain. The major helped her loosen her coat and gently pulled down the back of its collar, to enable her to pass the chain around her neck. He fastened its clip for her, then sat back with an admiring smile.

Whatever next? she thought, but she did not say it.

The carriage halted outside the tall, looming house. It was midnight, but she saw that the hall lights were still on. Major Farjeon escorted her to the area gate. He shook hands, with a little bow, and wished her goodnight. She heard the carriage clopping away as she opened the area door with her own key and went through to the kitchen region, which she found was also lighted.

Mr Trotter was alone in the kitchen, smiling expectantly.

'What you been waiting up for, Mr Trotter?' Louisa asked, surprised.

'It's my job to wait up,' he said, and indicated a decanter of wine and two glasses on a tray. 'Fancy a drink, Miss Leyton?'

'Cor, no thanks,' she said. 'But I'm famished. Haven't eaten anything the whole blessed evening.'

She went to the larder and came back with a plate of sausage rolls. She began stuffing them into her mouth while the butler poured himself some wine.

'Went well, then, did it?' he asked.

'Yeh. All right.'

She answered in so casual a tone that he looked at her sharply and asked, 'Nothing went wrong?'

Chewing hungrily she hooked a finger under the pendant and held it forward for him to see, replying with her mouth full, 'Got this to prove it, haven't I?'

He examined it without comment, then stepped back and raised his glass to her. 'I see it did go well. Clever girl. To the future, eh?' He drank, then added, 'With your looks, talent…'

'You ain't done so bad yourself, Mr Trotter. Butler to a lord, at your age.'

He nodded and said slowly, 'That's true. We make rather a good pair, don't we? Oh, Mary tells me you're studying French.'

It was true up to a point. Louisa had acquired a French-English dictionary and had been memorising the meanings of some of the French culinary expressions she had seen on menus and in recipe books.

'Monsieur Alex was very impressed when I told him,' he added.

'Oh! I was going to surprise him.'

'You did. *Very* impressed.'

'So he should be. Daft bloomin' language, anyway.'

Mr Trotter put her to a little test of his own. *'Bonjour, Mam'selle Leyton. Comment allez-vous?'*

Louisa frowned and said, 'Oh, I can't speak it or understand it. Just some of the names of dishes and things.'

This emboldened him to go on, *'Mam'selle, vous êtes très belle. Je pense que je suis amoureux de vous. Je pense que je vous aime. Voulez-vous m'épouser?'*

She had finished the last of the sausage rolls and was now only conscious of the tightness of her boots and of her general tiredness. She yawned. 'Look, stop babblin' all that stuff, Mr Trotter. I'm goin' to bed. Goodnight.'

She went wearily up the stairs. He remained standing where he was, the glass of wine in his hand. When she had passed out of sight he took a reflective sip, poured some more, and sat down to finish it in thoughtful mood. It was quite some time before he, too, sought his bed.

Later that week Major Farjeon came once again to the house in Charles Street. This time he came by appointment to see Lord Henry Norton. It was at noon, and they sipped Madeira together in the library.

'Something of a triumph, then?' Lord Henry commented after his friend had reported on the success of the dinner party.

'Absolutely. HRH was captivated. So was I, I may say. We all were. By the cooking *and* the cook.'

'Really? To think I had a pearl under my own roof and never knew it.'

'Come now, Henry,' Farjeon chided. 'Surely you haven't lost your eye for a pretty girl?'

'Damned if I have! Just that I've scarcely seen her. Come to think of it, I believe she is rather good-looking.'

Farjeon laughed, then asked with an elaborate casualness which even the vague Lord Henry noted, 'She must have a fair number of admirers, I should imagine?'

'Eh? Oh, I haven't the faintest idea. I don't believe we permit followers.'

'Even so, an enchanting girl like that … I mean to say, there must be someone.'

'Well, if there is I don't know.' He gave the younger man a sly look and added, 'You interested, by any chance?'

Farjeon didn't reply, but persisted, 'Your housekeeper would know. They always do.'

'I suppose she might.'

'Henry, would you mind asking her for me? I'd be most grateful.'

Lord Henry stared back at him. 'You serious, Johnnie?'

The answer was a nod. Almost reluctantly, Lord Henry walked to the bell beside the fireplace and gave its handle a sharp turn.

The footman who appeared was sent away to fetch Mrs Catchpole. Meanwhile, Lord Henry poured more wine for them both. Farjeon volunteered no more particulars of his interest in Louisa, and his friend was too well mannered to press him. Inwardly, he was chiding himself for not having taken more notice of this paragon he appeared to be harbouring.

When the housekeeper appeared he diplomatically consulted her about arrangements for accommodating a General Murray who would be arriving for an overnight visit. That settled, he allowed Mrs Catchpole to get halfway to the door before saying, as if from an afterthought, 'Oh, by the way…'

She stopped and came back a few paces. 'Yes, m'lord?'

'That young cook of ours … what's her name…?'

'Leyton, m'lord.'

'Ah, yes. How's she settling down after all that excitement the other evening?'

'Very well, m'lord. She's a level-headed sort of girl.'

'Good, good. Pleasant nature, I thought.'

The housekeeper concealed her surprise that he should be aware of anything about the young woman, except that he paid her wages, and he would have no idea how much they were. She was even more surprised when he continued, 'Tell me, you don't happen to know if anyone is … interested in her? Romantically, I mean. Any, er, runners in that department?'

'Well,' Mrs Catchpole managed to reply after a moment's quick thought, 'the only person I can think of with … that sort of interest in her, since you mention it, m'lord, is … is Trotter.'

'Trotter? My butler?'

'I have noticed he's been rather attentive to her lately.'

'Good lord! And what about her? Feelings … reciprocated, are they?'

'Oh, I wouldn't go so far as that, m'lord. I think she quite likes him, but I wouldn't care to say there was any strong interest. Not at the moment, anyway.'

'Hm! But from Trotter's side you think there might be … something serious?'

'Well, m'lord, if I may put it this way, I'd say he's got his eye on her, certainly.'

'I see. Just enquiring, you understand? Like to keep the staff's welfare in mind, you know.'

'Thank you, m'lord.'

Mrs Catchpole went away, pondering deeply the certainty that, whatever the truth surrounding this sudden interest, it had no connection with staff welfare. Her aloof employer left that department entirely to her.

In the library, Lord Henry turned to his friend. 'Well, Johnnie,' he said with a quizzical upturn of his eyebrows. 'You heard. Sorry to disappoint you, old man.'

To his surprise, Farjeon was beaming at him. He replied, 'But that's splendid, Henry!'

'Eh?'

'Now, this butler of yours. Trotter. Is he reliable? Discreet?'

'Of course he is. You've met him often enough. Dammit, Johnnie, what *is* all this about?'

Major Farjeon tapped the side of his nose. He said, 'It, er, would be a great help if they were to get married. Do all you can to push them into it — eh?'

For all of a quarter of a minute Lord Henry Norton gaped back at him, his mind churning. At length he said weakly, 'You … don't mean…?'

Farjeon's only answer was a nod. Lord Henry's response was to pour himself another glass of Madeira and drink it at one swallow. The major grinned at him. 'Not a word, naturally, Henry.'

'No, no … No, of course not.'

'HRH and I leave for Balmoral in the morning. Couple of weeks' shooting. Nice to have some news on our return. Put us all in a good humour for Christmas. Eh?'

He put his glass down and departed. Lord Henry Norton, most imperturbable of men, looked at his own empty one, filled it again, and sat down to drink it slowly, deep in wonderment.

CHAPTER SIX

'*Married?*' Louisa echoed explosively, then sneezed with equal violence. She had gone down with a sudden streaming head cold and had been sent back to bed by Mrs Catchpole, who now sat in the wicker chair, plying her with handkerchiefs. 'What do I want to get married for? I want to be a cook, not a wife. That's the last thing I want.'

Mrs Catchpole had anticipated a difficult task. It was proving to be one. 'Yes,' she pretended to agree. 'Only, you can't be a cook ... I mean, you can't go *out* to cook for important people ... unless you're married. That's the point.'

'Who says I can't?'

'Well, Lord Henry, for one. It's not suitable for you to go on like men do, my dear. It's a question of respectability. Of course, if you were married, all doors would be open to you then.'

'But I haven't done nothing wrong.'

'I know you haven't. But it's generally felt to be better, for all concerned, that you should have a husband.'

'But I'm not in *love,* Mrs Catchpole. And there's nobody in love with me. So that ends it.'

She was surprised to see the housekeeper smiling at her, saying, 'I think you're mistaken there, you know. I think there's someone more than a little fond of you.'

'*Who?*'

'Mr Trotter.'

Louisa lapsed into a further paroxysm of sneezing. Mrs Catchpole unbent so far as to pat her hand and tuck the sheets beneath her. Then she left the room to wash and change and find an omnibus that would take her to Wanstead, where she would be expected for afternoon tea, following a letter she had written on Lord Henry's crested notepaper to Mr and Mrs Leyton.

At the little house in Camden Road she found Mrs Leyton in her best, with sandwiches and bought cake and scones set out on the sideboard of the minute parlour. Mr Leyton was present, too, asserting his independence from the proceedings by carrying on working on the movement of a carriage clock. He kept a watchmaker's glass screwed into one eye, enabling him to be concentrating on what he was doing while leaving his hearing undistracted.

'We couldn't believe it when we heard, could we, dear?' his wife said in his direction. He grunted noncommittally.

'We're very proud, too,' Mrs Catchpole assured them both, referring to the royal dinner party, whose success she had just recounted.

'I mean,' Mrs Leyton went on, 'there's no telling where it might lead, is there? Invitations to cook in all the big houses. She might end up marrying a lord. Way to a man's heart is through his stomach, they always say.'

It was the cue Mrs Catchpole might have prayed for.

'How odd, Mrs Leyton!' she was able to say. 'That was one of the very reasons why I wanted to come and talk to you myself.'

Louisa's mother looked at her blankly. Mrs Catchpole continued.

'The question of marriage. You see, if your daughter does want to get on — and I believe she really has every prospect before her now — well, then, it would be much more suitable if she had a husband.'

Without raising his head, Mr Leyton asked, 'Why?'

'Because, Mr Leyton, it is a stamp of respectability. Cooks in charge of a household are always known as Mrs, as a recognition of their responsible position. But those who go out and about in society do well to be really married. It gives less rise to talk, in any circumstances.'

Mrs Leyton had been considering. 'There's plenty of young men round here always been keen on her. Respectable tradespeople, you know.' She addressed her husband's bent head. 'That nice young Belling, f'r instance.'

'She's got no time for him,' he muttered.

Mrs Catchpole leaned towards Mrs Leyton. 'What I can tell you,' she said, almost as though Mr Leyton were an eavesdropper there, 'is that there's a young man in our own household. I don't know whether she's mentioned him to you in her letters…?'

'No. No one.'

'Well — it's our butler. Mr Trotter.'

'Butler?'

'A very superior person, if you take my meaning.'

'Oh, I'm sure. You hear that, Ernest?'

'It's only my opinion, of course,' Mrs Catchpole reinforced her disclosure, 'but I think they'd make a very handsome and capable pair.'

Once again Mr Leyton spoke. 'Might I enquire if they love each other?'

'Well … they're both quite shy people, Mr Leyton. But given a little encouragement…'

'Our Louisa? Shy?'

But his wife snapped at him, 'Why don't you leave Mrs Catchpole and me to talk this over … dear? You could take your cup and your things into the kitchen.'

76

He ignored her. She turned eagerly back to the housekeeper and resumed, 'What ... sort of encouragement did you have in mind, Mrs Catchpole?'

'Well, I was thinking it would be quite nice if you asked Mr Trotter to tea. I'm sure he'd consider it a great pleasure and privilege to meet Louisa's parents.'

Mr Leyton gave one of his rare laughs. 'And what d'you suppose she'd have to say to that?'

His wife replied, 'If I ask Mr Trotter to tea, Ernest, it's no business of Louisa's.'

'I reckon it is. You can't force the girl to get married — not if she doesn't want to.'

'We're not forcing anything. It's a matter of arranging — for her own good.'

'That's quite right,' Mrs Catchpole was quick to agree. 'I've already explained to her the difficulties of unmarried cooks working out. I can assure you, Mr Leyton, from all my years of experience, it's most advantageous for girls like Louisa to get married as soon as possible. She wants to get on, and this is the best way of helping her. Lord Henry quite agrees, too.'

This was a certain clincher where Mrs Leyton was concerned.

'Lord Henry as well!' she exclaimed. 'You see, Ernest? It's very nice of you to be taking so much trouble, Mrs Catchpole. We'll speak to Louisa ourselves the very next time we see her and make her see it's for the best. And if Mr Trotter would care to drop us a line about coming to tea, we shall be only too pleased to receive him.'

She glared at her husband, ready to crush any defiance. He bent resignedly over his work and said nothing.

'Married?' echoed Monsieur Alex after a much-recovered Louisa had told him what Mrs Catchpole had said to her. 'You are far too young. You take my advice, my child, and concentrate on cooking.'

'That's what I want,' she said. 'But isn't it true that you need to be married if you want to get on?'

'Of course not. It's nonsense. Now, we continue with our lesson. *Crevettes à l'Indienne. Salmis d'Alouettes.* And you put all that stupid romantic stuff out of your head. Understand?'

'Yes, Monsieur Alex,' she promised, feeling much relieved. 'It wasn't in my head, anyway. It's in Mrs Catchpole's.'

Unknown to Louisa, though, Mr Trotter was at that very moment on his way to Wanstead, where Mrs Leyton was fussing over her tea table yet again. Her arrangements this time were more formal and considerable than on the previous occasion, and Mr Leyton had been commanded into his best suit.

The youth and dapper appearance of the butler impressed Mrs Leyton. She thought him positively handsome, and so polite to her, considering that he worked for a lord. Nor did he fail to give Mr Leyton his share of deferential interest.

'My word,' he said, stooping to examine the face of one of the clocks. 'Louisa has told me all about your skill with clocks, Mr Leyton. Is this one of yours?'

Mr Leyton shook his head. The maker's name was there on the face. Evidently the visitor hadn't noticed it. 'No,' he admitted. 'That's by a very famous French maker. This is one of mine. And this,'

Mr Trotter stooped again to examine the two clocks. He looked from one to the other, and then back at the first he had commented upon, and said, 'To be honest, Mr Leyton, I prefer your work — if I may say so.'

Louisa's father was not impervious to flattery. 'It's very good of you to say so, Mr Trotter. I'm hardly in the same class, though.'

'Well, of course, I'm no judge. But as a man in the street, so to speak, I'd say your work was … less fussy. I always think the best taste is the simplest.'

When Mrs Leyton brought in the teapot she was agreeably surprised to find the two men chatting freely. 'I was just telling your husband how fine I think his work is, Mrs Leyton,' their visitor said.

'Oh, yes. I'm so glad you think so, Mr Trotter.'

'This face here is very, very similar to one in Lord Bouverie's house in Eccleston Square. I understand it's by a most celebrated maker, but I'd be hard put to it to tell it from this.'

'There, Ernest! That's a compliment for you.'

'Yes, it is.'

'Now, come along, both of you. You sit there, Mr Trotter, please.'

'Thank you, Mrs Leyton. What a grand sight indeed! You wouldn't see many teas like this in Mayfair, I can tell you.'

'Oh! Wouldn't you?'

'No, you wouldn't.'

'Well … it's nothing, really. Do take a scone. They're fresh home-made.'

'I can see that at a glance, Mrs Leyton.'

Mr Trotter proceeded to do justice to everything set before him, praising the baking, the brewing of the tea, even the slicing of the bread for the sandwiches. As they all ate, he submitted himself willingly to their interrogation.

'Now then, tell us all about yourself, Mr Trotter,' Mrs Leyton began by inviting him. 'You seem quite young to be a butler in a lord's house, if you don't mind my saying so.'

'Ah, well, there's a story behind that,' he answered with an enigmatic smile.

'Oh! I hope you'll tell us it, then.'

'Well … you see, I never knew my mother and father … not for certain, that is. My sister and I were brought up on a big estate in Yorkshire by a lodgekeeper and his wife. They were childless, so it was an arrangement that suited us all. My mother, too, I presume. I was given to understand later — you know how people talk in a village — that my mother was the daughter of the titled lady of the big house, and she'd formed an attachment with one of the young grooms. Yes, and ran off to Italy with him. I was born in Naples. And then *her* mother went out and brought her back, just in time for my sister to be born. And that was that.'

Mrs Leyton was clearly riveted by this romantic narrative. Her husband asked, 'What happened to your father, then?'

'I'm led to believe he met an untimely end. Drink, they say, pining for his lost love. Who can be sure, though?'

Much moved, Mrs Leyton asked, 'And your mother, Mr Trotter? Did you never see her?'

'It's a strange thing, Mrs Leyton, but I remember vividly an incident on my twelfth birthday. I was playing in the park with Norah, my sister, and we saw a lady on horseback, quite close by, just watching us. I remember clearly she was wearing a … a pale-pink dress. Very beautiful. Then she rode away, and we thought no more of it at the time. But, looking back, I think *she was* my mother.'

'And that was the last time you saw her?'

He sighed. 'That's right. But ever since then, pink's been my favourite colour.'

Mrs Leyton glanced down at her own pink dress and thought how many happy coincidences you got in life. 'Do have another scone, Mr Trotter,' she said. He accepted readily.

'How did you get up to London, then?' Mr Leyton was asking.

'Soon after that time I was put into service as a hall-boy at a colonel's house nearby. Then he came to London and I was footman with him. Then footman to Lord Henry. Then, some years later, I was made his butler.' He gave them a conspiratorial smile. 'I seem to have noticed some ... hidden hand in my advancement.'

Mrs Leyton said, 'Well, I'm sure you've fully deserved to have got where you have, Mr Trotter.'

'It's very kind of you to say so, Mrs Leyton.'

'Not at all. And it's a great comfort to us, meeting you, isn't it, Ernest?' Her husband agreed sincerely. Mrs Leyton went on, 'You hear such stories about young women like Louisa all alone in big London houses. It's nice to know she's got you watching over her.'

'Oh, we're all devoted to her, Mrs Leyton. She's such a willing and pleasant girl. I'm sure she'll get on extremely well if she wishes.'

There was an awkward little pause, the Leytons hesitating to raise the matter Mrs Catchpole had come to see them about; he, apparently, wanting to say something which he was finding it hard to bring out. Eventually, he looked Mrs Leyton fully in the eye and said, 'As a matter of fact, Mrs Leyton, with, er, your permission, that is ... in the not-too-distant future...'

'Yes, Mr Trotter?'

'I ... I wish to propose marriage to her.'

'Marriage!' Mrs Leyton said, succeeding in hiding her pleasure under the feigned surprise.

'I'm extremely fond of Louisa, Mrs Leyton. I understand that Mrs Catchpole has said something about it to you?'

'Oh, not in so many words, Mr Trotter. She just said it would be a good thing for Louisa to be married, and she dropped a hint about yourself.'

'Ah. Well, there is that practical consideration to it, of course. But it's a more personal matter with me. I ... I'm devoted to Louisa for herself.'

Mr Leyton cleared his throat and asked parentally, 'Have you spoken to her at all?'

The butler shook his head. 'Not yet ... sir. I thought it more proper to speak to her parents first. I can assure you I'll do everything in my power to make her happy. But I may have trouble convincing her of that, if you understand me.' He gave a little nervous-sounding laugh.

'She'd be a fool to turn *you* down, Mr Trotter,' Mrs Leyton said emphatically.

'Well, it all depends whether my feelings for her are reciprocated. If I might have your permission to ask her, Mr Leyton?'

Urged on by the concentration of his wife's gaze, Mr Leyton replied, 'Well, she's always reckoned she wasn't the marrying kind. But speak to her, by all means. I'm sure her mother and I wish you the best of luck.'

Mr Trotter got to his feet and went round the table to shake his host and hostess gravely by the hand in turn. Mrs Leyton was tempted to draw him down and give him a kiss, but thought it might be a little forward and premature.

Shortly afterwards he took out his watch, made a joke about the ridiculousness of having done so in a room containing so many clocks, and declared that he must be getting back to London. Mr Leyton walked with him to the omnibus stop and shook hands warmly with him again before he boarded the vehicle. When he got back home he found the tea table uncleared, except for enough space to enable Mrs Leyton to work busily on a letter she was writing.

The letter reached Louisa the following day. Recognising her mother's hand, she didn't trouble to read it until her day's work was over. When she did, she flushed angrily and seized her hat and coat.

'You going out, Miss Leyton?' Mary asked, surprised.

'You bet I am.'

'But it's not your night off.'

'Who cares? I've had a letter, and it needs answering — in person.'

'But what shall I tell them…?'

'You can tell 'em there's a conspiracy goin' on!'

She slammed out of the area door. Mr Trotter heard the crash as he came down the kitchen steps.

'Was that Miss Leyton?' he asked Mary.

'Yes, Mr Trotter. She seems very vexed. She's had a letter.'

'A letter? Who from?'

'She didn't say. Just something about a conspiracy going on.'

Mr Trotter cursed inwardly that he had been putting off until this evening the carefully planned speech he proposed making to Louisa in the privacy of his pantry.

At Wanstead, an hour later, Louisa railed furiously at her parents. She had not taken off her coat and hat in the urgency of her fury.

'Bloomin' cheek! Askin' him here behind my back. What's goin' on, that's what I want to know?'

'There's nothing going on,' her mother protested. She had fully expected some stubbornness on Louisa's part, which was why she had thought fit to prepare the young man's way for him by writing the letter, but this was pure fury, and no mistake.

'What was he doin' here, then?' Louisa was demanding. 'The sneaky devil…!'

'Now! That's not a very nice way to speak of your future husband.'

'Future husband? Over my dead body!'

Her father ventured, 'Listen, Louisa. He told us he wants to marry you, and we think it's a very good idea.'

She sat defiantly, keeping her back very stiff. 'Do you? Well, he ain't said nothin' to me about it.'

'Because he knows the proper behaviour, that's why. He wanted to know our feelings first.'

'Your feelings. His feelings. The whole world's bloody feelings, except mine. Nobody asks about *them*, do they?' She turned to her mother, her tone changing to one of appeal. 'Look, Mum, he's all right. I don't *mind* him. But I don't love him, and I certainly don't want to marry him. I want to be a cook. I'm good at it. Just a cook, that's all.'

'But it'll help you at that,' Mrs Leyton said. 'Mrs Catchpole explained —'

Louisa shook her head hard. 'That's all bunkum. I asked Monsieur Alex.'

'Well, be that as it may, Mr Trotter's not just an ordinary butler, you know. He's a gentleman. His mother was a titled lady. He'll go far in the world, and if you've got any sense you'll go with him.'

'Oh, come off it, Mum. He's not all that much cop.'

'You tell me someone better, then. You should count yourself very lucky, catching his eye. If you keep him waiting he'll look elsewhere. There's plenty of girls better placed than you who'd queue up to marry somebody like him.'

'Let 'em, then. I don't need him.' Louisa got up again and went to the door. 'I'm not marryin' him, or anybody — and that's final.'

For the second time that evening a door slammed in her wake.

The butler was waiting for her when she got back, but Mary and Ivy were also in the kitchen. Before he could contrive to be alone with her she had bidden them all goodnight and gone upstairs. It gave him just the chance he needed.

'Louisa,' he called quietly from outside her bedroom door a few minutes later. There had been no answer to his knock.

'Go away,' he heard her muffled voice.

'Louisa, we ought to have a talk,' he said. 'We really ought. Please.'

He was relieved to hear movement, after which the door opened. She looked agitated, but there was no flush of anger in her cheeks.

'I suppose you'd better come in,' she agreed, then turned from closing the door to ask him, 'Look, haven't my mother, or Mrs Catchpole, or anyone else who's been pushing you at me told you the answer is no? No, no, *no*.'

'I just wanted to explain,' he said. 'I hadn't planned it to happen this way at all. It's … just that I do have sincere feelings towards you, Louisa, and I think we could be happy together. Happy and successful.'

The latter word perhaps made more impression on her than any of the others. She couldn't help being pleased that he seemed to feel something genuine for her. He was certainly a nice-natured man, superior in every way to any other who had ever wanted her to be theirs.

But she answered quietly, 'I don't love you. So just let's forget all about it.'

He merely nodded, the disappointment in his eyes quite touching her. To her relief, he made no attempt to persuade or argue, but left her room.

Two days later one of the footmen came to Louisa and told her that her presence was required in the library. This was, for her, unexplored territory. She had no direct dealing with Lord Henry. Instructions from him were given to her superiors, and sometimes delegated to her. Anything she was ordered to prepare for him to eat — even the merest plate of sandwiches — was served by a footman. She had not been summoned to the library before, and it seemed portentous.

To her surprise, she found the only occupant of the musty, book-crammed room to be her semi-confidant, Major Farjeon, dressed in morning clothes. He seemed really pleased to meet her again.

'Come in, my dear,' he greeted her. 'How are you?'

'Very well, thank you, sir.'

'You're still enjoying your cooking? Y'know, the Prince of Wales continues to talk about your accomplishments. I can tell you, he holds you in very high regard.'

'Thank you, sir,' Louisa said again. The compliment delighted her in a way that few others would have done.

'So much so,' Major Farjeon went on, 'that I'm sure he'll be asking for you again in the near future.'

'Very pleased to oblige, sir.'

He walked about a few paces after that, then clasped his hands behind his back and inflated his chest in military fashion.

'Yes,' he said. 'Now, er, we, er, come up against a problem which I'm sure we can overcome between us. Sit down, won't you?'

She obeyed this seemingly impulsive invitation. He himself remained standing as he continued.

'You see, in cases of this kind, there are certain … how shall I put it? … certain rules we have to observe. I'm sure you appreciate that. The prince feels … and I must say I absolutely agree with him … that it would be in everyone's best interests if you were not to remain a single lady. Now, I understand that the butler in this household —'

Louisa interrupted him, leaping to her feet agitatedly. 'Oh! Not you as well!' He seemed mystified. She explained, 'Everyone's trying to marry me off to him.'

The tall equerry seemed to her to be less than enthusiastic about his errand. He had to make a visible effort to continue.

'My dear Louisa … if I may call you by your name? We know each other well enough, I think … I hope … for me to be absolutely frank with you. You see, the fact is … the prince's interest in you is not confined to your cooking.'

He fell silent and looked at her, as if hoping for her help. But she didn't understand, and he had to go on.

'It extends to you *personally*. Do you follow?'

She thought she was beginning to, though it was unbelievable. 'To … *me*?'

He smiled reassurance. 'Well, you can't be so surprised, can you? You're an extremely pretty young woman. That's no secret. And the prince has let it be known to me that he'd … well, very much like to get to know you better.'

It was lucky for Louisa that she had not moved away from the vicinity of the chair on which she had previously sat, for she now sank back on to it automatically. 'Oh, no!' The room seemed to be going round.

'It doesn't alarm you, does it?' she heard Major Farjeon's voice. 'It's a very great honour, you know. When you consider that he's had the pick of the most beautiful women of European society. To have singled you out... However, he's above all things a gentleman, so he's entrusted me with the delicate task — for which I apologise sincerely, my dear Louisa — of finding out your feelings on the matter. Now, most importantly, I do hope that I have your trust, as well?'

'Yes, sir,' she answered numbly. 'But ... I don't think I could. Honest...'

'Yes, yes, I know how you must be feeling. It must seem like some fairy tale come true.'

'No!' she retorted, to his surprise. 'I mean, I don't *know* him.'

'My dear ... I can assure you that he's the most charming and courteous of men. You've met him...'

'I'm sure he is,' Louisa assented readily. 'But I ... I just want to be a cook. I'll *cook* for him any time.'

Major Farjeon looked even more unhappy. He said, as if having to force himself, 'I'm afraid that wouldn't be possible.'

Louisa shrugged. 'There's other people to cook for, then. I've already been asked —'

'My dear,' he interrupted her gently, 'you don't understand. If you were to ... fall from favour with the prince, you could hardly expect further invitations from his circle of friends. On the other hand, if you were to ... consent, your future as a cook — as anything you might wish to be — is assured.'

'I see,' she said flatly, as the whole notion sank in. 'Have I got any choice?'

'Of course you have! Good lord, I haven't come here to threaten you. If you refuse, I'm sure the prince will understand.

There will be no further word spoken on the matter. I'm perfectly sure you will find someone else to employ you on very favourable terms.' He sighed. 'But, if you want my private opinion, it would be a sad waste of talents indeed.'

Louisa sat unhappily silent for some minutes, while he stared out of the window, thankful to leave her to her thoughts. He did not turn round when she whispered at last, 'Why do I have to get married, though?'

'Because, my dear, the prince would never compromise a single lady.'

'Only married ones?' she retorted more spiritedly.

He turned to her again. 'After the … interlude is over they can return to the security of their family lives.'

Louisa suddenly began to laugh. She shook with it, and leaned forward, putting her hands to her sides. Farjeon watched her with an uncertain grin.

'That's how society carries on, then, is it?' she was able to ask at last.

'Most successfully,' he said. 'I promise you. Look, Louisa, Trotter's not a bad chap, is he? He seems awfully fond of you.'

She asked sharply, 'Does he know about all this?'

He swallowed, and answered, 'Lord Henry is telling him at this very moment. No one is attempting to deceive anyone.'

'I see,' she said, as a further sensation of numbness swept through her.

Major Farjeon came over to her. He stood looking down at her as she herself studied the carpet. There had been a moment, in the carriage returning from the royal dinner party, when she had suddenly wondered if he was going to put his arm round her and kiss her. If he had, so suddenly, at such a moment of anticlimax after the drama of that evening, she would probably have yielded. She didn't know that that very impulse had stirred in him, but that he had made himself hold back because he had recognised the all-too-familiar look in his royal master's eye as he had held the curtseying young woman's hand.

'My dear Louisa,' he said sincerely, 'we're all very fond of you. I give you my word that no harm will come to you. It ... can only be to your advantage.'

She raised her eyes to his. There was no contempt in hers. There were no tears. If there was anything he thought he could read in them, it must be sheer wonderment.

She nodded slowly.

CHAPTER SEVEN

'Here we are,' Major Farjeon told Louisa, who was sitting between him and Mr Trotter in the carriage.

They were pulling up in front of an unassuming little house in a pleasant Chelsea terrace, Regency or very early Victorian in its dignified modesty. They got out of the carriage to stand on the pavement, looking up at it. There was an air of unease about them all, which Mr Trotter tried to break by saying half-jokingly, 'We could take in lodgers, eh? Put up a sign over the transom: APARTMENTS TO LET.'

Louisa made no answer. Farjeon, taking him seriously, frowned and said, 'No, I think for the moment that won't be necessary. Shall we go inside?'

He held up a key and turned to the front door. Trotter glanced anxiously at Louisa, who didn't return his look, but followed, silent and unsmiling, after the equerry.

The house was charming inside, a bijou counterpart of some of the bigger ones past which they had driven in the previous minutes. It was elegantly decorated, in good feminine taste. To any eye, its carpets, curtains, wallpapers, furniture and ornaments were expensive, and there was in the atmosphere a sniff of new paint and paste and polish.

'Well?' Farjeon asked in the parlour, after showing them all round the house. It was Louisa whom he addressed, but her features remained unmoved.

Trotter said, 'It's lovely, sir. Thank you very much.'

'Good,' the major said. 'Well now, I, er … I'll leave you two together. I'm, er, sure you have a lot to talk about.'

'Thank you, sir,' Trotter repeated. Louisa still said nothing. She sat down, ignoring Farjeon entirely. He gave Mr Trotter a last apologetic glance and went briskly out. They heard the front door close.

Louisa roused herself at last. 'How dare they?' she demanded. 'How dare they do it to us — that's what I want to know. Pushing and shoving us around like we was sacks of bloody coal.'

He made no answer. She looked up at him challengingly.

'Well? Knowing what's behind it all, are you prepared to go through with it?'

He replied carefully, 'It's nothing to do with us, really, is it? That ... side of it. It won't last for ever.'

She stared contemptuously at him and echoed angrily, '"Nothing to do with us"? Don't you mind? About me?'

'Of course I mind,' he assured her. 'I wouldn't be human if I didn't mind very much indeed. But look at it another way, and there's honour attached to it. I mean, my wife ... the envy of...'

'Oh, come off it! Don't give me that guff. That was his line.'

But he had detected some sign of resignation in her eyes, sufficient to embolden him to urge her, 'Let's play their game, Louisa. We haven't any other choice, have we?'

He let her reflect in silence for some minutes. Then she said slowly, 'As long as it's their game, we'll make it *our* game.'

A relieved smile spread across Augustus Trotter's face. He knelt down to bring his face level with hers, though he didn't dare try to touch her.

'That's the spirit, Louisa!' he said. 'I ... I am very fond of you for yourself ... you know. And to prove it, I'm going straight round to the registrar's office to get a marriage licence.'

He was surprised to hear her say indignantly, 'Registrar's office? I'm not gettin' married in no registrar's office.'

'But … I thought … quick and simple.'

'Did you? Well you can bloody well think again. If I'm going to get married, I'm going to get married proper.'

'The Church of St Saviour, Pimlico, m'lord,' Mrs Catchpole was able to report to Lord Henry Norton in his library two mornings later.

'Good,' he told her. 'No last-minute snags?'

'Oh, no, m'lord. I think Leyton lost all her doubts, once she'd seen round that house.'

'Ah, yes. Marvellous opportunity for a young couple, you know. I'll be sorry to lose Trotter, though. Good fellow.'

'Will your lordship be going to the wedding?'

'What? No! Must I? I'm fishing on Saturday. Tell you what, Mrs, er… Champagne downstairs. That'll excuse me, won't it?'

Mrs Catchpole beamed. She was fond of a drop of champagne. 'I'm sure that will be much appreciated, m'lord.'

She turned to go, but he remembered something and called her back to his desk. After a little moving of objects and feeling under papers he at last located a small box. He handed it to her.

'Small token … for your part in all this. From all of us.'

She opened it. Inside lay a small but obviously costly brooch. She snapped the little box shut.

'Thank you, m'lord,' was all she thought it proper to say before leaving him.

Mary was ironing a plain cotton frock for Louisa, who was sorting through her cupboard and drawers, discarding some things and packing others. It was the evening before the wedding.

'Are you getting married in *this*, Miss Leyton?' Mary asked, indicating the cheap garment.

Louisa answered defiantly, 'What's wrong with it? It's white, isn't it? Do for a wedding dress.'

She took it from Mary and tossed it with deliberate carelessness on to a chair. The astonished Mary managed to say, 'I'm sorry you're going. This house won't be the same without you. Or Mr Trotter.'

'It's not what I want, Mary,' Louisa said quietly. 'It's other people.'

'But you do love Mr Trotter, don't you?'

'He's … all right. He's kind and he's done well for himself. It's not him. I just don't fancy marrying, that's all.'

'But it gets you out of service.'

Louisa laughed. 'That what you think?'

'Well, I wouldn't mind a nice, kind man looking after me. Having his children.'

Louisa made a noise of disgust. 'Cor, I don't want any of *them*. Haven't got time for 'em. Too much I want to do. Anyway, they always disappoint you.'

'But … you're sure to have them, aren't you?'

Almost to herself Louisa answered, 'Not if I can help it.' Aloud to Mary she said, 'Why couldn't they just have called me Mrs Leyton, and have done with it?'

The wedding was over. The servants had been joined in the kitchen of Lord Henry's house by Mr and Mrs Leyton. Champagne and beer were present in ample quantities, and plates of delicacies prepared by Monsieur Alex's own hands occupied every surface in the big room. Even Louisa, who had been quiet and pale beforehand, was now pink and animated under the effects of the wine.

'Just admiring your brooch, Mrs Catchpole,' said Mrs Leyton, also pink-faced and overjoyed. 'Looks new. Special for the occasion?'

'That's right,' the housekeeper replied, smiling outwardly and inwardly.

'Very becoming,' Mrs Leyton said. 'Oh, I can't tell you how glad I am — Mr Leyton and me — that our Louisa suddenly decided to accept Mr Trotter — Augustus.'

'A nice man, Mrs Leyton. Such a wise decision.'

'I'd have thought, though, that his lordship would have wanted to keep him on here. And Louisa, too, I mean.'

'Oh, no, that wouldn't quite do. In some households nowadays butlers are allowed to be married. His lordship is one for the old traditions.'

'I see.' Mrs Leyton still looked worried. 'What I'm wondering, though, with such a nice house to go to, is what they'll live off.'

Mrs Catchpole was careful not even to hint. Mr and Mrs Leyton had, of course, been told nothing of the truth.

'Don't worry about that for one moment, Mrs Leyton,' she said in her most disarming way. 'As I told you before, Louisa's best future is going out cooking in society. Much more chance for her than staying in employment here, or in any other one household. Now that she's married, she'll be free to accept any engagement offered her — even by bachelor gentlemen — with complete propriety. And Mr Trotter, with his manners and skill, he'll make a perfect partner for her at functions. You mark my words, before long they'll be in demand all over London.'

Mrs Leyton's face cleared. 'Oh, well, that's all right, then,' she said, and turned towards a new commotion attending Ivy, who was entering, a trifle unsteadily, with a modest-sized but beautifully piped wedding cake bearing a single candle.

Applause and enthusiastic shouts greeted it as it was laid carefully on the big table. Monsieur Alex, imposing in his black coat and grey trousers, held up a hand for silence.

'Today,' he began to address them all, 'is a happy day. Also, it is a sad day. Louisa —' his voice trembled slightly now — 'Louisa, my little *protégée* who is like a daughter to me … today she is taken into the holy state of matrimony. A most solemn state. Lucky is the man who has wooed her and won her heart. Lucky is our friend Mr Augustus Trotter.'

This produced renewed applause and cries. Glasses were poised ready to drink the toast, but he was going on.

'Louisa is a beautiful young woman, no one can dispute that. She is also a princess of the culinary arts, born with a rare and delicate touch for a cabbage, a chicken — for what you will. I know this because I, too, possess these gifts. But rarely have I seen them in one so young, and a woman, too.'

He smiled at Louisa, who gave him a little smile back, but who also thought of the time he had tried his best to dissuade her from her career.

You see, girl! she told herself. *You always knew you could do it. And, by God, you will, too, when this lot of nonsense is over.*

Monsieur Alex was coming to his peroration. 'She can, if she wishes, become *une reine de cuisine* — a queen among cooks. And now, I bestow on her and her husband my most tender and deeply felt blessings for a long and fruitful life together. I ask you all to drink to Mr and Mrs Trotter.'

'Mr and Mrs Trotter!' the cry went up from all around her, and Louisa thought how ugly the name was, when you came to listen to it properly.

Monsieur Alex was blowing his nose emotionally. Louisa went to him and said genuinely, 'That's very kind of you, Monsieur Alex.'

Ivy turned to say, 'He had to bake it secret. Didn't yer, Monsewer Alex?'

He made a deprecatory gesture. 'Though I do say it myself, it is a cake fit for a princess … and a prince, of course.'

'Thank you very much, Monsieur Alex,' said Mr Trotter, who had come forward to stand beside his bride. 'Much appreciated.'

'Now,' the chef instructed. 'First you blow out the candle together.'

They bent their heads and blew. The flame wavered, recovered, then went out.

'*Bravo!* Now you take the knife together. No, you must hold it together,' he said to Louisa, who was trying to get away with just placing a finger on it. 'So … and cut, while all of us wish.'

As she felt the knife going in Louisa looked round almost desperately for her father. He was standing near her, watching with what she read correctly as a mixture of sadness and concern. *Wish for me, Dad,* she almost begged. He gave her a little smile of encouragement and closed his eyes. Louisa closed her own, and wished fervently.

There was more clapping after the cake had been cut. Monsieur Alex then took the knife and swiftly carved half the cake into perfect slices of exact uniformity, which were passed round by Mary and Ivy while more drink was poured. Mr Trotter made a short speech, which was much applauded, and Mr Leyton, pressed from all sides, mumbled a few words which hardly anyone could distinguish. When his fainter applause had subsided, Louisa suddenly said loudly, 'Right, that's done. Got to go now, I'm afraid. Cookin' dinner for Lady Margaret Duff.'

The hubbub diminished into the silence of surprise.

Monsieur Alex said, 'But … tonight is your wedding night.'

Louisa was putting on her coat. Augustus Trotter, not liking the prospect either, grinned at the others and tried to make a joke of it in his wife's support.

'Keeping her at it, you see, Monsieur Alex. Not letting your teaching go to waste.'

'That's right,' Louisa said. 'Plenty of other nights for us. Whole bloody lifetime. Bye all. Thanks for everything.'

Without pausing to make any individual farewells she strode out, followed by her husband. The silence they left behind them continued until the door was heard to close. Then excited conversation broke out.

Monsieur Alex looked at Mr and Mrs Leyton. 'But … plenty of other nights to cook,' he said, shaking his head uncomprehendingly.

And there were plenty of other nights to cook, indeed. To Augustus Trotter's frustration Louisa accepted almost every engagement she or they were offered. The only ones she declined were those which clashed with ones already accepted, or those which she declared were not up to her standard. Every night saw them out making and serving. The dinner parties invariably ended late, and there were things to be done in the visited kitchens after them, so that it was the small hours of the morning before they returned to the pleasant little house which was becoming to Trotter to seem more like an office of an employment agency than a home.

Louisa would share a few minutes with him in their kitchen while he had a nightcap and she sometimes sipped a hot drink.

Then she would get up, give him a little peck on his forehead, and go yawning off to bed. He took the hint and did not try to trouble her, or even persuade her that he was, after all, her newly wed husband.

Louisa's name, as a cook, had spread in London society with what seemed to be almost magical rapidity. It was only a matter of months since she had been reluctantly taken under Monsieur Alex's tutelage, yet she was now acknowledged a mistress of her art. He had not exaggerated in his farewell speech: she had an instinct for it which surpassed anything she could have learned from anyone else, or out of books. Her memory was perfect. She had only to be shown something once for every detail of it to implant itself in her mind. Having learned the classic way of preparing and garnishing a dish of which she might never have heard before, she could thereafter do it exactly right herself, without recourse to notes. And she would add to its preparation some indefinable touch which transcended her employers' expectations.

Hostesses told one another. Pleased diners gossiped about this exciting new discovery. And, unbeknown to Louisa or her husband, word-of-mouth advertisement for her was discreetly but deliberately put about by one or two people in very high places, in part payment for the extra-culinary services she had committed herself to render.

Those services were not commanded immediately. Several weeks passed without any message reaching her. She gradually began to lose the fear, on waking each morning, that this would perhaps be the day. She relaxed and concentrated on her work, hoping against hope that she would be totally reprieved to get on with it in peace.

She was also able to get on with training her own cook, Mrs Wellkin, a pleasant-looking woman in her late thirties. From the moment of entering the house as resident Louisa had made it clear that she was not going to do any cooking for Trotter and herself. She would cook like a queen for other people in the evenings, but she would live like a lady during the days, waited upon by a general maid, Ethel, and a younger one named Dolly. Mrs Wellkin cringed under the lash of Louisa's blunt criticisms, but improved rapidly and almost hero-worshipped her teacher.

For his part, Augustus found the daytime an increasing bore. Deprived of his employment, except as a sort of temporary footman in the evenings, he had nothing else to fall back upon. He also felt acutely the loss of dignity. His career seemed to him to have gone into reverse, rather than to have taken the leap forward he had expected. And he couldn't prevent himself feeling a growing jealousy towards Louisa and her mounting fame.

One morning he wandered idly into the parlour to find her at her small desk, carefully writing out a menu in her beautiful hand. The French words no longer troubled her. She knew their spelling and meanings better than most of her clients did.

'Going to be long?' Augustus asked pleasantly.

She didn't trouble to look up, but replied offhandedly, 'Don't expect so.'

'Nice day,' he tried again. 'Thought we might take a walk by the Serpentine. Maybe a music hall this afternoon.'

'All right,' she answered, still writing. 'Don't mind.'

He stood watching her for some minutes, longing for her to throw her pen down and spring into his arms. She seemed to have forgotten he was in the room with her.

'Louisa...' he ventured at last, moving a step towards her. 'Dearest...'

He was about to touch her hair, but her sudden movement made him draw back swiftly. 'There!' she said, putting down the pen and getting up. 'Finished.' She gave him her charming smile. 'Get me coat, shall I?'

Before he could reply the door had opened and the little maid had entered. 'Excuse me, madam,' she said, 'but there's a gentleman at the door. To see Mr Trotter.'

Annoyed at the girl's having addressed this to Louisa, as though he were not to be entrusted with it direct, Augustus snapped back, 'Well, who is it, then?'

'A Major Farjeon, sir.'

He and Louisa exchanged glances. He could read plainly in her look that she was thinking the same as he — that the time had come.

He told the maid, 'Show him into the sitting room, Dolly. I'll see him there.'

The girl gave a little bob and went out. Louisa and Augustus regarded one another in silence for some moments. Then she shrugged, sat down at her desk again and drew up a blank menu card to resume writing.

They had not been wrong in their surmise. After the briefest of pleasantries the equerry came to the point. He named a date on which Augustus knew for certain Louisa had a dinner party booking. There could be no question of putting this to the equerry. Augustus didn't even try. He merely assented on his wife's behalf, and the go-between went away.

Augustus braced himself to pass the news on to Louisa. She heard it without stopping writing. When he mentioned the necessity of cancelling the booking she only shrugged again.

Four evenings later she sat before her dressing table, carefully making up her face. She was fully dressed in an evening gown which she had had specially made and which had been waiting several weeks for this occasion. Her hair had been done at a salon that afternoon. Much as she liked to play the lady at home, Louisa refused to let any maid dress her, nor even touch any part of her. In so far as she could hope to remain, she was herself alone.

She was carefully making up her face, conscious of the fact that her husband was downstairs, in his butler's garb, waiting to open the front door to her royal visitor. It was the greatest irony she could imagine in life. At least the Prince of Wales had made a point of sparing her from having to give him a meal. She had often imagined that sort of an evening: herself in her cook's garb, hot-faced in the kitchen until all was nearly ready; then rushing upstairs to change into finery; then going to join him in the parlour, where her own servants — her own husband, even — would gravely serve them the meal she had cooked, while they sipped champagne and looked on.

She knew, of course, about the prince's penchant for ladies, and had occasionally wondered how it was all managed. She had always imagined that he took his choice from amongst high society, where things could move straightforwardly, watched only by the blindest of eyes. But why her? Well, it had been said often enough to her that a man's heart was to be won by way of his stomach. She didn't believe for a second that she had won this man's heart, but it had certainly been his stomach that had introduced her to his attention.

As to what she would be expected to do for him, she had tried not to think about it. He would know and she would obey. It had to be as simple as that. She felt no more nor less revulsion than she did in regard to Augustus Trotter's advances — except that Augustus was certainly a more agreeable figure of a man. What she would just have liked would have been to be left alone by both of them. Plenty of other women had the talent, and no doubt the eagerness, to do for them what she was so reluctant to do, but how many women could match her as a cook? None, she reckoned, and thought miserably about the unfairness of life.

She had finished making up. She inserted the earrings through her recently pierced ears, then sat up and looked at the overall result in the mirror. 'God, girl,' she told her reflection aloud. 'Why'd you have to be born a good-looker as well? Cooking'd be more than enough.'

And then she heard the doorbell down below, and knew she was on duty.

As it turned out, the ordeal was not terrible. For all his grossness, the Prince of Wales, aged almost sixty, was both a gentleman and a gentle lover. There was nothing to embarrass her; nothing beyond what she knew to be 'ordinary'. It was all over before she had fully appreciated what was going to happen, and she thought she sensed a sort of apologetic relief about his manner, as if he had been ashamed of what he was doing, but unable to prevent himself, and was glad, too, that it was over.

He paid her the compliment of staying for more than an hour longer, just talking to her. Again, she was surprised. Without saying as much, but through his manner of saying what he did, he gave her the impression that he wanted friendship more than anything else — and even, it struck her, the kind of friendship a mother would give freely to a loved son. Everyone knew how coldly Queen Victoria and the late Prince Consort had behaved towards him. Perhaps he had to spend his days trying in vain to make up for it by eating himself into ill health and searching for the woman who possessed some quality which he had obviously never found in his lovely wife, the Princess Alexandra.

When he had gone, she went straight to the bathroom and took off the fine clothes with a feeling of relief. She bathed and put on a favourite old nightdress. Then she went to bed, knowing that Augustus would not want to come hanging around her that night.

She lay in the dark and thought about it all. About how absurd it was, a woman of her independence letting herself be hooked into a situation as tangled as this.

It can't be long, she assured herself again, thinking, with a little pity for him, of the prince's corpulent figure and his hacking cough. *Stick it out, girl, and you never know but what it'll all be for the best in the end.*

Before she fell asleep, her last thought was a regretful one. If she'd only played her cards right, she could have had a house equal to this one, and servants and money and all the trimmings. And she could have had the charming and handsome Charlie Tyrrell, too. At least she'd have known just where she stood then.

Ah, well…

CHAPTER EIGHT

Having survived the dread of her initiation, Louisa settled down happily into the process of furthering her real career. On at least five nights a week, and sometimes seven, she would be booked to cook dinner in some noble or rich household, with luncheon engagements in between. It became apparent to her how few inspired cooks there were in London. Good reliable ones still abounded, but their employers seemed to be only too eager to give them an evening off and engage Louisa for the most important functions.

Inevitably, she cooked on a number of occasions for the Prince of Wales, though never in her own house. Whenever he was the guest of people for whom she was cooking he would send for her to be congratulated. With an extra pressure of his soft hand around hers and a significant look into her eyes he affirmed his pleasure at their special relationship. On a number of occasions she was told by her employer that in accepting the invitation His Royal Highness had stipulated that she be engaged.

His visits to her house were infrequent, at intervals of several weeks. They amounted to only half a dozen in all. He was unfailingly kind and courteous to her. Her affection for him grew. She made the effort to be more ladylike in her speech for him, but he noticed it, laughed, and told her he liked her as she was. They laughed a lot together. He encouraged her to call him Edward, though she was careful to do so sparingly. She had heard tales of people of higher rank than she being misled by his cordiality into taking liberties with him, and how he had promptly put them in their place.

He kept a few belongings at her house — mostly items of bedroom attire and toilet things. She thought he felt a special pleasure about this little token of permanence. And whenever he visited her he brought a gift.

So she had become quite reconciled to the arrangement: pleased that so few demands were made on her, but not resentful when they were; and glad of this golden opportunity to establish herself on the highest plane of her true profession.

Augustus Trotter remained less happy. True, they were prospering under the arrangement, but that was all he could say for it. Egged on increasingly by his acidulated spinster sister Norah, who had taken to seeing much more of him — and, without Louisa's knowledge, borrowing regularly from him — he nurtured his resentment at the way things had worked out.

The century ended. And three weeks after this symbolic turning point the longest reign in British history finished when, on January 22, 1901, Queen Victoria died at Osborne House, on the Isle of Wight, after a brief illness.

It did occur to Louisa to wonder what it might mean to her personally, if anything. But she was so busy catering for the more raffish hostesses who saw the ending of the era as a blessed relief, and had hastily organised dinner parties in secret celebration, that she had little time to concern herself. Culinary matters were the only ones which raised her emotions.

'Call this a bleedin' mayonnaise?' she demanded of Mrs Wellkin in her own kitchen, one rare evening at home. She had been dining alone with Augustus, or 'Gus' as she had come to call him. As always at home, she had dressed superbly for the ceremony of the meal. Ethel had served the fish and offered the mayonnaise. Louisa had taken one look, flung down her napkin, seized the sauceboat, and stormed downstairs.

'It's curdled!' she accused her cowering cook.

'I … I followed the recipe you gave me exactly, madam,' Mrs Wellkin faltered.

'In a pig's ear you did. I'll tell you just what went wrong. The oil you used was cold. Straight from the pantry.' She had had no doubt of that, though her cook's expression was confirmation enough of it. 'When it got too thick, you bunged in some vinegar, and then more oil, and you beat it all up at once. Right?'

'I was in a hurry … madam. I thought it would save time.'

Louisa banged the sauceboat down on the table. The mayonnaise was too solid even to quiver. 'You can save time on most things,' she said. 'But not when you're making a mayonnaise.'

'I did my best, madam,' the humbled cook muttered, but her mistress was relentless.

'No, you didn't. That's the whole point. You mind wasn't on it.'

'I'm sorry,' the miserable woman replied, wondering whether a quick death might not be preferable. 'I'll be more careful in future. I'll pour it away.'

'Hold on, hold on,' Louisa told her, the quick anger gone just as speedily. 'Waste not, want not. Fetch us an egg.'

Mrs Wellkin obeyed. Watched by her and the awestruck Ethel, Louisa cracked the egg, separated it into a bowl, then proceeded to drip the curdled mayonnaise into it, drop by drop, beating the mixture vigorously with the wooden spoon she had seized in her other hand.

'Slow and steady does it,' she intoned, her eyes never leaving her task. 'And you can't beat it too hard.'

In the ensuing silence, Ethel took the chance to ask something which had been preoccupying her for some days. 'Excuse me, ma'am...'

'What, Ethel?'

'We was wonderin' if we could go and watch the funeral procession at Windsor? There's ever so many kings and princes and such to be there.'

Louisa went on beating concentratedly. It had not passed her thoughts that the man who would be walking immediately behind the queen's coffin, at the head of an entire Empire's mourning, would be the same one who kept a pair of his slippers in her wardrobe.

She knew she could easily ask for a privileged place to watch the unique procession herself. But she answered Ethel, 'You go and gawp if you want to. See the old girl off.'

'Won't you be going to watch, madam?'

'I take no pleasure in funerals.' She threshed the mayonnaise harder. 'See how much beating it needs, Mrs Wellkin? Oh, go and answer that, Ethel. It's Dolly's night out.'

The front doorbell had rung. Ethel hurried up the steps. Louisa beat the mixture for some time longer, then handed it over to her cook, wiping her hands dismissively on a cloth. 'Right,' she instructed. 'Now, keep beating. Add the rest, drop by drop. And let's have it livened up with a bit of tarragon, eh?'

Hitching up her evening gown, she went back up to the dining room. It was empty. She heard voices in the parlour and went in. Major Farjeon, in evening dress and retaining his hat and cane as a sign that he did not intend to linger, was chatting with Augustus. As soon as she entered the room, Louisa could sense an uneasiness in the air.

'Ah, my dear,' her husband said. 'Here's Major Farjeon. I'll leave you together.' He went out.

'Just passing,' the equerry explained to Louisa, shaking hands with her and looking at her searchingly. 'I've apologised to Mr Trotter for not having come by appointment, only I have to go to Windsor tonight. His … Majesty wants me to oversee some of the funeral arrangements.'

'Always pleased to see you at any time, Johnnie,' said Louisa, who had come to be on semi-comradely terms with him. 'Ooh!' she corrected herself, with a hand to her mouth. 'Sorry. It's *Sir* John since the New Year, isn't it?'

He smiled. 'Johnnie will still do,' he said.

'I thought you'd be on the Isle of Wight.'

'I just crossed today. My word, there are tremendous arrangements going on. Can you imagine ten miles of warships, Louisa? The pride of the British Fleet. They'll be lining the whole of the way across the Solent when the royal yacht passes with the coffin.'

'Phew! Takes your breath away a bit, doesn't it? Takes a bit of getting used to. How is … His Majesty?'

'He's stood up to it surprisingly well. He's not a … young man, and he's waited longer in history than anyone to become king.'

She smiled. 'I've heard him say he'd got used to the waiting. Some days he hoped it would never come.'

'So did many others, I'm afraid,' Farjeon said.

He was quite surprised by the indignation with which she retorted. 'They'd better not say that near me, then! Who are they? Who thinks like that?'

'Many in society — and the government. They see him only as a man of pleasure.'

'Huh! Blind asses!'

'Exactly. They don't realise how devoted he is to his people and country. He's waited so long to serve them, and never been allowed to.'

'What's he going to call himself? King Edward, or King Albert?'

'Edward, I'm glad to say. It will be the more popular choice.'

'I'm glad. Couldn't think of him as Albert. It'd seem like … someone else. Well, I suppose they'll all have their telescopes trained on him from now on.'

Farjeon met her look fully. 'Every minute of the day. He must be extremely careful from now onwards not to give ammunition to those who expect him to prove unworthy of his high position. That … that is really why I'm here.'

Louisa realised at once and replied, 'So he won't be calling for a while?'

He shook his head and his gaze slipped away. 'Not for the foreseeable future.'

She could not have failed to recognise his embarrassment. 'Come on, Johnnie,' she said softly. 'You don't have to go all round the houses with me. Let's have it straight, eh?'

'Louisa, he asked me to say that he will always cherish the fondest memories of your kindness — your friendship. But in the new circumstances, I'm afraid that the special relationship between you must regretfully be considered as over.'

Louisa was too sharp not to have sensed from his manner that something of this sort had caused him to be 'just passing' her house in the middle of dinner time. Her feelings were a bewildering mixture of relief and regret. She might have preferred the liaison she had not welcomed, but had learned to accept with some pleasure, to have ended less abruptly.

'I just won't see him again?' she asked.

'I'm sorry, Louisa. He hopes you will still meet as friends — in society. The lease of this house is yours, of course, and all the furniture and movables. If in the future you are ever in financial difficulties —'

She stopped him with a shake of her head. 'He's been kind enough already. I don't want to sponge off him.'

'All the same, times change. In case of need, remember you can always call on him. And now, I really must be on my way. Don't bother to see me out. Thank you for making my mission so painless … Mrs Trotter.'

She smiled reassurance at him. '"Louisa" will do fine still. I hope we're going on being friends?'

He smiled back. 'You know, Louisa, after two weeks of full mourning it's a blessed relief to spend a moment or two with someone as refreshing as you.'

'Go on!' she laughed at his solemn compliment. 'You've been taking lessons from him, Johnnie.'

'Well — if you'll kindly collect his things together, I'll send one of the valets round to collect them in the morning.'

He bowed and went out. The interrupted dinner forgotten, Louisa remained in the parlour. She wandered over to the mantelpiece. Amongst a profusion of ornaments and the gilded clock, flanked at each end by a coloured cut-glass lustre, there stood a pair of photographs in matching silver frames. One was of Edward, looking masterful and assured. The other was of his late mother, old, sharp-nosed and disapproving of everything.

Louisa addressed the latter aloud. 'Well, old girl. You tried all your life to change him. The only way you could do it was by poppin' off.'

'So it's all over then? You're free.'

She turned sharply when she heard her husband's voice behind her. He stood a few paces inside the room. His smile annoyed her.

'How do you mean, "free"?'

'You know. I can't tell you how I've prayed for it, Louisa.'

A retort was on the tip of her tongue, but she bit it back. 'I don't want to talk about it now, Gus,' she said. 'Some other time, eh? Just … leave me alone, and I'll see you in the morning.'

He went out disappointedly. She turned back to the mantelpiece, regarding the other portrait with the heavily lidded eyes and the jauntily held head. For a few moments she felt more emotional than she could remember ever having done in her life. Then she picked up the photograph in its frame and carried it to the middle drawer of her little desk. She locked it in there and took away the key.

A few days before the queen's death Louisa had had 'words' with Augustus's sister Norah. The women had little in common; Louisa's downright and open manner was in complete contrast to Norah's deviousness. Their different ways of looking at any subject often brought them into dispute, with Augustus nervously occupying the middle ground and trying to restore a pretence of amity. On this occasion he had failed and Norah had swept out of Louisa's house, declaring that she would never be seen there again, even if wild horses dragged her.

Early one evening, two days after Major Farjeon's visit, though, she was round again. She had known about her brother's and Louisa's circumstances all along — it would have been impossible to have kept them from her prying mind, anyway. Ever since the news of the royal death had reached her she had been speculating with increasing curiosity about its significance for the household in Chelsea. Now she could no longer restrain herself from calling there.

To her relief, Augustus, as she always called him in her stiff manner, was briefly alone, already changed for dinner. She demanded point blank to know what was going to happen. Reluctantly, he told her half the truth and had the rest bullied out of him. When she asked what financial provision had been made in recognition of the couple's services, and he admitted — after some hedging — that Louisa had refused to accept anything, Norah treated him to some abusive observations.

'It was up to Louisa,' he kept defending himself. 'She didn't want anything more from him.'

'Then what about you? How much did you get?'

'N … nothing.'

'*Nothing?* You're too soft by half, Augustus. Always have been, that's your trouble. You're the man. It should have been you dealt with it, not her. You should have made sure you got something out of it — to make up for the humiliation. But oh no, can't stand up for yourself — as usual.'

'Listen, Norah,' he almost dared to shout back. 'Listen! All I can feel is that I'm glad it's over … that I have Louisa to myself at last…'

'Huh!'

Louisa walked in at that moment, in a long plum-coloured gown and some of her jewellery. At sight of Norah she struck an astonished pose and said with coarse provocation, 'Wotcher, Nore?'

Norah drew herself up and turned down her mouth. 'Good evening, Louisa,' she nevertheless managed to say.

'And what brings you round here?'

'Surely I can visit my own brother?'

'Ooh! Seems to me the last words I heard you say were something about never darkening this doorstep again.'

'That's just Norah's way, my dear,' Augustus intervened hastily, earning a disdainful look from his sister and a pitying one from his wife. 'It doesn't mean anything, really. She just has to speak her mind.'

'Oh, I see,' Louisa said mildly. 'Well, let bygones be bygones. I've no objection to people speakin' their minds. I've been known to do it meself.'

She delighted in roughening her way of speaking in the presence of Norah, who never failed to react with a contemptuous stare which made her lean features even more sour and amused Louisa greatly.

'The, er, news from the Cape seems better,' Augustus resumed hopefully. 'Kitchener's pushed De Wet and his army right back across the Orange River.'

'Hoo-ray,' Louisa responded flatly.

'You must be longing for your brother to come home, my dear,' he ploughed on.

'Not much. No doubt he'll turn up one of these days, though. Looking for a hand-out.'

This was excuse enough for Norah. 'Yes, Louisa,' she said, with an attempt at cordiality. 'I was wondering what you were going to live on now.'

'Now?' Louisa said sharply. A glance at her husband told her that the matter had been under discussion before she had come in.

'After all,' Norah was saying, 'this must be an expensive house to run.'

'We'll manage.'

'But how? If you ask my advice…'

'I never ask, when I know I'll get given it anyway. You mind your business, Norah. We'll mind ours. Sorry we can't ask you to dinner. They're only cookin' for us two.' Louisa marched out of the room.

'Well!' Norah fumed.

'Please, Norah,' Augustus begged. 'Don't go on.'

She turned on him furiously. 'You married beneath you! You were one of the youngest butlers in the country. You were highly thought of — in a fine position, with a great future. She put an end to that. She dragged you down.'

He tried to speak to defend his wife, but she was relentless.

'You were always too trusting. Well, if you're to have any hope of leading a normal married life with her you must put your foot down.'

And to his intense relief she, too, left him. He went to the brandy decanter and poured himself a good measure. When he had finished it he poured another.

Louisa knew that he had been drinking rapidly by the way he walked into dinner soon afterwards. He quickly made inroads into the sherry and the wine, only playing with his food.

'Come on, Gus. Eat up,' she tried to rally him in a friendly tone. 'Mrs Wellkin'll be walking out in a huff if we send all that back.'

'I'm not hungry,' he said.

She was trying her best for him. 'Look, I'm sorry if I upset Norah,' she said, with rare apology. 'You know how she gets my goat.'

'She means all right,' he replied. 'She's ... she's a good woman. She's only concerned for our welfare.'

'Welfare, my Aunt Fanny! She wants to know you're still good for a touch.'

'How did you…?' he began to blurt out, then checked himself. He had never told Louisa that he was giving his sister money.

'Think I'm blind and deaf? *And* I can add up accounts.'

He turned on a wheedling tone. 'She is part of my obligations, dear. My mother would expect it.'

This was trying Louisa's sympathy too far. She ordered Ethel out of the dining room before resuming. 'Your mother! I'm sick and tired of hearing you and Norah going on about your great connections. You can't even put a name to them.'

He took some more wine and, after a few moments' silence, made the effort he had been working himself up to ever since the effects of the pre-dinner brandies had begun to make themselves felt.

'Louisa … love,' he said, a trifle thickly now. 'I've been meaning to say … that we're just starting all over again now. Everything's starting again. The past — it's over. I … I draw a veil over it.'

She raised her eyebrows. 'What d'you expect me to say to that? "How decent — how generous"?'

'I'm prepared to forget.'

'You're offering forgiveness. *You're* prepared to forgive *me*?'

'I married you and … and turned a blind eye.'

'You knew perfectly well what was going to happen. I was married off to you to make me available to him.'

'But I wanted you, Louisa. I'd have done anything. Anything to get you.'

She replied more gently, 'You knew how it would be, Gus. I did fight against it.'

He was becoming maudlin. 'I kept waiting. Hoping. No one would believe what it's been like for me. Never knowing when it would end. I hoped once he'd let you go we'd have a chance together.'

'Well, we are together.'

'*Really* together, I mean. Man and wife. I thought, all this time, maybe you'd get to like me a bit. Be ready to settle down. Maybe realise I could make you happy. And I could. I know I could.'

He drained his glass and filled it again. She looked at him anxiously. It was not like him to drink to excess. 'We get along fine,' she tried to console him. 'Nothing's changed.'

'I don't *mean* it like that. I want you, Louisa.'

She sighed heavily. It was a confrontation she had been fearing for a long time.

'We had a bargain, Gus,' she answered. 'I told you straight, I didn't love you. I still don't. I'm fond of you, but I don't belong to you, or to anyone. So, as to anything else, I can't promise, Gus.'

He shook his head in despair. His eyes were glazing now.

'There's no chance, unless you stay at home. If you're going to go on working out in other houses I won't be able to stand it. Wondering…'

'What do you mean?' she asked tensely.

'I'm not having you going to other people's houses. Meeting other men. They take advantage. The women are fair game. I know what goes on. I know what happens.'

He was starting to rave now and it annoyed her. Also, she could feel no respect for men who couldn't hold their drink.

'For God's sake!' she hissed. 'You always go with me. I'm always busy in the kitchen. What d'you think could happen to me? And get this straight. There won't be no one else. Ever again.'

'Only me, then,' he shouted across the table. 'It's my right. I've waited. I'm your husband.' The growing redness of his face suddenly turned to near purple. He lurched to his feet, knocking over his chair, and stood swaying, holding on to the edge of the table. 'I'm your husband,' he threatened, 'and it's my right to make you.'

A cold wave of revulsion swept through Louisa. She sat still and regarded him steadily.

'You're stronger than me, Gus,' she said quietly. 'You can force me. But if you do, it'll be the only time. And you'll never see me again.'

She got up quickly and walked straight out of the room and down to the kitchen, where she felt sure he would not so demean himself as to follow in his state. She heard the front door shut with a crash.

CHAPTER NINE

When Louisa reached the kitchen, Ethel, sensing displeasure, said nervously, 'There's a person been waiting to see you, ma'am.'

'What kind of person?' Louisa snapped back.

'Young. A servant girl, sort of.'

'Where is she, then?'

'Walkin' up and down in the street, ma'am. She wouldn't come in.'

'Why didn't you tell me before, then? In this cold! Fetch her now, before she's perished.'

The maid hurried out by the area door and returned some minutes later with a girl who was wearing a thin cape over her dress. She was shaking with the cold from head to foot. Louisa recognised her at once as her little Welsh friend Mary, from Lord Henry Norton's.

'Mary!' she cried, taking her by the shoulder. 'Here. Come over to the fire. Why didn't you say who you were? Why didn't you come in?'

'I … I didn't like, Miss L — Mrs Trotter,' the girl answered through chattering teeth. 'They said you and the master was busy.'

She swayed in Louisa's arms and burst into tears. Louisa jerked her head at Mrs Wellkin and Ethel, who were looking on intrigued. They caught her message and began bustling about heating up the remains of the soup and fetching a bowl and spoon.

Louisa forced Mary into a chair beside the fire and knelt to chafe her hands. 'You're frozen to the bone, girl. And so thin! What's happened? Here — you're not in the family way?'

The crying girl could only shake her head.

'What, then? Did you get the push from Lord Henry's?'

Mary rubbed at her eyes. 'No,' she sniffled. 'I ran away. Two days ago.'

'Two days? Where've you been sleeping?'

'Under the railway arches. But there's awful people there. I was afraid to go back.'

'Why didn't you come straight here?'

'I did. I walked past … hoped you'd see me. I was afraid to come in.'

'You daft ha'porth,' Louisa said, taking the bowl of steaming soup from Mrs Wellkin. 'Bet you haven't eaten for two days, neither.'

The girl shook her head.

'Then get yourself round this. Mind — it's hot as a jockey's breeches. Take it slow. Cor, I can't for the life of me think why you, of all people, didn't just knock at the door.'

Mary raised the spoon in a shaking hand, but had, indeed, to recoil from the scalding heat of the soup. She answered, 'Ivy said you were all different. You wouldn't want to see anyone you'd … been in service with.' She cast a furtive glance at the listening servants. 'She said you were a grand lady and wouldn't want to be reminded.'

'Did she, now? Well, there's some people I don't want to be reminded of, and she's one of 'em.'

'It … it was because of her I ran away.'

'Did she bully you?'

'It never stopped. It's never been the same since you left — you and Mr Trotter. And Monsieur Alex's gone, too. Couldn't stand the atmosphere any more, he said. They made me do everything — cleaning, washing, and fetching and carrying. Ivy hit me for being slow. And I got so tired…'

Louisa gently guided the spoon to the girl's mouth. This time she managed to swallow.

'Why didn't you tell the housekeeper?' Louisa asked.

'Oh, I wouldn't dare do that,' Mary answered, looking fearful.

'Wouldn't you, indeed?' Louisa said, her face hardening.

The next morning she was round at Lord Henry Norton's. She swept a protesting Ivy aside and marched into Mrs Catchpole's room with only a token rap at the door. She found the housekeeper markedly frailer than she had last seen her, on her wedding day. She noted a wheeze in the older woman's breathing when she spoke.

'I'm so glad she came to you,' Mrs Catchpole said, when Louisa had told her what had happened. 'Poor girl. I couldn't think what had become of her.'

'Your Poison Ivy's been up to her tricks again, that's what,' Louisa answered.

'Oh, dear!'

'Yes. But what're you going to do about it?'

The housekeeper replied mournfully, 'What *can* I do? I've not been well. The house has been so difficult to run since you and Mr Trotter left — and then Monsieur Alex. We've had a whole series of cooks on a month's trial each. Two of them were quite good, but only competent, really…' She made an effort and pulled herself together, even managing a little smile. 'But never mind my worries. I'm so happy things have worked out well for you, Louisa. I expect you were … provided for.'

Louisa shrugged. 'I've a house in one of the best parts of town. Servants to look after me. A bit in the bank…'

'And a devoted husband.'

Louisa merely nodded.

'Most women would envy you,' Mrs Catchpole said warmly.

Louisa shook her head this time. 'They'd be wrong,' she answered, to the older woman's surprise. 'I knew it at the time. From the minute I realised what was behind all the attention — all the special kindness I had from … the prince. Not that I wasn't flattered, mind. Quite cocky for a while. But the price was too high.'

'Too high? But knowing the prince must have … well, helped you … professionally.'

'In a way. Only, now he's gone — and he has gone, Mrs Catchpole — I'm beginning to wonder where it'll leave me. Too exclusive, maybe? "By Royal Appointment", sort of?'

'I don't think you need fear about that.'

'Well, I can't help doing. It's not only the big success that makes your name, you know. It's going on building up your reputation. *Keeping* it up, all on your own. Everything perfect all the time. It's a lot to ask, and no doubt there's plenty in the know who'd be only too pleased to see me make a slip.'

Mrs Catchpole smiled and seized an opportunity which Louisa's unexpected visit seemed to have sent miraculously her way. 'Lord Henry's giving dinner to the King of Portugal next Tuesday,' she tried to say casually. 'He's in town incognito.'

Louisa grinned. 'Oh, Carlos is no problem. He likes good no-frills English cooking — and lots of it. Give him oxtail or oyster soup, halibut, lark pudding, venison patty and three kinds of roast, and he's happy.'

'You see!' Mrs Catchpole cried excitedly. 'Who else would have known that?'

'Lord Henry'll probably get a decoration out of it,' Louisa said.

The housekeeper leaned forward and looked hard at her. 'And so might you, my dear, if you were to come back and cook dinner for him — just that once.'

Louisa had not seen this coming. She considered, then asked, 'How many for?'

'Twenty.'

'Tuesday's not much notice. Anyway, we're forgetting why I came to see you. What about Mary?'

A cunning gleam shone in Mrs Catchpole's eyes. 'Say yes, Louisa, and I'll make sure she's taken back,' she cajoled.

This time Louisa was ahead of her. She smiled back. 'Don't worry. I'll keep her myself. If I'm going to go on cooking I'll need someone to help me, won't I?'

With a civil nod to her old ally she got up and left. When she got home she reported her news to Augustus. Having had nothing to drink herself she immediately detected the spirits on his breath. She made no comment about it, though.

'You'd never believe the change in the place,' she said of the house in Charles Street. 'They've only learned to appreciate you in your absence.'

To her disappointment he only grunted ungratefully.

'It'll seem funny to be back where it all started,' she added.

He roused himself sharply. 'I don't want you going there again,' he said.

'Why ever not?'

'I won't have my wife in a menial position in that house, that's why. I mean it, Louisa. I won't have it.'

'But Gus, Mrs Catchpole was only asking me to do her a favour,' she explained gently.

'Then she should ask me. Must I keep reminding you that you're my wife?'

Disconcerted by this new and worrying facet of Augustus's character, Louisa got up to leave the parlour. He said in a hard voice, 'I haven't finished talking to you. We have to discuss our future.'

'Not now, Gus.'

'*Now!* We keep putting it off, but it can't be put off any longer.'

'All right,' she submitted, sitting down again. 'Let's hear what you've to say. You and Norah, I expect. I knew I'd get it sooner or later.'

He ignored the jibe and assumed a businesslike tone. 'We have to take stock. We live in a house that's much too grand for us. Everything we make — almost — goes to keeping it up.'

'You want to sell it, then?'

'Of course not. It's our only asset. All we got out of... We should use it.'

'How?'

'In the most sensible way. Let the spare rooms.'

Louisa gaped at him. 'Open a boarding house?'

'No, no. *Private* rooms — with service. For gentlemen.'

She tried to make a joke out of it. 'Oho! You get all huffy about me occupying a menial position, and then you want to give up our house to strangers, with me skivvying after 'em.'

He scowled. 'We have servants to do that. Don't you see? It will give us independence. A chance to keep up our station in life.'

'St Pancras or Waterloo?' she quipped again, but he was clearly in no mood for attempted wit. She became serious. 'All right, let's be practical, then. How much would we make out of letting three or four rooms? Precious little. There's no money in it, Gus.'

'There could be, if we budget carefully. And we wouldn't need Mrs Wellkin if you did the cooking.'

'Over my dead body! Locked up in this place all day and night, catering for a handful of mouldy lodgers who wouldn't know what they was eating? Just one booking like Lord Henry's, and I'd earn more than out of ten lodgers for a month.'

'But you don't know you'll go on getting bookings.'

She opened her mouth to retort, but had to reflect that this was what she herself had said to Mrs Catchpole that very morning. Would the king ask for her cooking in the way that the prince had done? If not, would it be noticed in society, that narrow world in which every snub or imagined fall from favour was so quickly seized upon and voiced about? To what extent had her popularity been due to the knowledge that she cooked 'By Royal Appointment', as she had put it? It cost far more to hire her for an evening than to pay a resident cook a little extra to buy some special materials, and until her advent society hostesses had managed their entertaining perfectly well.

All the same, she answered Augustus, 'All right, love, so we have to be practical. I know it's difficult for you. You're a butler by profession, and you can't very well keep it up and live in your own home. But letting lodgings wouldn't help that, would it? And it's different for me. I'm a cook who can go anywhere. So long as I'm wanted I'm prepared to work hard — all the hours…'

'You're my wife,' he reminded her weakly, and then spoiled his case completely by adding, 'Anyway, Norah says…'

Louisa jumped up. 'Norah can go and…!' She just managed to restrain herself because Ethel had come into the room. 'Anyway,' she added low to Augustus, 'I'm taking Lord Henry's booking, and we'll see how things go after that.'

In fact, things went splendidly. The afternoon following it Louisa had to call on Mrs Catchpole to collect her fee. She found the housekeeper much happier than at their last interview.

'It was a triumph, thanks to you, Louisa,' she beamed. 'His lordship was too ill to get out of bed this morning.'

'Ill?' Louisa echoed. 'You don't mean food poisoning?'

'Oh, no. Evidently the King of Portugal had so many helpings that he nearly passed out — and his lordship had to match him plate for plate.' They laughed together. 'Still,' Mrs Catchpole said, 'he said to thank you most particularly.'

She opened her drawer and brought out the envelope in which the money lay. She didn't hand it over at once, but looked at Louisa, sitting at the other side of her desk, and said, 'I won't beat about the bush with you, Louisa. He was overjoyed to hear that you're available again — if you won't misunderstand me. He's asked me to offer you the position as cook here, at the same salary we paid Monsieur Alex.' She sensed what Louisa's reply was going to be and added hastily, 'Don't refuse till you've thought about it, my dear. He'd expect you to work for him only during the season. The rest of the year you'd be free to take any work you liked. And he's prepared to take Mr Trotter back as his London butler on the same terms — living out.'

'Blimey O'Reilly!' Louisa murmured. It was a handsome offer indeed.

'Talk it over with Mr Trotter,' the housekeeper was urging her.

'No,' she replied decisively. 'I can make up my own mind. It's a generous — more than generous offer, and I'm tempted. But you see, Mrs Catchpole, if I'm ever to make a real go of my career I can't work for just one person — even for only part of the year. It would lose me my word-of-mouth, and it wouldn't be me, anyway. I'd be Lord Henry Norton's cook, not Mrs Louisa Trotter, special cook to all the best households. I can't go backwards, you see.'

Mrs Catchpole sighed and handed the envelope over. 'I was afraid you'd say that,' she said.

'Ta,' Louisa smiled, putting the envelope into her bag. ''Course, I don't know that anyone else is going to want me any more.'

Mrs Catchpole smiled sympathetically and produced another piece of paper. 'I could have told you that was so and you might have accepted his lordship's offer,' she said. 'As a matter of fact, though, I had enquiries about you from several of the other evening's guests. I made a list.'

She passed it over. Louisa stared and read out, 'Lady Paget. Sir Ernest Cassel! *Admiral Fisher.* Crikey! Half *Debrett*!'

She went home excitedly, having to suppress a childlike desire to skip. Only when she reached her own gate did her high spirits plummet, to be replaced by anger. On the front door was secured a long white piece of cardboard bearing the words ROOMS FOR GENTLEMEN.

Louisa ripped it off savagely and stormed into the parlour. Augustus was in his fireside chair, a glass of brandy on a small table near him.

'What the 'ell's this?' she demanded, flourishing the notice.

He had been anticipating this reaction and fortifying himself against it, though not to excess. 'It's obvious, isn't it?' he countered. 'I've decided to go ahead.'

'Go ahead?'

'It makes sense. Our savings won't last for ever. We have to have a regular income to keep our heads above water.'

'Just now, Gus Trotter, you could do with your head *under* water. We've already discussed this idea and decided against it.'

'*You* decided, Louisa. I say every little helps. From four rooms we could net, maybe, twenty pounds a month.'

'"Rooms for Gentlemen" indeed!'

'Discreet, Louisa. Only for the best people.'

Ethel made one of her untimely entrances just then, bearing the tea tray. 'Out!' Louisa ordered her. 'Out you get. We'll ring when you're wanted.' The girl backed out hastily.

'Now, you see here…' Augustus protested to his wife.

'Don't you "see here" me,' she snapped back.

'I … I don't understand what you're objecting to,' he said, less assuredly.

'That's what worries me, Gus,' she said without heat. 'You're always on about your dignity, your position in life. When you start putting signs like this up you're throwing it away.'

'I want us to be independent.'

'You were ready to work. Ambitious. Now you won't lift a finger. This whole idea is a way for you to sit at home and do nothing — except that.' She gestured towards the brandy glass. Her speculation had been made impulsively, but it flashed into her mind now that there might be some truth in it, whether he realised it or not. She suddenly felt sorry for him and wanted to help him. 'Gus, I told you I'm keeping my business on. I need you to help me run it. That way we can be independent. We can be together, as you want.'

He looked into the fire and muttered, 'I'm not a kitchen hand.'

'There's plenty of other ways you help. And prospects *are* looking up. Honest.'

He returned to his old theme. 'You're a good cook, Louisa. None better. But it's time you learned how to be a housewife.'

She flared up again. 'I'm *not* a housewife! Or a housekeeper! Or a house-anything! And don't keep trying to turn me into one. Let me tell you, when my business really gets organised — busier than now — it'll bring in fifty or sixty quid a week. That'll go into a bank account for both of us.'

'Sixty pounds!' The figure had shaken him.

'So, you see, we don't need to let rooms — because I deal with the *real* best people. And some of them will come here to consult me — to make bookings. Which is another reason I don't want this starin' them in the face!' Louisa bent the cardboard notice and snapped it in two. She tossed the pieces on to the small table, nearly hitting the glass.

She grinned at Augustus. 'An' you can put that where the monkey puts the nuts,' she said with finality.

With the addition of the willing Mary — being trained as Mrs Wellkin's assistant, and ready to work herself to exhaustion, if need be, in her gratitude to Louisa — she had a strong and capable team. Mrs Wellkin was by now capable of doing all the basic cooking to Louisa's own high standard, leaving her free to add the special touches and do the organising.

She had devised a system by which as many dishes as could be prepared in advance in her own kitchen were got ready during the daytime preceding a dinner party, or the day before where the engagement was a luncheon. Then she and Mrs Wellkin would go by cab to the house concerned, conveying it all in hampers and containers, thereby saving much time and flurry on the spot and enabling Louisa and her assistant to concentrate on the hot cooking.

Some of the kitchens and their equipment were already familiar to her, their deficiencies too, and they would also take in the cab any implements which Louisa knew she would want and would not find awaiting her. Whenever they worked in a house for the first time she took no chances and armed herself with a whole selection of her own assorted knives, mixing spoons, moulds, and even pans and an assortment of spices.

In counterpart to these positive changes in her arrangements there had been a major negative one. That was the defection of Augustus.

After Louisa's flat refusal to accept his scheme he had helped her on two or three more occasions. But he had put so miserable a face on things, and been so gloomy an influence on everyone, that she had told him candidly that he had either better make the best of things or stay at home. Genuinely unable any longer to play second fiddle to his wife and sustain the role of her serving-man, he had opted for this alternative — except that 'at home' in her absence now usually meant the Grenadier public house round the corner from their road.

'Come on, come on,' Louisa chivvied her helpers as they prepared to set off on one of these occasions. 'The cab'll be here any minute.'

'The sauce is nearly ready, Mrs Trotter,' Mrs Wellkin said.

'It'd better be. Mary, you sure you put everything in that box?'

'Yes, madam.'

'Good. Crikey, look at all these things! We'll start needin' two cabs if we go on at this rate.'

'You need a bigger kitchen, madam,' Mrs Wellkin said. It was only in proportion to the small house, although equipped with every necessity.

'Yes, we do,' Louisa agreed.

'Oh, what about the master?' Mrs Wellkin remembered to ask.

'There's something cold he can get if he wants it, isn't there?' Louisa asked offhandedly. 'Oh, hang it! We've forgotten the pâtés. Ethel, get 'em, quick.'

'I have, ma'am,' Ethel said, indicating another cardboard box.

'Good girl.'

Ethel seized on this congratulation to make a bid she had been preparing for some days. 'Please, ma'am — please, I could do more. I bin watchin' how you do things … an' now that the master doesn't go no more, I could help with the servin' and…'

'Hold on, hold on!' Louisa laughed. 'Let's take a look at you. Turn round … slowly. Mm! You're not bad looking, Ethel, I'll say that for you. Quite presentable. If you can pick up a bit of style — learn how to control yourself in all situations — I might be able to use you.'

'Oh, ma'am!' the ecstatic girl gasped. 'Oh, ta! Ta ever so, ma'am!' While the others giggled at her delight — except Louisa, who merely smiled — she glanced hopefully down at herself and said, 'Will I do like this, if I run and get a clean apron?'

Her pleasure faded as Louisa shook her head.

'No, dear. You won't be coming with us tonight. When you work in other people's kitchens they watch you — extra critical — and I don't want any of my girls showing herself up. You'll start with the basics, like Mary, tomorrow morning at six sharp.'

'Yes … ma'am.'

And so Ethel, who despite this initial disappointment could hardly get to sleep for excitement that night, joined Mary in the kitchen in the chill dark the next morning and began following her about, watching and copying every move in her routine.

With so many busy late nights to keep, Louisa had got into the habit of staying in bed until mid-morning, when she would be served her light breakfast with the newspaper. Then she got up, put on a decent enough dress to receive any chance callers in — though not so good that it might be spoiled in the kitchen — and went down to that part of the house, where her clean, crisply laundered apron would be awaiting her in its appointed place.

Since she and Augustus had separate bedrooms, and he followed no set pattern of life, she didn't know whether he was in the house or out of it, unless she asked the servants or chanced to meet him. It mattered little. He had almost no contact with the business side of things any more. She had asked him at least to deal with the bookings and other paperwork for her, but he had made no move to do so.

When Louisa came into the kitchen one morning at eleven Mrs Wellkin was standing, preparing a mixture for an egg custard, while keeping an eye on Ethel who was chopping parsley on a board. Mary occupied the end of the long table, sorting with her limited reading ability through a pile of correspondence and consulting the engagements book. The two girls got up at Louisa's appearance. She waved them down.

'I've been going through the bookings, ma'am,' Mary said. 'There's one for the 14th. Could you please quote for a dinner party for thirty-six, wines included. Lady ... Lady Beeo ... Byoo '

Louisa took the letter from her. 'Beauchamp,' she explained. 'Got it?'

'Beauchamp. Thank you, ma'am.'

'Who else?'

'The Markis ... Marquis of Thorne.'

'That randy old beggar!' The girls giggled and Mrs Wellkin flushed slightly. 'What's he want this time?'

'He's willing to pay up to three hundred guineas for a private supper for two. He says … ooh!'

Mary had realised that she was running headlong into a gaffe. She handed that letter also to Louisa, who scanned it scornfully.

'I might have expected. He wants me to be the other one — and at his own apartment. Six delicious courses, with a *bombe surprise* to follow. I'd give 'im a *bombe surprise,* all right. Nothing doin'!'

The front doorbell rang.

'Who can that be?' she mused. 'Is Dolly up there?'

'She's doing the bedrooms, ma'am,' Mrs Wellkin said.

'I'd better go, then,' said Louisa, who had not yet put her apron on. 'Where's Mr Trotter?'

Ethel said, a little apprehensively, 'He's at the Grenadier, ma'am.'

This early? Louisa thought as she went up the kitchen stairs.

The caller was a surprise to her, and a pleasant one. He was Major Sir John Farjeon.

'How nice to see you, Johnnie!' Louisa exclaimed. 'Come on in. The maid's working upstairs.' She made to take his hat and stick, but he held on to them.

'Just passing, Louisa,' he said.

She led the way into the parlour. 'Whenever you say that I get a very funny feelin',' she said, making him smile.

'It's a great pleasure to see you, my dear,' he said. 'As lovely as ever, too.'

'Thank you, kind sir. Well, sit down. Something to drink?'

'No, thank you.'

He appeared to be rather less than his usual easy self. A thought struck Louisa suddenly.

'What's up?' she asked. 'Not another visit?'

'No, no. Nothing like that. I, er, wonder if … if Mr Trotter is at home?'

'Matter of fact, he isn't. He's out this morning.'

'Ah. Most mornings, I gather. And evenings.'

'Johnnie,' she said meaningfully. 'Come on. Out with it.'

'Well, I'm sorry to say this, Louisa, but word has reached the palace that your husband spends much of the day in a public house near here. And that when he's had a few drinks he starts talking … about things he shouldn't.'

'Oh, no!' She had never suspected this.

'Apparently it's nothing malicious,' the equerry hastened to reassure her. 'It's partly boasting, partly feeling sorry for himself. He tells anyone who'll listen how his life has been ruined. Oh, I don't mean he gives the details, but there are … hints, you know. Enough to be dangerous, especially if they get stronger.'

Louisa sat in silent horror.

'So far the king hasn't heard,' Farjeon said. 'But if he does … His Majesty is completely discreet himself and demands discretion from others.'

She managed to say, with dry lips, 'He knows I wouldn't do anything to hurt him. Neither would Gus … not meaning to.'

'I'm sure. I admit I have a certain sympathy for Mr Trotter, and I realise this puts you in a very difficult position. But if the greatest possible damage is not to be done you must find a way to stop him.'

Louisa reached a decision there and then. 'Don't you worry, Johnnie,' she promised, getting up. 'I will.'

She saw him out, then went to the pass door and shouted down to the kitchen that she was going out and would be back in an hour or so. She quickly got her coat and hat and went out into the cold February morning, shouting for a hansom in a voice which caused a number of well-dressed passers-by to look at her with curiosity.

'Charles Street,' she called up to the cabbie through the little square hatch. 'I'll tell you just where.'

Not long afterwards she was again seated across the desk from Mrs Catchpole in the housekeeper's room, but her manner this time was less self-assured than on the previous occasion. Mrs Catchpole was shaking her head seriously.

'No, I'm afraid it's out of the question, my dear,' she said.

Louisa said, 'But you told me Lord Henry was keen to take 'im back.'

'Yes, but not without you. It was really you he wanted. A good butler's easier to find than a first-class cook, you know.'

Louisa's shoulders sagged a little. 'I'll be honest with you, Mrs Catchpole. I'm desperate,' she confessed.

'I'm sure it must be dreadful for you, my dear. I wish I could help.'

'I mean, *I* don't matter so much. It's the palace. Think what some of them scandal sheets could make of it.'

'I tell you, you must speak to Mr Trotter. Warn him.'

'I know. Only I don't seem able to talk to him any more. He gets on 'is dignity. If you try to lay down the law to him it only makes it worse.'

'He's been hurt very badly,' Mrs Catchpole explained. 'The fact that since you both left here he's not really worked at anything … I mean, been living off you, so to speak … He must have lost all belief in himself.'

'I asked him to take over running all my business for me. He wouldn't hear of it.'

'Because that would make you his employer. He'd be all the more convinced he was a failure.'

Louisa flapped her gloves exasperatedly. 'I'm fond of him, and I'm sorry for him,' she said. 'But it's no use if he won't even try.'

'I think you know the answer,' Mrs Catchpole said, rising. 'He has to be given back his self-respect and pride. My dear, I only wish I could help.'

Louisa made her way back to Chelsea on foot, wanting to think, scarcely noticing the people and vehicles about her, the incessant rumble of many wheels, the smell of horses, the verbal exchanges of their drivers. What did penetrate to her consciousness, though, was the shrill cries of the newsboys. There had been some particularly sordid murder in Camden Town and they were making the most of it to boost the sales of their halfpenny editions.

She went into a shop where a whole range of morning and evening newspapers was laid out on the counter and selected almost a dozen different ones, as well as some weekly journals specialising in small advertisements. Then she went on her way more briskly, and soon reached home.

There was no cooking engagement that evening. Louisa told Mrs Wellkin she would take the chance to get a good rest and ordered lunch to be sent up to her room at half past one. Then she locked her door, pulled up a chair to the bedside, and spread the first newspaper open on the counterpane. She turned to the 'Situations Vacant' columns and perused the likely entries with care. She spent the entire afternoon doing the same with all the other daily papers and periodicals, making separate piles of those containing nothing to interest her, and those others — the majority — in which she had made pencil markings.

Then she went through the latter again, reconsidering and eliminating. It was evening before she had narrowed down the possibilities to just a few.

Partner in Dairy — capital investment and share of profits.
High class Grocery requires manager with prospects of partnership.
Gentlemen's club seeks a Head Steward. Highest testimonials essential.

There were a handful of others. As she compared them yet again, wondering which she might have the best chance of persuading Gus to consider, her eye strayed quite by chance to an adjoining column in one of them. The advertisement stood out because it was boxed for prominence. Louisa read:

HOTEL FOR SALE.
Long-established Family Hotel for sale. Excellent position in Centre of West End. Permanent residents. Small, experienced staff. Present owner retiring. Lease and contents subject to negotiation. EXTENSIVE, FULLY EQUIPPED KITCHENS.

Her heart began to pound with strange excitement. She read the advertisement again, and then again. Then she took up her pencil and made on the paper the boldest of all the marks she had made that day.

CHAPTER TEN

'Well?' Louisa asked Gus. 'What d'you think of it?'

He didn't answer at once. His mind was awhirl with thoughts, calculations, uncertainties, fears, hopes.

They were standing on one of the pavements of Duke Street, gazing across the roadway at the mid-Victorian buildings opposite. The lower parts of some were shops; the upper, offices or apartments. But it was on one building in particular — the one immediately opposite where they were standing — that their concentration was focused. It was of modest appearance and a little dingy. It had no shop front and its function would have been difficult to determine had it not been for the small sign above its door: BENTINCK HOTEL.

It was the day after Louisa's search through newspapers. She had gone out early in the morning on an unexplained errand, leaving word with the servants that they were to request Mr Trotter to stay in for her, as she might be wanting an important word with him when she got back. He had waited accordingly, a little apprehensive about what might be in store for him. But she had come in again all smiles, and told him to get his coat and hat and come somewhere with her. She wouldn't say where, or give any sort of explanation. He had thought it best to obey, and a few minutes later a cab had dropped them outside the hotel.

They had gone in — Augustus thoroughly mystified by now — and Louisa had given the porter a letter which she had produced from her bag, and asked him to take it to the proprietor. A few minutes later that person himself had appeared. He was a stout, ageing man who looked unwell. He had greeted Louisa and Gus courteously and then asked them to follow him. To Gus's stupefaction the man had proceeded to show them all over the place.

The Bentinck had seen better days, that was for sure. The carpets on its stairs and landings were worn, the paintwork dingy with age, the plaster cracked and flaking in places. The sitting room looked as though it were never used, and, curiously enough, there was no dining room. There were only two bathrooms and few bedrooms, but a surprisingly large number of suites, each consisting of a sitting room, bedroom, bathroom and in most cases an extra small room, which the owner explained was usually occupied by a guest's own servant.

All the suites they were shown into were unoccupied. The others — about half the total — had permanent or semi-permanent residents, or were retained by gentlemen or married couples who kept their own furniture and possessions in them, ready for their use at any time. They kept to their own quarters and had all their meals served to them in their sitting rooms.

Having started the tour of inspection from the top of the building, which was much larger than its frontage suggested, the party reached the below-stairs region last. Louisa had given Gus's arm a squeeze of excitement when they set eyes on the kitchen. It was large and light and well equipped. A servants' hall adjoined it, and leading off it were a scullery, a larder and several small wine cellars, all well stocked. Like the rest of the premises, though, there was a run-down air even here.

'Well, Gus?' Louisa said again, and he turned to look at her eager face.

'A good class of premises,' he admitted. 'But gone to the dogs.'

'You'd be the boss,' she told him. 'I'd stick to the kitchen side.'

'It'd need a deal of modernising.'

'We could do that bit by bit. It can go on as it is for a while. Seems to be doing well enough.'

'He's made us a good price, I'll say that. Sixty years' lease *and* contents.'

'Poor old fellow,' Louisa said. 'I reckon he's not long for this world. Maybe the money doesn't matter all that much anyway.'

Gus stared back at the hotel. 'It's still a lot for us to raise,' he said.

'It'd be worth the effort, though, wouldn't it? What I can get for my house, plus the bit we've got put by. And it'll start giving us an income right away, and I can run my cookery from there. Anyway, Gus, it'll give you something to do — that's what matters. I don't like to see you moping so.'

He swallowed and said, 'If ... I do agree ... there'd be a condition.'

'What?'

'I'd need a housekeeper to assist. I'd want Norah.'

Louisa didn't answer. She stood looking across at the hotel, wrestling with her thoughts. At length she said, 'All right, then.'

He hailed a cab and they went home, by way of the estate agency from whom Louisa had obtained the letter of introduction that morning. A partner of the agency accompanied them back to the house in Chelsea. He was visibly impressed by its appearance and location, not having seen this couple as the kind of people likely to be living so stylishly. The interior of the house impressed him even more. He quoted a better price than Louisa had hoped even in her most optimistic moments.

When he had gone she and Gus sat down in the parlour with pencils and paper and worked out the sums. They found that the price for the house and the amount they had in savings would, as Louisa had hoped, just cover the cost of the hotel. But only just.

'Lucky he isn't asking more,' she said. 'We couldn't have managed then.'

He reminded her, 'They did promise you … if at any time you needed…'

'No!' she replied emphatically. 'I'd never accept that.'

He shrugged. 'Well, it's up to you.'

'No, Gus. I want you to take the decisions. That's half what it's about.'

'Well…'

He stared about the comfortable, elegantly furnished parlour. His thoughts travelled uneasily back to the shabby contrast of the hotel. And then he saw himself, important and busy, a man of property dealing on almost equal terms with gentlemen, instead of idling his days away with other servants in the Grenadier.

'All right,' he said at last. 'Done.'

The period of transition was not a long one. As Louisa had suspected, the owner of the hotel was mortally ill. She discovered subsequently that he could have asked, and probably got, twice the price if he had chosen to. London at the turn of the century had relatively few hotels. Gentlemen from the country needing a base in town more often than not owned apartments, or even a house, of their own. Their counterparts whose principal homes were in London had their secondary houses in the country, chiefly in the hunting and sporting shires or in Scotland. The diners-out tended towards places where they could meet *en masse*, where there was coming and going of both sexes and clamour and noise.

The residents of the Bentinck were mostly the kind of men who preferred privacy or indolence, and would tolerate slow service and shabby surroundings more than disturbing restlessness and efficient bustle.

Although Augustus was nominally in charge of the establishment, once it had changed hands, Louisa determined that it should retain its present character. She recognised its uniqueness and saw that this must be maintained. Some of its occasional occupiers she could not even identify from the 'Mr Smith' and 'Mr Brown' aliases under which their apartments were held. She thought she understood what lay behind this, and decided to ask no questions.

She made a point of introducing herself to those actually on the premises. They proved reticent and aloof; but gradually, by talking them round to the subject of food, she managed to draw them out, evidently to their own surprise. It seemed that the cuisine at the hotel in the past had been of about the standard to be found at any gentleman's club — baked, boiled, roast and grilled. Once she and her imported staff had thoroughly cleaned and re-equipped the kitchens, Louisa began to cater for her residents in a way to which they had plainly not been accustomed. She started a menu book, with a variety of favoured dishes against each name, and submitted a list of suggestions to each room every day.

This new regime was obviously appreciated, but it depended very much upon Louisa's own presence, as she discovered one afternoon on her return from cooking for a house party outside London. She found Mrs Wellkin in tears and mumbling threats of leaving. Louisa stormed up to the general office and confronted Augustus and Norah.

'I go away for only two days, and I come back and find Mrs Wellkin upset and ready to leave,' she shouted. 'Why?'

'All I did was send back her menus,' Norah answered, with a lift of her chin.

'You *what*?'

'It seemed to me that with only sixteen people staying in the hotel they were needlessly extravagant.'

'The hell you did! That was none of your concern, and you know it. Besides, she'd got my approval for everything.'

Norah smiled her chill smile. 'In view of the financial situation, Louisa, I should have thought that even you would have seen the need to economise.'

'No! The last thing we ought to economise on is the service we give. That's just where we can make our name.'

'You will go on playing the great cook, won't you? All you seem to be concerned with is your precious kitchen. I thought it was agreed that general decisions regarding this hotel should be taken by Augustus — and that I am the housekeeper.'

Louisa controlled herself with a great effort. 'All right,' she said, before stamping out. 'But I'll have no more interference with the kitchen arrangements.'

On her way down to the kitchen, she gathered up the porter, Jessop, an ingratiating man in his forties whom she instinctively didn't like, and Merriman, the waiter, lanky and antique, and herded them down with her.

'Trouble brewing,' Merriman muttered to Jessop. 'Knew it all along.'

'What trouble?' Louisa demanded, rounding on him.

'Couple more guests left this morning,' he told her. 'If many more go the shutters'll be up and we'll all be out on the street.'

Louisa stamped ahead into the kitchen. She picked up a rolling pin and banged on the table top, freezing everyone into attention.

'Now listen, the lot of you!' she commanded. 'This hotel is goin' to be a success. And it's going to make its reputation on its cuisine. Whether there's ten guests, or a hundred, they'll get the best meals in London. In six months we'll be turnin' bookings away. As for my own business outside, it's going to go on growin'. So whatever happens, no one's going to be idle. Everyone'll be treated fair, and there'll be no sacking. So carry on. And, Mrs Wellkin…'

'Yes, ma'am.'

'The menus stay the same as we arranged.'

'Yes, ma'am.'

'Right.' Louisa jerked her head towards Jessop and Merriman, the gesture taking in the stairs back to the hall. 'Get on with it.' They shambled away, and Louisa turned to her female helpers. 'Ethel, you'll take over the preparations for the German Embassy dinner.'

'Yes, ma'am. Only … I … I wanted to say that the kitchen at the Embassy's so small. Last time we had ever so much trouble keeping things hot. And when there's fifty or more places…'

Louisa had to agree. 'It's a problem we keep running into. I've been thinking about it. We'll use hay boxes.'

'*A* boxes?' asked Ethel, who had never heard of such things.

'H — *hay*. When I was a little girl my grandma used to put the porridge into hay boxes overnight,' Louisa explained.

'But we don't make porridge for the German Embassy.'

'You daft ha'porth! It's the process. You start the food in a big iron pot, then put it into a box packed with straw on the bottom and sides. It goes on cookin' in its own heat and in twenty-four hours it's done to a turn. For bouillons and fricassées and things it'd be perfect.'

'If you say so, ma'am,' Ethel responded doubtfully.

'At any rate, we'll try it out on the Kaiser's nephew.'

And they did; and it worked perfectly. Louisa kept the hay boxes in use after that and was able to cut down further on the amount of cooking needed to be done *in situ,* often under unfamiliar and inadequate conditions. Her freelance business survived the change of headquarters easily and began to pick up as Mrs Wellkin, Ethel and Mary became more proficient.

The same could not be said for the prosperity of the Bentinck Hotel, however.

Perhaps self-deluded by the nobly mysterious background he had created for himself, Augustus had assumed a most superior air. He spoke familiarly to the residents, and while a few of the more raffish of them appreciated this and enjoyed exchanging betting tips and risqué sallies with him, others resented it extremely. The two residents whose departure had caused Merriman's forebodings had gone because they regarded Augustus as a bounder and Norah, now dressing like a lady of fashion and trying to talk like one, as a jumped-up snob.

Louisa forced herself not to interfere in the running of the hotel. She had begun to fear that the arrangement had not had the beneficial effect on Gus which she had intended, and Norah's airs incensed her almost to screaming point. She concentrated all the harder on her cookery, and told herself that it was all that really mattered.

Inevitably, she sometimes had to be away from London for several days at a time, to cater for house parties in the shires. After one such engagement, she and Mary, who had gone with her as assistant, came back a day earlier than expected. It was evening when they arrived. They went straight down into the kitchen and found Mrs Wellkin and Merriman seated on either side of the range, their expressions reflecting each other's gloom.

'Evening!' Louisa greeted them cheerily, as they got to their feet.

'Good evening, ma'am,' Merriman said. After an initial period of suspicion of Louisa he had become quite attached to her. Unlike Norah she never upbraided him for his slowness and hardness of hearing.

'We weren't expecting you back till tomorrow, madam,' Mrs Wellkin said.

'We found we could catch the afternoon train,' Louisa answered, taking off her coat. Her glance fell upon a tray on the dresser containing two small chickens. She went over and looked critically at them, giving them a contemptuous prod with a forefinger. 'What are these?' she demanded of Mrs Wellkin. 'I told you never to buy anything but the best poultry. Anything else is a waste of money in the long run.'

'They were … the best I could get, madam,' her assistant said.

'Rubbish! Mather & Rudd's don't even keep stuff of this quality.'

'We don't buy from them any more, madam. They … won't give us any more credit.'

Louisa stared, astounded. 'No more credit? Why?'

'I went round to see Mr Mather himself,' Mrs Wellkin explained unhappily. 'He said our bills haven't been paid for ever so long.'

'What?'

'He said he and the other tradesmen have only been supplying us on your reputation, madam. But they can't any more. At least, not for the hotel side of things.'

Merriman said, 'There's only two guests left in the hotel, ma'am.'

Louisa was rendered speechless by the news.

He went on, 'Begging your pardon, ma'am, but it's ruination, that's what it is. Staff gone 'cause they've not been paid. Guests gone 'cause there's no one to look after 'em. There's only Jessop and me upstairs.'

'Where's Ethel, and the girls we took over with the place?'

'All gone, ma'am. Ethel was turned out last week. Miss Trotter told her she'd have to go back to being a general maid and stop helping you. She said she wouldn't, so she was put off.'

Alternate waves of fire and ice had been passing through Louisa's veins in these last few moments. Her face paled. Mary watched her anxiously as she heard her ask, 'Where is Miss Trotter now?'

'Lying down with her novel, I shouldn't wonder,' Merriman replied. 'It's what she usually is — begging your pardon, ma'am.'

'And Mr Trotter?'

'Café Royal, I suppose. He dines there most evenings.'

'Does he, now?' Louisa said grimly. 'Mary…'

'Yes'm?'

'You come with me.'

She led the way to the stairs. Mrs Wellkin and Merriman exchanged glances. They had identified the battle signal.

Louisa, with Mary in tow, emerged from the pass door and made for the office bearing the label MANAGER. There was a stirring from behind the hall desk and the bleary, red-blotched face of Jessop peered over it. His eyes seemed not to be focussing properly.

'Where you goin'?' he challenged Louisa rudely as she put her hand on the doorknob. 'No one's allowed in there.'

'Is that so?' she asked, and her tone caused him to make the effort to pull himself together.

'Mr Trotter said no one was to go in … ma'am. I'm supposed to take his orders and Miss Trotter's only.'

'Well, you just try and stop me,' Louisa told him. She jerked the office door open and beckoned Mary to follow her in. Jessop scrambled to his feet and made his unsteady way in the direction of Norah's room.

In the office Louisa and Mary stood aghast. The once neat, comfortable room was a shambles. Papers were strewn everywhere, including the floor. Empty bottles and glasses were on every surface. Cigar butts filled ashtrays and saucers, and the air was thick with the fumes of a tap room. It looked as if several drinking parties had been held there in succession, with no one making any effort to clear up between them.

'Find the cash box,' Louisa ordered. She herself went to the desk and began pulling open drawers. It was not long before she located the leather-bound ledger in which the day-to-day accounts were kept. She turned to the most recent entries and her mouth fell open with dismay.

'It's not possible!' she exclaimed.

'I've got the box, ma'am,' Mary said, 'It was in the safe. Neither of them's even locked.'

'Count how much there is,' Louisa said. She picked up some bills from the desk top and checked them against the ledger. None had been paid.

'Seven pounds, six shillings and fourpence, ma'am,' Mary said at last.

'Then that's all we've left in the world,' she was startled to hear Louisa say. 'Here.' She thrust the ledger at the girl. 'Take this downstairs and hide it in one of the ovens. Then clear off to bed.'

Mary had only just passed through the hall when Norah and Jessop came hurrying down the stairs. At that same moment the street door opened and Augustus came in with another man. Both were smoking large cigars and were grinning with the foolish expression peculiar to drunks.

'Hello, Norah!' Gus called out.

She went to him urgently. 'Louisa's back,' she told him. 'She's in your office.'

His expression changed dramatically. Leaving his friend standing swaying, he hurried into the office. Norah went after him and closed the door behind her.

'I … I didn't think you'd be back so soon,' he said to Louisa, with an attempt at ingratiation.

'Obviously,' was the cold response.

'I … had a few friends in.'

'Drinking some of our best wines, too,' she answered, flourishing a champagne bottle. 'And according to the accounts you've signed half the bar bills for weeks, and given free meals to every sponger in London.'

'Hospitality, Louisa,' he said in a wheedling tone. 'Good contacts for the future.'

'You mean you wanted to act the big man.'

Norah stepped towards Louisa and said, 'You've no right to speak to him like that.'

'Right?' Louisa flared at her. 'You talk to me about rights when this hotel… Not a bill's been paid in… Everything we made — every penny I slaved for and handed over to be put into the bank has been spent. Why, Gus, why?'

'I had to … learn. It's not been easy, you know.'

'Oh? Not easy to pour it down your throat and theirs?'

'I tried, love. I tried. If only you'd been closer to me…'

'I should have known,' she said. 'I should've known you'd try to put the blame on me somehow.'

'Well, why not?' Norah intervened again. 'You've ruined his life. He gave up everything for you.'

'Thass right!' Gus said, emboldened by this support. 'Everything.'

'You've never appreciated my brother, Louisa. How could you expect him to succeed as a common hotel manager? D'you call that a profession for a gentleman?'

'Gentleman?' Louisa echoed scornfully. 'He's little better than a thief.'

'Don't you dare say that about him. That money was as much his as yours. He is the owner of this hotel.'

'Owner be damned! I put him in here to run it — and with your help he's run it into the ground.'

Norah demanded of her brother, 'Are you going to let her speak to your sister like that?'

'Louisa,' he tried feebly, 'if only you'd stood by me. We…'

Her response was to fling the bottle she was holding, to shatter against the wall between them. Norah shrieked and frantically dragged the door open. Louisa was picking up another bottle.

'Out!' she was crying. 'Get out of my sight, Augustus Trotter.' She followed them menacingly into the hall. 'Take your bitch of a sister with you. And him.' She pointed at the bemused drinking companion. 'Yes,' pointing at the cowering Jessop. 'And him as well. Clear out, the lot of you.'

'Louisa,' Augustus tried once more, 'how can you run the hotel without us?'

'The hotel can go to 'ell! If either of you two shows your face in here again I'll smash it for you.'

She accompanied her threat by flinging the second bottle. It smashed against the door frame. Splinters of glass flew everywhere. It took no further words to send the four hurrying out into the night.

Louisa stood for some moments looking at the door through which they had fled. Then her shoulders sagged and she went slowly back into the office. The contemplation of the mess there caused her face to crumple and a tear to start into each eye. But she banged her fist against her thigh, gave an angry brush at her eyes with the back of a hand, and sat down at the desk to start sorting things out.

CHAPTER ELEVEN

After she had worked for a time Louisa got up from the desk, gathered a pile of paper, and went down to the kitchen. Mrs Wellkin, Mary and Merriman were there, looking heavily apprehensive.

'Thought I told you to go to bed,' she said to Mary.

'I … I didn't like, ma'am. With all the noise and that. I was frightened.'

'Oh. You heard it, then. All of you?'

'We couldn't help it, madam,' Mrs Wellkin answered.

'Well, you might have heard far worse if they hadn't slung their hooks when I told them to,' Louisa said grimly. 'Anyway, that part of it's over and done with. What we've got to concern ourselves with is tomorrow, and every day after.' She addressed her assistant cook. 'That offer you had from Lady Croxley — did you turn it down flat?'

Lady Croxley was only the latest of the titled people to have approached Louisa to become their permanent cook. When she had refused, several of them had made alternative bids for Mrs Wellkin's services. She had admitted to Louisa that she was tempted. The late nights' working didn't suit her and, much as she admired Louisa as a mentor, she was finding the pressure of work too much.

'I said I'd make up my mind, madam,' she answered.

'Make it up and take it,' Louisa told her candidly. 'You'd be in sole charge. It's a first-class kitchen and they're nice people. The fact is, I'm closing this hotel.'

They all goggled. She held up the papers she had brought down with her.

'See these? Bills. Two thousand eight hundred and nineteen pounds' worth. Run up by my husband — *former* husband, as he's going to be — and his cow of a sister. You wouldn't think it was humanly possible, would you?'

'No, ma'am,' old Merriman said.

'Well, it seems it is. So now you know part of the reason for all that shouting. And, Mrs Wellkin, that's why I'm advising you to take Lady Croxley's offer. I'm afraid I can't afford to keep you on. I've got to pay this lot off. Every penny.'

'I'm sorry, madam,' Mrs Wellkin said. 'I'd offer to stay on for my keep, but it just wouldn't be possible.'

'Don't worry, dear. I know you'll be well placed, and that's all that concerns me.'

'Nearly three thousand pounds!' Mary said incredulously. 'But if you're closing the hotel, how can we hope to pay it back?'

Louisa looked at her sharply. '"We"? Look, it's nothing to do with you, Mary. It's not your worry. I'm sure you'll have no trouble finding a good place. You, too, Merriman.'

The old man cleared his throat. 'If it's all the same to you, ma'am,' he said, 'I'd like to stay on here. Thirty-five years my room here's been my home. If I was to try to start again somewhere else, apart from that no one would take me, it'd kill me off. I know it would.'

Before Louisa could answer him Mary said eagerly, 'I'll stay with you, too, ma'am. I've nowhere else to go. If you're going on cooking you'll have to have help.'

'What do you mean "if" I'm going on cooking?' Louisa snorted. 'I'm going to cook all the hours God sends. For anyone who wants me and who'll pay the right price. If they want a French banquet, then they'll get a French banquet. If they want sausage and mash, they can have that. Still want to stay?' she challenged.

'Yes, ma'am.'

'Good girl. You, Merriman?'

'Please, ma'am.'

Louisa grinned at him.

'Who else'd be barmy enough to take you on?' she said.

And so the Bentinck ceased to trade as a hotel. The remaining residents were not sorry to leave. The place had never seemed the same since it had changed hands. The food had improved markedly, they conceded to one another, but the new proprietor, and especially his sister, had become the cause of growing dissatisfaction.

Mrs Wellkin accepted Lady Croxley's offer and departed. Louisa, Merriman and Mary were left the sole occupants of the uncannily silent building. To the astonishment of the others, Louisa ordered her bed to be brought from upstairs and placed against a wall of her sitting room, off the hall.

'And the wardrobe and the tallboy,' she commanded. Seeing Merriman shaking his head in bafflement she explained, 'If I sleep downstairs I can spend more time in the kitchen, can't I? And the more time I spend in the kitchen, the sooner I can go back to sleeping in my bedroom. Got it? Sunk in, has it?'

He went away shaking his head.

This little economy in timekeeping characterised Louisa's determined approach to her mammoth task. She slept only a few hours each night and worked ceaselessly the rest of the time, helped loyally by Mary. The one thing on which she refused to let herself skimp was the quality of her ingredients. There was another way to economise on that, however.

Every morning at four o'clock she made her way on foot to Covent Garden Market. The streets of London at this hour were in that transitional period where night life ended and day life began, with some degree of overlapping. Occasional noisy groups of top-hatted revellers wove their way homewards, or clustered round workmen's breakfast stalls, bandying good-natured chaff with men in aprons and smocks. Scarlet-painted mail carts, milk carts laden with full churns, high-piled country carts bringing produce, and newspaper carts with their string-tied bundles of the early editions, dodged, trundled and raced along streets mostly yet devoid of pedestrians. Destitute men and women lay or crouched oblivious in doorways from where they would soon be moved on to nowhere.

Covent Garden Market, in Bow Street, was a bustle of carts, porters, warehousemen and buyers. Long before she reached it Louisa could smell the fragrance of its massed blooms and the fresh scent of newly harvested vegetables, set out on trestles occupying almost every foot of space in the great hall and the streets surrounding.

It was to the food stalls that she made her brisk way, exchanging grins and winks with the porters who scurried about with piled baskets on their heads, sometimes so many of them that their carriers had to have boys to guide them carefully between obstacles.

A poultry-stall keeper arranging his wares saw her coming and broke off his whistling. He nudged his boy assistant. 'Thought I was tempting bleeding providence whistling. Here we go again.'

Louisa had come up to the stall now and was already prodding the chickens.

'Have mercy on the merchandise, Mrs Trotter, love,' he pleaded. 'It's done you no harm. Now I ask you, what harm's that poor bloody chicken done you?'

'Morning, Mr Smythe,' was all Louisa answered, continuing to prod.

'"Morning," she says! Like butter wouldn't melt in her mouth. Mrs Trotter, why don't you ever go and torment any of the other traders? Why's poor Ben Smythe got to be singled out?'

'Because you give me the best prices,' Louisa grinned back.

'More fool me. Thank Gawd I get other customers who'll pay what they're really worth.'

He gave her a leer, leaning forward a little. 'You like a bargain. How about a quick kiss and cuddle round the back of the next stall? And while we're there I'll nick you the finest cauliflower this side of Bermondsey Flower Show.'

Louisa picked up a quail and looked at it from all angles. 'No one kisses and cuddles me,' she replied. 'Least of all for bloomin' cauliflowers. How much are the quail?'

'Oho! That's different, eh?'

'Gerron! How much?'

He sighed. 'A tanner. Cheapest in the market.'

'Tanner for two?'

'For one.'

'I'll give you fourpence.'

'Fourpence?'

'And I'll take half a dozen.'

'Mrs Trotter,' the stall keeper moaned in mock desperation, 'I got a wife an' Gawd knows how many kids to keep. Oh, well. Wrap 'em up, Jamie. She's got that look on her face.'

Louisa granted him her smile. 'Thanks, Ben. And don't forget the finest cauliflower this side of Bermondsey Flower Show. And I'll wait here while you slip and get it.'

The man obeyed and Louisa moved on to make a few more purchases before returning through the increasing London bustle to the gloomy, silent Bentinck.

Later that day she had another bargaining encounter. This time it was in much more fashionable surroundings — Mather & Rudd's shop, where the best game, poultry, hams, pies and other foodstuffs were delicately arrayed in parsleyed surroundings.

'Have you gone barmy, Mrs Trotter?' asked Mr Mather, who had quite different voices for the gentry and for the rest, especially those trying to sell him something, as Louisa was now. 'You want *me* to buy from you, when you're already up to the eyebrows in debt for what you're bought from *me*!'

'I know I am,' Louisa said again patiently. 'That's why I'm suggesting…'

The shopkeeper seized a ledger and began riffling through its pages. 'I'll tell you exactly how much you're in debt,' he grumbled. 'Just to prove I'm not the soft touch you take me for.'

'I can tell you how much,' she answered simply. 'Twenty-eight pounds seven shillings.'

He had found the entry at that exact moment and stared across the counter at her.

'Right,' she said. 'Thank you. Now, in the absence of an apology, the least you can do is give me a hearing.'

He threw the ledger down, spluttering, 'Mrs Trotter! It's *you* owe *me*!'

'All I'm suggesting,' she went on, 'is a way to pay it off —
since I can't with money. My way, no money'll change hands.
You just keep knocking it off my bill.'

Mr Mather regarded her suspiciously. He was a sidesman of
his church. Louisa read his thoughts and grinned.

'No wonder you got gout, if you get excited like that,' she
said. 'Now then — how much do you charge for cooked
quail?'

'Half a crown.'

'Right, then. How's this for a proposition from me to you?
Two bob cooked.'

'Two shillings cooked?' he repeated, more interestedly. 'By
you?'

'With my own clever hands. Taste better than yours, won't
they? And even if you sell 'em for only two and a penny you're
still making a profit. All you have to do is hand 'em over the
counter and rake it in.'

He searched her eyes for a few seconds. Her reputation as a
cook was well known to him. 'How many can I have?' he
asked.

'Half a dozen today. By tea-time. Many as you want to order,
other days.'

Before any deal could be concluded the shop was invaded by
a fierce woman in bombazine. Louisa recognised her as Mrs
Carradine, housekeeper to Lord Ealing. She turned away to
examine some foodstuffs intently. In any case, the housekeeper
had made straight for Mr Mather without looking at her.

'Veal and ham pies,' she snapped. 'I'll take two.'

'Sorry, Mrs Carradine,' the shopkeeper said. 'I'm afraid we've
sold the last today.'

'What! This is getting ridiculous. It's every day the same.'

'Perhaps if you could call a little earlier, madam…'

'Perhaps if you could save me some.'

'Well, if I knew in advance how many…'

'Really! I am a regular customer, Mr Mather.'

'I do apologise, Mrs Carradine, but…'

'There's nothing more to be said, then.'

The black-clad figure swept out of the shop, sniffing loudly. Louisa turned back to Mr Mather, who was holding on to the edge of his counter so hard that the white of his knuckle bones showed through his skin.

'Not the most satisfied of customers,' she remarked wryly.

'I'm in the wrong trade, far as she's concerned,' he said. 'Need to be a bloomin' magician.'

Louisa eyed him. 'Why not be, then?'

'Eh?'

'You could have veal and ham pies coming out of Mrs Carradine's hat. Or her bloomers, too, by way of an encore.'

'What are you talking about now, Mrs Trotter?'

'Veal and ham pies, pork pies — any sort of pies you like.'

'You're not selling them, too?' he asked eagerly.

She nodded. 'As many as you'll take. I'll buy the pork, the veal and the ham, and I'll make the pies. All you do, Mr Mather, is smile at your customers and knock it off my bill.'

He asked cautiously, 'How much a pie?'

'What weight?'

'Say, a pound. Veal and ham.'

'Elevenpence-halfpenny,' Louisa answered without hesitation.

'Ninepence,' he countered. 'I can't go a farthing over that.'

'And I can't go a farthing under elevenpence-halfpenny.'

'I'd need a lot,' he said. 'Dozen of each.'

'All the more profit for you, then.'

'Tenpence-farthing,' he said suddenly.

'Done! Tenpence-halfpenny it is.'

'You said "Done",' he accused her.

'And they will be. Very well done, Mr Mather. Remember, we're talking about pies made by Louisa Trotter.'

Mr Mather suddenly held up his palms and smiled capitulation.

The Bentinck-based pie industry went into immediate production. Louisa had not delayed in buying her materials that very afternoon. Soon, every gas ring in her kitchen was occupied by a steaming pan, the ovens were heating, and the big table was piled with beautifully wrought pie cases. When Mr Mather received his first consignment promptly at eight o'clock next morning he sighed at the aroma, doubled the order, and carried off one of the pies into the back of his shop for a second breakfast.

So Mr Mather happily paid his price, and kept increasing the order as his customers' taste for the pies grew. But a different sort of price was exacted from Louisa herself. She was young, she was healthy, and there was no more physically and mentally resilient young woman in all London. But the strain on her was tremendous. Little by little the amounts owing on her bills went down, but new expenses inevitably cropped up. At times, when lack of sleep and excess of work and worry combined to press her spirits down to their lowest level, it seemed to her that she was merely managing to survive, and that new debts were replacing old ones. She juggled with her accounts desperately, followed the tried principle of settling with small traders first and leaving the bigger ones, who could afford to wait. She knew that some big shops gave more respect to a customer with a long-standing bill than to those who paid cash. All the same, it was a wearying period for her.

'Yes?' she called tiredly from her desk, early one spring evening, in answer to Mary's tap at the door.

The little Welsh maid came in. Glancing up, Louisa noticed that she, too, seemed gaunt about the features.

'What is it, love?' she asked gently.

'I came to see if you'd finished your tea and toast, ma'am,' Mary said, approaching the desk. 'Oh, look! You haven't touched either of them. It's stone cold.'

'Is it?' Louisa responded vaguely. 'Never mind. I didn't want anything, anyway.'

'You never *have* anything,' the maid retorted spiritedly.

'That'll do, Mary,' Louisa said in a less kindly tone. 'I'm not in the mood for arguing.'

When Mary had gone, with the cup of cold tea and the rack of untouched toast, she went back to her accounts. But after a time her eyelids drooped and she was soon asleep at her desk.

One afternoon Merriman opened the Bentinck's locked front door to a middle-aged couple, respectably dressed. 'Sorry,' he said in his brusque, deaf manner. 'The hotel's closed till further notice.'

The man said something to him. Merriman leaned closer, cupping a hand to his ear. The man repeated, 'We're Mr and Mrs Leyton. Mrs Trotter's mum and dad.'

'Mother and father,' Mrs Leyton corrected him.

Merriman stepped back and motioned them into the musty hall. 'If you'll wait here a moment,' he said, 'I'll see if she can see you.'

Mrs Leyton flicked distastefully at the dust on a chair before lowering herself on to it. She and her husband eyed one another with a look of unease.

Feeling like a child suddenly, Louisa threw on a clean apron and ordered tea to be served in her room. She went up and greeted her parents, whom she had not seen for a long time, and took them off into her overcrowded room. After some conversational skirmishing she learned that Augustus Trotter, back in service as a butler, had been to see her parents recently. Her mouth tightened as she listened to her mother's account of the interview.

'He adores you, Louisa. He really does,' Mrs Leyton concluded.

Louisa sighed. 'Yes. Makes it all the worse, doesn't it? He should never have come snivelling to you, though.'

'I think it was his sister's idea,' her father said.

'Everything's his sister's idea. Did she tell him to tell you what a bitch I am?'

'He just seemed to apologise mostly. Look, Louisa, girl. You can't pay it all off. Not on your own. You can't do the impossible.'

'I'm not on my own,' she retorted, making a stubborn chin.

'We don't count servants, dear,' her mother said.

'Well, I do.'

Mrs Leyton asked carefully, 'Hasn't ... hasn't *he* offered to help?'

'Who?'

'You know, Louisa. Your ... friend.'

Louisa stared. 'Here!' she demanded. 'What's that bloody Trotter been telling you?'

'Language, girl!' her father admonished her.

Her mother said uncomfortably, 'He didn't tell us anything. Sort of hinted that there was someone...'

'All right, Mum,' Louisa said. 'If there was someone ... and I'm not going to say if there was or there wasn't ... and that someone offered to help, I wouldn't accept. I'll be beholden to no one. Is that plain enough?'

'We'd help you ourselves,' her father said hastily. 'Only you know how things are with us.'

Louisa looked at him keenly and understood with regret why they had come visiting her. She had not been writing home lately, and the contributions she had been in the habit of making towards their living costs had been discontinued. It wounded her much to recognise that, even though they could see what difficulties she was in, they could still bring themselves to sponge.

She opened a drawer and took out her cash box. 'By the way,' she said, as casually as she could. 'I've been putting a bit by for you. I meant to send it on sooner.'

The glance which passed between her parents confirmed her suspicion.

'We couldn't take anything from you, Louisa,' her mother said, but she did not look her daughter in the eyes.

'No,' Mr Leyton said. 'I mean, it wouldn't be fair.'

Louisa held out the notes. She saw his hand twitch before he restrained himself from putting it out.

'No,' he said again. But she leaned over and put the money into his hand. He nodded silently.

'Well, since you insist,' her mother said.

'You're a good girl. Thoughtful,' her father put in huskily.

There was a knock at the door and Mary came in. 'Excuse me, ma'am,' she said, 'the veal's done now, and…'

Louisa got up. 'Thanks, Mary,' she said. 'I'll come straight down.' She turned to her parents. 'Have to go now. Thanks for coming. See you sometime.'

She went off to the kitchen, glad that the interview was over. But it had taken its toll. On top of the labour and stress of the past few months, not to mention the uncertainty about what Augustus might take it into his head to do one of these days, she felt suddenly vulnerable and alone in the face of the crippling debt. She had thought more than once of selling the lease of the hotel, but she would have to pass a share of the proceeds on to him, and she would still not have anything like enough to clear her debt. Besides, she would be depriving herself of her kitchen headquarters. Nothing smaller would suffice. She seemed to be trapped, hemmed in from all sides.

Autumn passed. The approach of the Christmas season brought an increased flood of catering engagements.

'Three more enquiries, madam,' Merriman said, referring to a piece of paper. 'The Duchess of Launde on January the second, luncheon for twelve. Lady Blackwater, also on the second, supper for four. Mrs Lionel Watson, fifth, dinner for —'

'Accept,' she interrupted, going on working at the kitchen table.

'Which?' he asked.

'All of them. All three.'

The old man protested. 'I don't see how you can. On the fifth you're already doing a luncheon for twelve at the —'

'Accept them. We'll manage.'

She turned at an unmistakable sound and saw that Mary had slumped into a chair in tears.

'All right, Merriman,' Louisa said with a jerk of her head. He went off back to the hall. She wiped her hands and went to comfort the girl.

'Go and rest, love,' she said when the worst of the crying was over.

'I can't, ma'am,' the girl muttered desperately. 'There's the pans to scour, the fish to clean, the veg to do, and we've —'

'Go and rest. Go on. Forty winks. Well, thirty-nine.'

'*You* don't rest. You never rest.'

'Even just ten minutes' lie-down will do you good.'

'I could have cleaned the fish in that time.'

'You're a good girl, Mary,' Louisa said, touched and a little emotional. 'I don't know what I'd do without your help. I don't truly. And it's all for my benefit. It's *me* we're working for. What'll you ever get out of it?'

A large pan began to boil over. Louisa went to the stove and grasped the handle. To her dismay she found that she couldn't lift the pan. Suddenly panicky, she turned appealingly to Mary. The girl jumped up and hurried to perform the task for her. Then she guided Louisa to a chair. She sank down, and shook and shook.

CHAPTER TWELVE

'How long has this suicidal business been going on?'

The question was put sharply to Mary by the elderly doctor she had called Merriman to fetch when Louisa had crumpled down to the floor from the kitchen chair in a complete faint. She herself had carried her mistress to her bed, undressed her and got her tucked in. Mary was anything but Amazonian in strength, but she had found Louisa surprisingly easy to carry. She felt like nothing more than a bundle of skin and bone, and Mary saw, when she had got her clothes off, that that was about all she was.

'All winter, sir,' she told the doctor. They were talking outside the closed door. 'Working herself day and night, hardly eating, hardly sleeping. Is she ... very poorly?'

'Completely exhausted,' he answered. 'By the looks of you, child, the same isn't far off for you. Come on, get that blouse unbuttoned and let's have a listen.'

He had taken the stethoscope out again. He sounded Mary and grunted, then took her pulse and grunted again.

'Well, you're not so bad,' he admitted, putting the instrument away.

'Oh, I get more rest than she does,' Mary explained. 'She makes me. Besides, she's got all the books to do and the early-morning buying and that.'

'I see. You'll have to watch yourself, though. You may be more tired than you feel. Living off your nerves. How are you going to manage while she's in bed?'

'How long will that be, sir?'

'She shouldn't get up for two days at the very least. Preferably, I'd keep her there for a week, but from what you tell me I doubt whether I'd succeed.' He scribbled on a prescription pad. 'I'll call again tomorrow. Get this made up at a chemist's and make her take it three times a day. And above all, make sure she rests and eats properly from now on. Those are strict orders, you understand? She might not be so lucky another time.'

Mary answered doubtfully, 'I'll try, sir. I can't imagine trying to give Mrs Trotter orders.'

They heard Louisa's voice calling weakly from within the room. 'Mary! Mary!' The doctor lingered outside while Mary went in, leaving the door ajar. He heard Louisa say, 'Mary, with all this palaver we forgot to put brandy in the chicken liver pâté. Bring me the livers and a cheap bottle. I'll mix it in here.'

There was a moment's silence before Mary answered resolutely, 'No, ma'am.'

'What the hell do you mean, "no"?'

'I mean no, ma'am. The doctor says you're to have complete rest and that I'm to see you get it. So I'd like that to be understood, please.'

'Well done, nurse,' the doctor said to himself as he went away.

Louisa found herself too weak to resist Mary's ministrations. Through eating so little over a long period she had lost the capacity for it, but Mary managed to force some game soup into her and a slice of toast. Merriman got the bottle of tonic made up and Mary administered the doses. She was pleased to hear Louisa say drowsily that she thought she would have 'just a little nap'. This was at eight o'clock in the evening — fortunately, one without any engagement. Mary left her and went down to the kitchen to carry on making the pâtés and Mr

Mather's pies. He would just have to go a bit short for the time being, she decided.

It was getting on for midnight before she was free to go to her own bed. She crept into Louisa's room and was relieved to see that she had not moved in the bed, and to hear the steady drone of her relaxed breathing.

As usual, Mary was up at five o'clock next morning. She thought of going straight in to see Louisa. She put her ear to the room door and listened hard. She could hear nothing. She decided it would be best to let her mistress sleep on as long as possible. She would probably be enough of a handful once she woke up feeling a bit rested.

By six o'clock, though, Mary was beginning to worry. 'Mr Merriman,' she said to the old man, who was reading the morning paper over a cup of tea.

'I'm reading the paper,' he said without lifting his eyes from it. 'When I read, I read. I don't talk as well.'

She had long since learned to be persistent with him. 'What is it that I'm in sometimes? When I don't know what to do, and you say I'm in a something? It's a word.'

'Quandary,' he answered, still not looking up.

'That's it. Well, I'm in one again.'

'Good,' he murmured.

'It's gone six o'clock,' she went on. 'Before she took poorly Mrs Trotter would have been up and about by now. But the doctor said she's to stay in bed all day. Well, my ... quandary is, if I don't take her her morning pot of tea in soon, she might get up and come looking for it. And then what chance would I have of ever getting her back to bed again?'

Merriman turned a page without answering, so she extended the question.

'Only, if she's still asleep and I take it in to her, I might wake her up. And that'd be a pity.' A new thought struck the little Welsh girl. 'Mr Merriman … if she rests and does less cooking and earns less money, it's all over, isn't it? Everything. For all of us. It'll all have been for nothing.'

The old man spoke at last, though without looking at her. 'One of the attributes of old age is wisdom,' he pronounced. 'In my wisdom, I've always said it was a mad idea. And I'm right.'

'You said no such thing in my hearing!'

'I thought it, then.' He gave his paper a dismissive shake.

Mary got up and went to get the tea caddy. 'I'll take her the tea in quietly,' she decided. 'If she's asleep I'll slip out quietly.'

When she entered Louisa's room a few minutes later she found with a shock that her ruminations had been over nothing. Louisa wasn't there.

She was, in fact, in a lamp-lit street on the route from the Bentinck to Covent Garden Market. Only she was travelling the reverse direction to that. She was pushing the small barrow she used for her marketing. It was laden with produce. Every step she took was an effort and she tottered occasionally. She was willing herself on by counting her steps.

'Two thousand one hundred and twelve, one hundred and thirteen, one hundred and fourteen…'

A tall, handsome young man in evening dress came out of a house she was nearing. He stood on the pavement and waved to a young woman peeping from a corner of a bedroom curtain. She smiled, blew him a quick kiss, then ducked back out of sight.

The young man started to walk briskly up the street in Louisa's direction. He saw Louisa, but in the semi-darkness merely registered a pale, undernourished woman heaving at a burden that was obviously beyond her strength. It was not an uncommon sight, though. What he did realise was uncommon about it, a few seconds later, was that the woman looked extremely like a worn Louisa.

He went and stood in her path. She raised her eyes from the roadway and looked at him dully.

'I know you, don't I?' he said.

'I shouldn't think so,' she replied and prepared to push the barrow again. He stood his ground and said, 'It's Louisa...'

'Is it, now?' she responded with some of her characteristic sharpness, and the tone confirmed his belief for him. 'Well, I don't know you from Adam or Eve or the serpent, so shift your carcass and let me...'

His face had grown puzzled and serious.

'Louisa, stop it. You know me perfectly well. Charles Tyrrell.' In her bemused state she hadn't recognised him, but she did now. He tried to lighten things by asking, 'Any chance of a lift to Piccadilly Circus?'

But she said coldly, 'Mr Tyrrell, please. Just get on your way and let me go mine.'

'"Mr Tyrrell"?' he echoed her. 'It was "Mr Charlie" when we first met.'

'Not the first time, it wasn't. If I remember right it was rogue, vagabond, rake and seducer of innocent young kitchen maids.'

'*Attempted* seducer. *Failed* seducer. It was the second time you called me "Mr Charlie". Anyway, how are you, Louisa?'

'I'm well. Now, can I please go about my business?'

'And your husband?'

'No longer my husband.'

'You mean you're divorced — so soon?'

'As good as.'

He looked even more curious and concerned. 'Louisa, what on earth are you doing at this time in the morning, pushing a barrow of all things?'

'Well, in the first place I'm minding my own business. And in the second place, whatever I'm doing is a damn sight more respectable than *you* — still in your evening suit at this time of the morning.'

'I don't think you are well, actually,' he said. 'You don't look well.'

Louisa decided that the conversation had gone on long enough. She felt the great need to get back to her kitchen and her work. She took up the shafts once more and pushed the barrow forward.

'Where can I call on you?' he asked as he stepped aside to let her pass.

'At the Bentinck Hotel, if you want to,' she said indifferently, moving on. 'There's no guests any more. It isn't a hotel any more. You can please yourself.'

He walked beside her. 'You wouldn't object?'

'Suit yourself.'

'We *are* old friends…'

'Good morning, Mr Tyrrell.'

But the last colour swiftly drained from her cheeks. Her eyes widened with sudden alarm and then glazed. She slumped forwards between the barrow shafts and then to the ground.

Charles Tyrrell found her in a complete faint. He looked round, but no one else was in sight. For a few moments he stood feeling helpless, wondering what to do. He looked back at the house he had recently left, but knew that he could not take her there. At last he picked her up, surprised, as Mary had been, at her light weight, placed her on the barrow and took the shafts himself. He turned the barrow round and wheeled it off in the opposite direction to that which Louisa had been taking.

At any other time, the thought of herself being trundled through the streets of London on top of a barrowload of vegetables by a man in evening dress — complete with top hat — would have amused Louisa vastly. But no feelings of amusement came to her when the realisation of her new surroundings, and the recollection of what had caused her to be in them, dawned on her later that morning. She was in bed in a stark, old-fashioned hospital ward, aware of the coughing, hawking and moaning of several dozen other women patients, whose commonest feature — when she was able to take stock of them — seemed to be that they were toothless, whatever their age. The atmosphere was heavy with antiseptic and human smells.

A middle-aged nurse saw her stirring and came over. She explained how she had been brought in and answered Louisa's weak demand to be allowed to go home with a firm refusal. There could be no question of it for several days, it seemed.

'And don't you try getting up and doing a flit, young woman,' the nurse warned her. 'Or you'll end up one of those.'

She nodded towards a sheet-covered figure being wheeled out of the ward. The sheet extended over the face, Louisa noticed with a chill of fear. She had never seen a corpse before.

She was given nourishment and sleeping draughts alternately. After the initial impulse to resist the latter, she surrendered to the drowsiness and sank into deep sleep. Over the next few days this was the pattern of her existence. She thought sometimes of the Bentinck and wondered what was happening about her bookings and her supplies to Mr Mather, but strangely, although she wanted to worry about them, she was unable to do so.

After four days the sleeping draughts were discontinued. She still spent most of her time asleep, though. Her doctor had achieved what he had intended.

Fastidious and innately snobbish, despite her earthiness, Louisa shrank from contact with any of her fellow patients, most of whom were ignorant and coarse of speech and habits. It was a relief to her at length to see the trim and tidy figure of Mary approaching her bed. She carried a small parcel. After a hesitation she ventured to give Louisa a kiss. She held out the parcel.

'I couldn't think what to bring you … without spending money,' she said. 'I was in a quandary. So I brought quail in aspic.'

She went on to tell Louisa how a policeman had called at the Bentinck with the news of her collapse and admission to hospital. She had tried several times before this to visit her, but had not been allowed.

'Mr Tyrrell said it was horrible,' Mary went on. 'You collapsing in the street like that. He thought you was dying.'

'Mr Tyrrell?' Louisa asked, surprised. She was sitting up and looking, to Mary's relief, more rested and healthy than she remembered her. 'When did you see Mr Tyrrell?'

'He's called at the hotel every day since it happened, to tell us how you were. Oh, and I've managed to keep the pies going, ma'am. Mr Merriman helped as best he could. Only I had to send word to Viscount Stanley and the Honourable George Campbell that they'll have to whistle for their dinners.'

'They can all whistle in future,' Louisa said. 'The kitchen can blow itself up, for all I care. I'm going to chuck the whole thing in. To hell with my debts.'

'But, ma'am, if we don't pay the debts they'll take the hotel away from you. You'll have nowhere to live.'

'Then I'll just die, so the problem won't arise, will it?'

'You're not to talk like that!' Mary scolded her, but Louisa, now sufficiently withdrawn from the influence of the sedative drugs to be able to recognise the extent of her problems, rambled on into a wholly uncharacteristic vein of self-pity.

'Two patients died in here the other night. One was consumption. The other just didn't want to live any more. She was younger than me, and prettier. I shouldn't think she'd even heard of quails in aspic. Rotten, isn't it, how parents are always right in the end? If I'd just got decently married, the way they wanted, instead of wanting to play at being a cook, none of this bloody mess would ever have happened.'

'But you're the best cook in London,' Mary tried to reassure her.

Louisa shook her head fiercely. 'What's it all about, anyway? Banquets? Some people don't even get bread. Because I got above my station and stopped thinking about people like that, I suppose I didn't believe they existed any more. Well, look at 'em in those beds. And that's only a bloody handful.'

Try as she did, Mary couldn't talk her round. She had no comforting news to build persuasion on to. Feeling she was going to cry, and that this would upset her mistress even more, she said she would come back the next day, and left.

Immediately outside the ward door she met Charles Tyrrell. He was carrying a bouquet of mixed flowers.

'Hello, Mary,' he greeted her. 'Merriman said you'd been allowed to visit, so I came straight here. How is she? Does she seem any stronger?'

Mary fought back the tears. 'She's never been like this,' she answered miserably. 'Ever. Talking about wanting to die...'

She shook her head and hurried away with her handkerchief out. Charles Tyrrell stared after her, then went briskly into the ward. He saw Louisa immediately. She was still sitting up, but her eyes were closed.

'Louisa,' he whispered to her, thinking she might have dozed off. But she opened her eyes at once and he was pleased to see her give a little smile.

'Hello, Charlie,' she said. Her tone was dull, though.

He put the flowers into her hands.

'Who'd you buy them for?' she asked.

'The first pretty woman I bumped into. And I must say she's looking a great deal healthier than the last time I saw her. How are you, Louisa?'

'Sleeping my life away.'

'Well, it'll be time to wake up before long.' He sat on the edge of her bed and went on. 'Listen, I've been doing some thinking. I think you were right to make yourself responsible for those debts. It would have gone against your nature not to.'

She looked at him in some surprise. 'You seem to know a lot about me all of a sudden.'

'I've been talking to Mary about you, round at the hotel. She's a bright girl. She can recognise things.'

'Well, I hope she can recognise I've been a bloody fool, then.'

'She's devoted to you. But she does see — anyone with half an eye could see — that if you go on in this way you'd be dead before half your debts were paid. I can see it for certain, so I want you to listen to a proposition…'

'If it's money, the answer's no. I want no one's money.'

'Don't you think Mary's told me that? She repeated it over and over again, like a catechism.'

'Well, then, you know how things stand.' She changed the subject abruptly. 'How's Lord Haslemere these days?'

He replied a trifle impatiently, 'Oh, Father's all right. Keeping as fit as he can because he thinks I'm waiting for him to die. Now, listen —'

'And are you?'

'Of course not. Anyway, he'll live for ever. Now, this idea of mine —'

'Still living the same sort of life yourself, are you, then?'

''Fraid so. Like a fairground Johnny, wandering from one friend's house to another's.'

'Not changed have you, Charlie?'

'Not in one single respect,' he answered with a new earnestness, and plunged on through her diversionary defences. 'Louisa, how much would the lease cost on your hotel?'

'Why?'

'How *much*?'

She replied suspiciously, 'About fifteen hundred quid.'

'I'll buy it.'

'I told you, Charlie...'

'Just listen, please. You know I wanted a home of my own in town. Well, I still do. The Bentinck could be it.'

'A whole bloody hotel? Don't be daft.'

'Not the whole place at all. A suite of its rooms, furnished to my own taste, that I could regard as home. Where I can invite my friends instead of always having to visit them.'

She said crossly, 'I can smell charity a mile off, and I don't want it.'

He responded equally firmly. 'It isn't charity, for God's sake! If you don't want to sell, all right. I'll buy somewhere else. But I'm determined to have a place of my own.'

'You do that, then. My answer's no.'

'Please yourself.'

'I always do.'

'Louisa, you're stupid as well as stubborn, aren't you? That's one thing I'd never have thought of you.'

'Yes, I am stupid,' she agreed passionately. 'This past day or two I've come to see just how much. I've been stupid all the way along. But I'm not stupid to refuse help. It was being "helped" that got me where I am now. Death's door.'

The strength of his feelings surprised her. He struck the bedcover with a fist and retorted, '"Death's door" my foot! You'll live as long as my father. As far as anyone being helped is concerned, I'm asking *you* to help *me*. I'm asking you to sell me the best cook in London, kitchen and all.'

There followed a long silence while she took this in. At length she asked, 'You mean … you want me to be your cook?'

'If you're agreeable.'

'I told you, the only one I'll be cooking for'll be Saint Peter.'

'Blockhead! Look, you'd have no debts left. It'd be less work and a damn sight more money.'

With less conviction she said, 'No one buys a hotel just to get a cook.'

'*The* cook, Louisa.'

A longer silence followed. He could see her struggling with herself, and kept silent. It was fully two minutes before she said slowly, 'Rum sort of hotel. Just one guest and one suite of rooms.'

And then his heart leaped, because he knew she had succumbed.

CHAPTER THIRTEEN

A hooded leather hall porter's chair stood beside the dais of the auction rooms, with a man in a dustcoat leaning one hand against it. His thoughts were on a horse race and he took no notice of who was bidding.

That was the auctioneer's job. His eyes searched amongst the gentlemen and ladies seated before him. He saw no significant movement.

'Eighteen guineas, then?' he repeated. 'Do I hear nineteen? Nineteen anywhere, please?'

In the third row Louisa leaned a little towards her companion and half-whispered, 'Does he, Charlie?'

'Up to you,' Charles Tyrrell answered, but conveyed his opinion with a wink.

'It's terribly extravagant, isn't it?' she asked. 'I can't remember the last time I spent tuppence, except on food.'

'Going for eighteen guineas, then.' The auctioneer raised his gavel.

'Nineteen,' Louisa said clearly. Then she told Charles, 'That's my limit, honestly. I can't go higher.'

'Twenty,' a man's voice called from far behind.

'Twenty-one,' Louisa said automatically. 'And that's definitely it.'

Luckily for her, it was. She gave Charles an excited grin as the auctioneer terminated the bidding in her favour.

'Come on,' she said. 'We'd better go. I've got eight chairs, a dining table, a hall table, pictures … not to mention a hotel-full of old junk already.' She started to get up, but he restrained her with a hand on her arm.

'Just a moment,' he said. The porter had removed the chair from the dais, and three of his colleagues were pushing forward a rosewood inlaid grand piano.

The auctioneer was announcing, 'And now, ladies and gentlemen, we come to Lot Number 24 — a drawing-room grand piano, handwork of Messrs Bechstein. Beautiful to look upon, and I've no doubt beautiful to listen to. Messrs Bechstein, ladies and gentlemen, makers to the late Franz Liszt, Richard Wagner, Anton Rubinstein, to name but a few eminent names. This particular model would cost approximately a hundred and fifty guineas new. Now, who will start me at, say, seventy?'

There was no response, but Louisa felt Charles stirring. She looked at him in surprise.

'I don't want a piano,' she warned him.

'I do.'

'You! You don't even play — do you?'

'I could always learn,' he said and called, 'Fifty.'

He got it for sixty.

It was a month since Louisa's release from hospital. Mary had tried to persuade her to go and stay with her parents at Wanstead for a while, until she got her strength back, but the notion had been rejected. A new excitement seemed to have infected Louisa. Mary and Mr Merriman had been informed that the lease of the Bentinck Hotel was now the property of the Honourable Charles Tyrrell, who would shortly be moving into apartments there. She herself would still be in charge. She would cook for him, but had been offered the use of the kitchen for her freelance activities, which, however, would be on nothing like the previous hectic scale. Mrs Wellkin had been invited to return as her assistant, and had accepted. Mary and Merriman were welcome to stay on, if they wished. They did.

Charles had done more than completely refurbish the upstairs suite he had chosen for himself. He had insisted on the main hall being redecorated and its new, brighter wallpaper hung with pictures. Carpets, furniture and decorations elsewhere in the building had been renewed, to his satisfaction.

'I couldn't have lived with all that musty gloom around me,' he explained to Louisa, who had protested against his extravagance.

'Charlie,' she said tentatively. 'Since you've gone to all this trouble … I mean, I must be barmy to suggest it, but why don't I open the whole bloomin' hotel again?'

'That's not barmy,' he grinned. 'I was wondering how long you'd take to come round to it.'

'You mean, you did it deliberate?'

'Not actually. It seemed absurd to do up just a part of it and let the rest go to rot. Now that I look at it, I doubt if there's a more comfortable hotel in London.'

'What if it fails, Charlie?'

'It won't.'

'It might. And I'd be right back at the beginning again, slaving and sweating to pay off a new load of debts.'

'You won't let it fail, Louisa,' he tried to convince her. 'You've got what you wanted in life now, haven't you?'

'I suppose I have,' she admitted. 'I thought just cooking would be enough, but all this too…' She glanced delightedly round the transformed hall.

'*Is* it all you want in life?' he asked.

She didn't fail to catch the deeper meaning.

'Tell you what I've got for your dinner tonight,' she said lightly. 'Melon, followed by turbot, followed by roast beef, followed by cherries in brandy. That tempt you?' She gave him one of her more exasperating grins and went quickly off to the kitchen.

Later that day Merriman answered the front door to a man a good deal smaller than himself. He wore a carelessly brushed bowler hat with a curly brim and a suit whose shine showed its age. Squatting beside him, on a lead, was a mongrel dog of mixed terrier ancestry.

'Starr,' the man announced, 'Two Rs. And this is Fred. We've come in answer to the advertisement. Hall porter.'

Merriman looked from the man to the dog, which gazed expectantly up into his eyes, as if anticipating a doorstep interview. Instead, Merriman addressed the man.

'The … dog's with you, is it? I mean, wherever you go?'

'Day and night,' Starr answered resolutely.

'Well, you'd best come in,' Merriman said dubiously. He led them into the hall and left them there while he went to Louisa's parlour to tell her that there was a man and a dog to see her. Even she was a little nonplussed when the dog appeared, towing the man by the lead.

'Do, er, sit down,' she said, nearly adding 'both of you.'

'Thank you, Mrs Trotter,' Starr said civilly. 'Sit, boy. Sit. And no arguments, mind.'

'Now then,' Louisa said, 'where do I start? I'm not all that used to interviewing hall porters.'

'That's perfectly all right, madam,' Starr said. 'We are. I think we might begin by establishing exactly what remuneration you have in mind?'

'Thirty pounds a year, all found.'

He looked at Fred, as if for approval. Fred looked at Louisa.

'Plus tips, of course,' she added hastily.

'Of course, madam,' said Starr. 'You would, of course, be looking for a man of experience? A man with excellent references?'

'Yes, that's right. Have you, er…?'

'The very best, Mrs Trotter. I *am* my references. Yes, Fred? Isn't that so?'

Louisa was by now quite expecting the dog to speak out in his master's praise. She had never been interested in animals, but there was something oddly engaging in the relationship between this self-assured, inscrutable man and the dumb animal which seemed to serve as his companion, confidant and, for all she knew, adviser.

Since Starr made no move to produce any written references she tried asking, 'Where have you worked previously?'

'Here and there, madam.' His gaze met hers frankly as he gave her such answers as his laconic manner permitted.

'I see,' she said, not seeing at all. 'What doing?'

'This and that.'

'Oh. Did you fight in the war?'

'Very possibly,' was his remarkable reply. Then, to her surprise, he reversed the roles and almost loquaciously took over the interview. 'Well, now, madam, Fred and I would be grateful if you'd be as frank with us as we have with you, madam. What we'd like to know is: One, the number of guests to whom we are to be of service. Two, whether Fred, of course, would be welcome. (Correct, Fred?) Three, the number and character of the remainder of the staff. Four…'

The one thing he didn't request was a separate wage for the dog, but it wouldn't have surprised Louisa if he had. She engaged Starr, and, by implication, Fred, too.

While this conversation was going on Merriman and Mary were engaged in one of a very different sort in the hall. Without bothering to ring, two overdressed and over-painted young women had entered. Merriman recognised what they were immediately.

'Here! Who invited you in?' he demanded. Mary, emerging at that moment from the pass door, paused to look on curiously.

'This is the new hotel, isn't it?' one of the women asked in a cheeky East End voice.

'We're not open yet,' Merriman replied. 'In any case…'

'We was hoping there might be a bit of trade for us,' the other young woman said. 'Any single gentlemen staying…'

Mary stepped forward, flushing angrily. 'Out!' she cried. 'Go on, both of you!'

The first girl said, 'Who the 'ell are you talking to, little bloody skivvy?'

The other, milder-mannered, asked with what seemed to be genuine surprise, 'It *is* going to be a hotel, isn't it?'

'Not your kind,' Mary replied.

The first girl smirked superciliously. 'They're all our kind, dear. How long you been down from them mountains?'

Ignoring Merriman, Mary bundled the pair off the premises and slammed the door after them. She turned round from it to find Louisa at the door of her room. A man and a dog were behind her.

'What's going on out here?' Louisa demanded.

Mary's face was already red, but she blushed as well. 'It was two … two … um…'

'Tarts, ma'am,' Merriman finished the sentence for her.

'They had the effrontery to … I chucked them out, ma'am,' Mary explained. She was surprised not to receive any congratulations for it.

'No bones broken, then?' Louisa asked instead.

'No, ma'am.'

'That's all right, then. Mary, this is Mr Starr. Mr Starr's to join us as hall porter.'

'And Fred,' Starr said, indicating the dog.

'And Fred,' Louisa corrected herself, with a smile. Starr gave Mary a little bow, which pleased her.

Merriman was formally introduced and Starr and Fred left. When the door had closed again Merriman asked, 'He's … what you had in mind, would you say, madam?'

Louisa smiled. '*He* interviewed *me*,' she admitted. 'I don't know anything about him. I think that's why I engaged him. I like mysteries.' She stopped Mary, who was about to go. 'One little thing, Mary…'

'Yes, ma'am?'

'When you chuck ladies out in future, do it gently. Eh?'

'But they were *streetwalkers*, Madam.'

'Which is another word for working girls, Mary. There's not everyone able to keep a secure job in a nice situation. Never forget that, and don't be a snob.' She terminated the admonition with a smile, though, leaving Mary baffled but relieved.

A few days later, by which time Starr and Fred had joined the establishment and taken up their joint duty in the hall, Louisa displayed yet another side of her remarkably varied attitude towards strangers.

A middle-aged man, well dressed and with a commanding air, marched through the front door and up to the desk. Starr had his back to him, working out some dates on a wall calendar. The man slapped the palm of his hand hard on the desk top and barked, 'You there! Some attention.'

'Yes, sir,' Starr said, turning. 'Sorry, sir.' He had genuinely not heard the man enter.

Louisa, coming down the stairs, was just in time to hear the stranger reply, in a provincial accent, 'Never mind the "yes, sirs", I've a cabful of luggage out there. Get it in here, and sharpish.'

'Yes, sir. At once,' said Starr, assuming the arrival to have been expected. But Louisa stepped forward. She was fashionably dressed and ladylike and could be mistaken for nothing less than the housekeeper, if not the proprietress.

'Just a moment, Starr,' she checked him, then turned to the other man. 'For what purpose, Mr, er…?'

He crimsoned. 'For what purpose? It's a hotel, isn't it? I want a room, woman. The biggest and the best, and a damn sight less impudence. "For what purpose?" indeed!'

Louisa said calmly, 'I don't think I caught your name.'

'Well, in that case, I suggest "sir" will do.'

'Is "sir" your title?' she enquired, with deceptive innocence.

'No, it isn't. "Sir" just happens to be the custom when dealing with people who're prepared to give you their good money. My name is Atkinson, Josiah Atkinson, proprietor of the Atkinson Coal Mining Company, Northamptonshire, and I want a room befitting that position.'

Louisa raised her eyebrows, 'Oh, yes, sir. We have a very good coal cellar.'

'You … you *what?*'

'Otherwise, I'm afraid we have no rooms available. At least, not for the likes of jumped-up snotty-noses like you. Try some common lodging house. One of them might condescend to let you a back room.'

Mr Atkinson swayed, and it seemed for a moment that he might be going to slap Louisa's face. Starr came quickly out from behind the desk, followed by Fred, who began to bark.

'Scarper! Sling your hook!' Louisa ordered the startled industrialist. Fred advanced to snarl at his ankles and Starr ominously eased his wrists free of the cuffs of his jacket sleeves. Mr Atkinson turned about and left swiftly, without another word.

'Lovely!' Louisa exclaimed. She actually patted Fred, who licked her hand.

Starr said, 'He was a wealthy man, though, madam. And we've got all those rooms empty.'

'I'm just starting as I mean to go on,' she replied. 'My standards are mine, and everyone'll have to like 'em or lump 'em.'

A further example of what those standards could embrace was demonstrated that afternoon. Starr entered Louisa's room and informed her that a Major Smith-Barton, DSO, requested an interview with her with a view to becoming a long-term resident. She sent him to invite the major in. He proved to be the archetypal retired Army officer of modest rank: elderly, rather blotchy about the cheeks and nose, side-whiskered and sporting an eyeglass.

'Just back from the East,' he explained in a bluff voice after courtesies had been exchanged. 'Looking for somewhere to put up, don't you know? Been down in Suffolk, shooting with my cousin, Lord Dedham. Said he'd heard the old Bentinck had opened again, run by a damned fine woman who really knew how to cook. Asked me to stay on down there, don't you know, but the Dedhams live in a draughty old barrack of a house, and my blood's a bit thin after so many years in the sun, so I upped sticks and made for London.'

'Were you thinking of a complete set of rooms, Major?' asked Louisa, gratified to know that word of mouth was already spreading in good circles.

'Oh lord, no,' he responded. 'I'm an old campaigner. Don't like a lot of fuss. If you've got a boot cupboard somewhere, that'll do me.'

She liked him. 'I think we can do better than that for you,' she said and led him back into the hall. 'Starr,' she ordered, 'let them bring Major Smith-Barton's things in. I'm putting him in Number 11.'

'Very good, madam.'

'I say,' the major said to Starr. 'Wonder if I might have a loan of that *Sporting Life* of yours?'

'Certainly, sir,' said Starr, handing the newspaper over.

'Sure you've finished with it?'

'He's better off without it,' Louisa said. 'If you'll just follow me, Major?'

'You're very kind, ma'am,' the major said as he went up the stairs after Louisa. 'Nicest bit of London, this, too, I always think. Like an old armchair, don't you know?'

Merriman approached them, carrying a tray. Louisa stopped him and introduced them. The major said, 'I wonder if I might have dinner in my room? Cold pheasant and a bottle of claret — something like that?'

'Did you hear that, Merriman?' Louisa asked.

'I did,' was the laconic reply as Merriman passed on.

'Poor old fossil's as deaf as a post unless he chooses not to be,' Louisa told the major. 'Only keep him out of kindness.'

Down in the hall Merriman paused to survey the newcomer's possessions: a mixture of shabby, much-travelled cases, a black metal trunk bearing many dents and scrape marks, a hat box, two fishing-rods, and other odds and ends, bearing many worn labels.

'Seems to have got his feet under the table nice and quick,' Merriman remarked.

'He's the sort,' Starr replied sagely. 'Seen plenty of 'em. We'll never get rid of him, now he's here.'

Merriman launched into one of his rare monologues, usually precipitated by gloom or crisis. 'He'll want every meal carried up to his room, I suppose. Breakfast, luncheon, tea, dinner. I've seen 'em before, too. There was a day not so long ago when no gentleman would have had his luncheon at his hotel. What does he think his club's for?'

He sighed and went his way, thinking how different everything was becoming since the old queen's going. Starr picked up some of the baggage and began carrying it upstairs. Fred moved to follow him.

'No, you stay there and mind the desk, Fred,' his master instructed. 'Getting as busy as Charing Cross round here, all of a sudden.'

When they next encountered one another, Charles Tyrrell said, 'I bet you by the summer you'll be turning people away. Personal recommendation, that's how it's done. I'm doing my best. Every party I go to I become a positive bore about the virtues of the Bentinck Hotel. By the way, the Mastersons say they'll definitely be coming. They're people worth having.'

'Well, we get plenty of enquiries, but apart from one old major...' Louisa said. Today she was in a subdued mood; almost edgy. She had been like that since waking, and she knew why. The reason irked her. She considered it beneath her to let it, but there it remained.

Charles had informed her the day before that he would be wanting a special dinner *à deux* served in his room. 'She's an awfully topping girl,' he had added. 'Met her at a hunt ball in Hampshire last week. Dances divinely.'

'Married, I suppose, knowing you.'

'I should say so. Husband in the Army, conveniently on a mission to Egypt. Said she was coming up to London this week to do some shopping, so I asked her to dine. She agreed just like that, keen as mustard.'

Louisa grunted. Jealousy over a man was something new to her. She knew that Charlie was a considerable man about town where women were concerned, and she had had no doubt about why he had thought it convenient to set up his own quarters — a lair, almost. But this was the first time that he had invited one of his ladies to visit him. Louisa felt a little as she had done when Johnnie Farjeon had brought her her first summons from the Prince of Wales.

But she had no grounds for objecting, and was cross with herself for even wishing she could. She handed him a slip of paper now. 'I've done all the shopping for your little party tonight,' she said.

'Rather an occasion,' he said. 'My first at the Bentinck.' He read the pencilled draft of the menu. '*Pâté de Foie Gras, Croute de Cailles Bentinck … Bombe Surprise.* Oh, by the way, no garlic in anything, please.'

Louisa said, 'I'll see to it. I'm going to cook it all myself, anyway.'

'Thank you. Oh, by the way, she likes roses…'

'Does she? Well she can go on liking them. She won't get none here, not at this time of year.' It was February, 1902. 'I'll get some other flowers.' An edge of sarcasm sharpened her tone. 'Something nice and virginal.'

Charlie laughed, not noticing the little cut. 'And I'll go out now and buy a new waistcoat to impress her,' he said, and went gaily away.

That evening she supervised Merriman laying the round dining table she and Charlie had bought for his room. It was set back into an alcove off the sitting room. Louisa had arranged a centrepiece of early flowers.

'While they're eating the soup, put a light under the sole, but not before,' she ordered. 'And let me know in good time when they come to the quail pudding. I'll bring it up myself.'

He made no comment.

'Did you hear me?' she asked loudly.

'Yes.'

'Respect, please, Merriman.'

'Yes, madam.'

'That's better. And don't light them candles till Mr Tyrrell rings and says he's ready for dinner. And get done quick when it's over. He won't want you hanging around like a drunk at a wedding.'

'No, madam.'

Louisa stood back to admire the table setting. Well, he'd been good to her, so it was up to her to do him proud in return.

Even so…

CHAPTER FOURTEEN

Major Smith-Barton and Starr stood beside the porter's chair in the hall that evening, commiserating mutually over the racing pages of a newspaper. Fred paid them no attention. Dogs have more sense than to back racehorses.

'Fell three out,' Starr said.

'Probably brought down or interfered with,' the major said gloomily. 'Not the horse's fault, sure of that. Real good 'un. Oh, well, sorry, don't you know, but you can't always win.'

Starr, who had lost a small amount as a result of the major's 'certain' tip, asked cautiously, 'What's your fancy for tomorrow, Major?'

The old soldier's eyes sparkled again. 'Sultan's Kiss in the 2.15 at Sandown,' he said emphatically. 'Can't go wrong. Had it from a feller who —'

He broke off as the hotel door opened and a young woman came through and glanced about. She was about thirty, well and tastefully dressed, and good-looking. The major, who had removed his eyeglass to emphasise with a gesture his certainty about Sultan's Kiss, replaced it and looked at her appreciatively.

'Yes, ma'am?' Starr enquired, stepping forward.

'Mr Tyrrell's party, please,' the lady said in a somewhat affected voice with a slight lisp. 'Mrs Travers.'

'Ah, yes, ma'am. Good evening. Will you follow me, madam?'

He led the way up the stairs. The major looked down at Fred, who had decided not to bother to follow.

'Nice looking filly, that, Fred. Bit of blood there. Highly strung, I shouldn't wonder. Be all right with the right jockey up, eh?'

The dog wagged his tail.

Merriman disposed of Mrs Travers' coat and wrap in the small anteroom to Charlie's sitting room and announced her before retiring.

'My dear Belinda,' Charlie said, shaking her hand. 'How very nice to see you again.'

He was, he had just assured himself before his cheval glass in the bedroom, appearing at his very best, his fashionably cut new waistcoat giving a fresh look to his perfectly pressed evening suit.

'Good evening, Charles,' she said, not failing to notice how dashing he was looking. 'Ooh, it's cold out. Horribilino.'

'Champagne too cold, then?' he asked, indicating a bottle standing in a bucket of ice. 'What about some Madeira instead, perhaps?'

'Champagne, please,' she said. 'But don't open it specially for me.'

'Good heavens no,' he grinned. 'It's mother's milk to me.'

He opened the bottle expertly, the cork coming out with the merest sigh, and poured glasses for them both.

'What an unusual place this is,' she said, glancing about. 'Not a bit like an hotel, really.'

He gave her her glass and they drank together, raising the glasses in unspoken salute.

'That's the idea,' Charlie explained. 'You see, Mrs Trotter, who runs it, wanted it to be more like a country house.'

'How quaint,' Belinda said. Charlie could sense that she was becoming puzzled and changed the subject quickly.

'Great fun, last weekend.'

'Oh, yes. Really quite deevy.'

'Tubby Vernon dressing up as a footman and spilling the soup over old Admiral Squeezy Dick's shirt…'

'Yes. Quite a lark, wasn't it?' she agreed.

'I bet the old devil was playing footy footy with you under the table.'

'Yes, he was, actually. It was most awfully embarrassing.'

Belinda took a quick sip of her champagne. Charles said, 'I can't say I'd blame him. What did you do?'

'Oh, my mother taught me always to have a fork ready,' Belinda answered, sipping again.

'To repel invaders, eh?' Charles laughed. 'I must be careful.'

He picked up the bottle out of the ice bucket and advanced it towards his guest's glass, but she placed the palm of her hand over the mouth.

'You'll have me tiddly, you know,' she said, the lisp already rather more pronounced.

'Nonsense,' he insisted, pouring her a little more. 'But there's some rather nice claret ahead. Don't want to spoil our palates. I say, that's the most awfully nice dress you're wearing.'

'I'm so glad you like it,' she answered, talking more rapidly. 'It was part of my trousseau. My sister said she thought it was rather risqué. I'm staying with her in Paddington, you know. I always seem to be cuckooing with some friend or relation or other when Basil's away.'

An apt reply, pleasingly so to him, offered itself promptly to Charlie. 'I'm sure you're very welcome in any nest. That's … what's so nice about this place. One is so completely undisturbed. Private … if you know what I mean. One's own little nest.' He added quickly, 'I hope you're hungry?'

'Famished, actually.'

Charles went to ring the bell. From behind him he heard Belinda ask, 'Was I boringly early ... or is everyone else boringly late?'

Without turning, he answered as casually as he could, 'There isn't anyone else.' He turned to face her and indicated the alcove with its table laid for two.

Merriman entered and began lighting the candles on it, but Belinda had turned to Charles and was saying, 'I'd no idea, Charles. You asked me to a dinner party in an hotel. I couldn't possibly dine with you alone. It would cause an absolute scandalare. I mean, it simply isn't done in Basil's regiment.'

Charles looked round, to see Merriman drifting tactfully out of their presence. Of course, long experience had taught Charles that machinations such as his, which had involved an invitation that had not been a lie but had left out the essential truth, could sometimes be rewarded with disappointment. But on more than one occasion he had managed to overcome the initial setback by the application of his considerable charm, if necessary aided by liberal dispensation of champagne.

'My dearest Belinda,' he smiled now, picking up the bottle yet again, 'you *are* teasing me, aren't you? It's awfully unkind to play at tease, you know.'

She put her glass down on the table. 'No, Charles, I'm not. Really, really I'm not.'

'But there can't be any scandal if nobody knows. Nobody's going to know. Just one evening. Look, it's all ready ... and even cuckoos have to eat.'

He had replaced the bottle and now tried to take her hand instead. She drew back sharply and said, 'Please don't touch me, Charles. I never took you for ... for a cad. If Basil knew, he'd shoot you.'

'Shoot me?'

'He shot a man in Durban for less.'

What — killed him?'

'He only grazed his finger, actually. But that was because the man moved. You don't know Basil's temper.'

It was not so much the threat of retribution from Basil that told Charlie he was wasting his time. It was the expression on Basil's wife's face, and the rigid set of her body, and the glance she had thrown in the direction of the anteroom where her outdoor things lay. He gave in gracefully.

'Do forgive me,' he smiled with contrived wistfulness. 'It was a silly mistake on my part. You'd like to go home?'

'Yes, I would,' she said thankfully. But as he was helping her on with her wrap a sudden thought came to her. 'My carriage wasn't ordered until ten-thirty!'

Fresh hope glowed in Charlie. Perhaps she was a better and more teasing tactician than he had suspected.

'Then you'll stay! I knew you would.'

Her cheeks went pink. 'No, I will not.'

'I'll find you a cab, then.'

'I couldn't go home in a Hackney cab! Not at night.'

Even Charles's suavity was melted by a sudden flush of impatience. This was not tactics. It was female obtuseness. He almost rammed her coat on to her and said, 'I'm sure dear Basil wouldn't shoot you for that!'

They went coldly down to the hall. The major and Starr were still there, so for appearance's sake Charles said to Belinda, 'I'm sorry you couldn't stay longer, Mrs Travers. Sure you wouldn't like me to see you home?'

'No,' she responded in kind. 'Thank you, I'll be quite safe by myself.'

'Then I'll just take you down to the cab stand,' he said, and ushered her out.

'Well, I'll be damned,' said the major to Starr. 'Didn't even get her to the post.'

When he got back a few minutes later Charlie went straight up to his room. He finished the bottle of champagne in large gulps and opened another which had been chilling in readiness. He had failed similarly before, in other surroundings, but it was always a let-down and a bore when it turned out like this; and more especially on this evening when he had hoped to use for its truest purpose the apartment he had so carefully prepared and had even bought an entire hotel to obtain.

There was a soft knock at the door and Louisa came in.

'Stood up proper, were you?' she asked, not sarcastically, but with less than sympathy.

'Stupid woman!' he growled. 'Typical, stuffy, middle-class Army…'

Louisa raised an eyebrow. 'Retreated in the face of the enemy's advance, did she?'

'I didn't so much as lay a finger on her, damn it!'

'No, but you was going to, wasn't you? "No garlic!" Thank heavens there's some honest decent women in the world what are prepared to be faithful to their husbands and behave themselves.'

He said bitterly, 'Thank you for those comforting and consoling words. What are you laughing at? I don't think it's very funny.'

She stopped giggling and said, 'No, it isn't. Rather sad, really.'

He indicated the bottle. 'Have a spot of bubbly with me, Louisa.'

'Well … ta. Just a little.'

He poured some for her and another full glass for himself. 'Louisa, I do want to apologise after all the trouble you've taken. I really am most awfully sorry about the waste.'

'Cheers, love. Look, don't worry. You just forget the ladies for one night and sit down and eat my nice dinner.'

The idea had not occurred to him. Before she had come in he had been contemplating whether to go down and take his pick from the promenade at the Empire, or somewhere more exclusive. He smiled his gratitude.

'Just like you to take it on the chin without moaning,' he said. 'Thanks. You're a tonic —' He stopped suddenly and Louisa saw a curious look come into his eyes.

'What?' she asked.

'Louisa … will you dine with me?'

It came out with an impetuous rush. The silence afterwards seemed a long one.

'Me?'

'Yes. Do me the honour of dining with me.'

She flushed as she said, 'No, Charlie. I couldn't manage it. Not possible. I got another fifty pies almost due out of the oven…'

'Mrs Wellkin can manage that, for heaven's sake!'

'And I got all the bits and pieces to get ready for Lady Manton's dinner tomorrow night…'

Charlie gave her his most appealing smile, though it was sincerely done. 'That's tomorrow night, not tonight. Just relax for once. Enjoy yourself. Take a night off. No one's worked harder or deserves it more.'

'Eat me own poison?' she tried to joke it off. 'That'd be a laugh!'

'It would give me a lot of pleasure if you'd dine with me, Louisa,' he said earnestly. 'I need cheering up badly. Anyway, I'm your resident. What the guest orders he's entitled to get.'

He was pleased to see her grin and hear her say, 'All right, Mister the Honourable Misery, sir. I should be pleased to accept your kind invitation to dinner. I suppose I'll manage. Just give me a few minutes to tart meself up a bit.'

She went quickly. Charles picked up his glass of champagne again, but this time he merely sipped it, savouring it. Then he rang for Merriman and told him to go down as quickly as he could and fetch a bottle of the Clicquot Rosé '93 to be chilled.

In Louisa's bedroom, Mary finished lacing her mistress's corsets.

'Wish I had a nice tiny waist like yours, ma'am,' she said wonderingly. 'Can't be more than eighteen inches.'

'Comes of eating nothing but tea and toast for so long.' Louisa got up. 'Right, let's have the dress.'

Mary lifted it from the bed, where she had laid it out. It was the one Louisa had worn for her last visit from the Prince of Wales. It had never been out of the wardrobe since. As Mary helped her into it Louisa said, 'Haven't worn this for over a … well, not since we came to this place. It was made by a royal dressmaker, you know.'

'Will you wear your gold necklace with it, too, ma'am?'

'No. It's the jet one tonight. It's got to be.'

'Why, ma'am?'

'Proper brought up ladies' maids don't ask that sort of question, Mary. But since you have, Mr Tyrrell gave me it a long time ago, so it'd be only polite for him.'

When the dress was fully fastened, and the necklace in place, and the last adjustment made to Louisa's beautiful hair, which Mary had already swept up for her with combs and pins, revealing the perfect slender white neck, Louisa held her fan and gloves and twirled in front of her long mirror. The little Welsh maid could almost have cried in her admiration.

'You look beautiful, madam. You look like a real duchess — you do really.'

The compliment pleased Louisa, but she replied, 'I'm glad I'm not one. What a life. Nothing to do all day, 'cept change your clothes, eat too much, sleep too much, talk too much … Still, it feels nice as make-believe.'

Picking up the skirt of the long gown, she made her way back to Charlie's rooms.

'Pink champagne!' Louisa exclaimed when Charlie drew the bottle of Clicquot from the ice bucket and uncorked it. 'That's pushing the boat out a bit, isn't it?'

'It's a special occasion. A launching ceremony.'

'Didn't even know we had any in the cellar.'

'Ah, but Merriman and I knew, didn't we?' Charles said to the aged waiter, who was assiduously maintaining his deaf pose and made no response.

'Well, here's to a first-rate second-hand evening,' Louisa said as she and Charlie clinked glasses and drank.

'Merriman,' Charlie said so loudly that there could be no excuse for not being heard.

'Sir?'

'We will now taste this good lady's cooking.'

Merriman bowed slightly and moved to help Louisa into her place at the table. He did it gravely, with as much respect as he would have accorded a real duchess.

The *pâté de foie gras* was already set out. Merriman proffered a napkin containing toast he had been warming. It occurred to Louisa how long it had been since she had sat down to a formal meal, and been waited on, and in what unique circumstances and company those last occasions had been. A little of the mood she had felt then crept back to her now.

Charlie's starched shirt front and pearl studs glistened in the light of candles and subdued electricity. The perfectly arranged cutlery gleamed. The different-sized glasses twinkled.

A little nervously she asked Charlie, as they ate, 'What would you talk about to your lady if she was sitting here?'

'With the first course, the weather.'

'The weather? That don't sound very romantic to me.'

'It's a sort of way of breaking the ice. You know, how the fog stopped the pheasants flying well at Mentmore. That's if she likes shooting. At any rate, her husband seems to,' he remembered to himself.

'What if she doesn't?'

'Hunting, perhaps. We might consider together how many days the Belvoir has been stopped by frost this season. Then go through every yard of that splendid run we had with the Warwickshire in November. Never missed a fence. Or consider the merits of the big bay gelding…'

'What if she likes tiddlywinks?'

'Then we'd play tiddlywinks together — later. Just now, though, it is essential to return to the weather.'

'Why?'

'Because just when I am about to suggest that we should go skating on the Serpentine a thought strikes me. I am immediately all attention and apprehension. I must find out if the lady's tiny hand is frozen.' He reached across and took Louisa's hand.

'Here — stop it!' she rebuked him, and withdrew it. But she laughed.

Over the quail pie Charles announced, 'At this stage the time is ripe to embark on rather more serious subjects. Such important matters as where the lady is staying for Ascot.'

'That's easy,' Louisa said, putting on a 'posh' accent. 'Windsor Castle. If the queen'll weather it,' she added in her own voice.

'Louisa, I said "serious",' he mock-chided her. 'Such as what horribilino plays she has been to, and what deevy house-parties, and where she has been dinared before dansareing with that divine partnerino…'

She chortled at the society slang. 'And who's been poppying into beddies with who, I bet,' she suggested.

He was surprised. 'Put rather crudely — yes.'

They had finished their delicious main course. Louisa got up, saying, 'Well, if you'll excusare me?'

She went away behind the curtained-off serving alcove, from which Merriman emerged to clear away the plates and lay smaller fresh ones. Charles was surprised to see him switch off the remaining electric lights, leaving the table illuminated by the candles only, and then leave the apartment altogether. A moment later Louisa came back through the curtain. On a small silver tray she was carrying a perfect representation of a swan, fashioned from solid white ice cream and resting on a nest of creamy meringue. In the middle of the swan's back the blue flame of burning brandy flickered. It was a superb creation.

Louisa laid it in the centre of the table. 'And what do you think your lady would say to that?'

'She'd be enchanted — as I am, Louisa.'

'She'd say it seems a shame to eat it. They always do…'

'She would say that she'd heard this Mrs Trotter wasn't only the best cook in London, but a most beautiful woman to boot.'

He had spoken without the preceding flippancy and had looked at her very intently while doing so. He took her hand again, but she withdrew it again to enable her to serve them portions of the confection.

'Here, Mr Dishonourable Tyrrell,' she said, concentrating on what she was doing; 'you want to watch it, or you'll get a clip on your lughole.'

The strains of the song 'And Her Golden Hair Was Hanging Down Her Back' drifted downwards as far as the hall. The voices were Charlie's and Louisa's, and the uncertain, fumbling piano accompaniment, lagging several notes behind, was his.

Starr raised his eyes from the sporting form. 'High jinks up there, Mr Merriman,' he said, as the old waiter tottered to the foot of the stairs.

'High jinks it is, and no mistake, Mr Starr,' he replied. He sniffed disapprovingly and went through the pass door.

Starr lowered the paper to address his dog, at his feet. 'Bit perky tonight, our Mrs Trotter. Eh, Fred?'

Fred yawned and snuggled his muzzle again between his paws.

The song ended and Louisa, brandy glass in hand, let go of the piano and slightly stumbled into a chair. 'I think,' she said, speaking carefully, 'I think it's about time that lady of yours went back to her pots and pans.'

She sipped the brandy and held the glass up before her eyes. It had acquired two rims, and two levels of the spirit

Two Charlies arose from the piano stool and came towards her, melting into one as they moved into closer focus. He took the glass from her hand and then held both her hands in his.

'No. Not quite,' he said. 'Not till I have told her that her hair is like the finest gossamer seen at dewy dawn. That her eyes are like twin pools of rare delight. Her cheeks like blushing clouds.'

Louisa roused herself. 'What about her Hampsteads, then?'

'What? Oh, her teeth. A … a ring of precious pearls, culled from an Eastern crown.'

'Not bad,' she conceded, and hiccupped.

'Where was I?' he asked. His eyes, even to hers, were a shade glassy.

She pointed to her lips, with a wavering finger.

'Lips … like twin rosebuds, new … newly opened in June,' he managed. 'Neck like a column of the finest alabaster.'

They stayed there, he kneeling before her, for some minutes, just looking at one another. Then she realised that his eyes had become less blurred, both to her and to him. The double outline of his shoulders had merged into a single one. There was this one man, and this one man only, here with her. She licked her lips.

'That's … about far enough, isn't it?' she suggested.

'Yes,' he said, looking down, and then up again towards her eyes. 'Then … then I tell her that I love her.'

There were some seconds of silence.

'And the magic spell always works?' she asked.

'Lord, no. It's like … hooking a salmon. That's the real sport of the thing.'

She was not offended by his frankness. 'Just a sport, is it?'

'I suppose it is — usually.'

'And you always win in the end.'

Another lengthy silence fell. Then he shook his head and said, 'No. Sometimes the lady says her carriage is waiting…'

The candles behind them flickered. The piano keyboard stretched white and black behind him. The glowing embers in the fireplace rustled as a coal disintegrated into ash and fell.

'I haven't got a carriage,' Louisa said, very quietly.

Charlie raised himself from his knees, took her arm, lifted her from her chair, and guided her towards the dark room beyond those in which she had spent the evening with him.

CHAPTER FIFTEEN

'You want to watch it this morning, Mr Merriman,' Starr remarked next morning in the hall. 'Don't he, Fred? Proper tantrum she's in this morning, ain't she?'

Even Merriman was inclined to believe that Fred nodded agreement. The waiter paused with his tray, watching the porter assiduously getting rid of some paw marks on the floor.

'I spoke to her quite civil,' Starr went on. '"Your mail, Mrs Trotter," I said, and she bit my head off. "Why isn't it on my desk?" she said. "And what are all them dirty paw marks all over this floor? This is meant to be a hotel, not a dogs' home," she says. We don't stand for that sort of talk where we serve, do we, Fred? Seems she's got out of bed the wrong side, and no mistake.'

Merriman leaned across and imparted a rare confidence. 'Not her own bed, neither.'

Starr gaped, and even Fred cocked an ear.

'Is that what you think, Mr Merriman?' the porter asked.

'More than *think*, Mr Starr. Ssh!'

Mary was coming downstairs. 'Old Major Whiskers is still in bed,' she told them brightly. 'As I was making up his fire he was telling me about how he fought the fierce pythons of the north-west frontier of India.'

'Pathans,' Starr corrected her.

'That's what I said. He said if they didn't have us to fight, they'd fight each other for the fun of it.'

'Just like the Welsh,' Starr commented. Mary put out her tongue at him.

'Anyway,' she told Merriman, 'he'd like some biscuits and a glass of light port at eleven. Oh, and the loan of your sporting paper, Mr Starr, if you'd be so obliging.' She went through the pass door, leaving the two men respectively making gestures indicative of the bending of drinking elbows and the tugging of horses' reins.

Charles Tyrrell breezed in through the front door. 'Morning!' he greeted them. 'Morning!' he also greeted Louisa in her parlour moments later.

'Hullo,' she said flatly, not looking up from her desk, at which she was attending to papers.

'Will you come out to lunch with me?' he asked.

Unexpectedly snappily, she responded, 'How can I? I'm meant to be running a hotel, not waltzing round the West End with you.'

Astonished to find her in such a mood so few hours after what had happened between them, he perched on her desk and tried to put his hand against her cheek. She drew back, but let him hold her hand instead.

'Oh, Charlie,' she said. 'What have we gone and done? What will people say? What will they think?'

'"They"? They won't know.'

''Course they will. Servants always find out everything. You wouldn't understand things like that. They'll find out, then everyone'll know.'

'Well, does it matter, anyway?'

'Oh? "Have you heard about that Mrs Trotter at the Bentinck? Tucks up with her customers." It's my own fault, I expect. I oughtn't to drink.'

A hurt look came into his eyes. 'You mean … it was just that … and to be kind to me?'

Her grip tightened on his. 'No, Charlie, I don't mean that at all. You know very well I don't. Your … magic spell wouldn't have worked unless I'd wanted it to. It's just that … I feel in my bones it's dangerous.'

"We can't go back now, Louisa. What's done's done — and it was wonderful. Truly wonderful, my dear.'

'I know. But we can take a pull back. A real pull.'

'You mean, stop?'

'Yes.'

'Is that what you really want?'

She almost cried out, 'No, of course it's not what I want. But you can't always have what you want in life. It hardly ever comes to that. I don't know, I don't know. Hell, I got all the accounts to do, and the dinner at Lady Manton's for twenty-four tonight…'

Charles Tyrrell had found himself in many situations with many women in the course of his young life. There was a formula solution to most of them, sometimes facile, sometimes painful, sometimes costly in emotional or financial terms. This, though, was something new. No unwritten textbook solution presented itself. Louisa Trotter was unique, and his feeling for her, so newly conceived, seemed to fit none of the familiar patterns.

She released his hand, picked up her pen in one hand and an invoice in the other. He quietly left her room.

When she returned to that room, long after midnight, tired but victorious again after a surpassing banquet at Lady Manton's, she saw in the centre of her blotting pad a cut-glass vase containing red roses. A white rectangular card leaned against it.

Even without picking it up she could read the handwritten message: I LOVE YOU.

In his sitting room, Charles Tyrrell drew on his pipe, but produced no smoke. He glanced into the bowl and leaned forward to knock out the last shreds of dottle into the waning fire. He glanced up at the mantelpiece clock. It showed half past one. He considered whether to refill the pipe and the brandy glass beside him. The temptation was strong, but his mouth was sour and dry and he contented himself with draining the last quarter-inch of spirit.

Rarely for him, he had stayed in all evening. He had eaten the cold supper Merriman had served, had begun to dress to go out, then had thrown his evening things aside and put on instead his dark-blue silken dressing gown with the quilted collar and lapels. He had glanced through two evening newspapers, without edification, and started a novel, which he had given up after two pages. Nothing outside his own life seemed meaningful or real any more. The hedonistic Charles Tyrrell, wealthy, popular, handsome man about town, suddenly felt himself to be some sort of hermit in a well-appointed cell in the cavernous depths of this half-empty hotel.

He made the effort to get up and place his pipe on the mantelpiece. He wound the clock, a habit he preferred to reserve for himself, and replaced the key behind it. He turned towards his bedroom door.

Louisa was standing between it and him. She had entered his apartment soundlessly, barefoot and wearing nightdress and dressing gown. Her superb hair hung abandonedly loose about her shoulders and down her back.

They stared at one another for a full five seconds. Then, with a little ecstatic cry, she ran across the carpet to him and pulled his face into the depths of her hair.

The word-of-mouth advertisement for the Bentinck's accommodation, as well as for Louisa's cookery, was by now widespread about London and as far away as the Shires. More apartments had been let. It was well known that Louisa had no objection to what her residents chose to do in their own quarters, in the matter of the opposite sex; but the carefully scrutinised visitors had to be ladies in the true sense (single or married made no difference), or at least so fashionably regarded in the theatre, the opera or other such spheres as to be acceptable in the best society. Professional ladies of the town, however elegantly got up and pleadingly vouched for by their patrons, got no further than the scrutiny of those literal watchdogs of the hallway, Starr and Fred.

A few mornings after Louisa's willing surrender to Charlie she returned to the hotel in high good humour, smartly dressed and accompanied by her lover who carried a big cardboard hat box. She held out the lilac-gloved little finger of her right hand to Starr, indicating that he should unloop from it an expensively wrapped small parcel.

'Little something for Fred,' she smiled.

'Oh, thank you, Mrs Trotter,' the porter said. 'Say thank you, Fred.'

The dog indicated gratitude to the best of his ability.

'Er, Merriman's wanting to see you urgent, ma'am,' Starr said. 'Oh, here he is now.'

Louisa jerked her head towards her room. Charlie went on upstairs with the hat box.

'Excuse me, madam,' the old porter said, 'but there's a message come round from the German Embassy. Can you do dinner for thirty, Thursday night?'

'No, I can't,' she answered, to his surprise. 'Not an earthly. Mrs Wellkin can.'

'It wasn't Mrs Wellkin they asked for … madam,' Merriman ventured to correct her.

'I dare say it wasn't. Only, I'm going to the theatre that night to *The Country Girl.* So you can tell 'em it's no good. It's Mrs Wellkin or nothing.'

'Very good, madam.'

'Thirty for Thursday?' Mrs Wellkin echoed some minutes later in the kitchen. 'She's gone barmy, and no mistake. I suppose she's forgotten there's people staying in this hotel who have to be cooked for as well. And more due. She's gone barmy, Mr Merriman. I mean, there's no one I ever worked for who looked after their servants better than Mrs Trotter. Really thoughtful, she's always been. Granted, her temper's never been good, but what's an argy-bargy every so often? But this business of going all spoony over *him!* I dunno. I really don't.'

And she proceeded to take out her anguish upon the dough she was kneading, with the result that when the German Embassy did, of course, get its dinner provided a day or two later, the pastry was commented upon by all for its exquisite lightness.

The perplexity below stairs at the Bentinck did not diminish, however. Even Mary had caught its germ.

'Mr Merriman,' she said to him, in one of his more receptive moods, 'this … passion Mrs Trotter has … it's changed her. I mean, she seems to have gone all flighty. I suppose it's marvellous for her being in love, and all that, but…'

'It may be a marvel for her,' the old man grumbled, 'but it's not for us. More like sitting on a powder keg.'

'You mean … some sort of explosion's coming; Mr Merriman?'

'Any second of any day, mark my words. Order and sense out of the window. Confusion reigns. *The Country Girl* instead of the German Embassy, if you get my drift.'

'Not entirely, Mr Merriman.'

He sighed. 'There was a chef in an hotel where I worked once. A real touch with fish, he had. Could make a common piece of hake taste like turbot. But when he had a passion on him — and, being a Spaniard, he had one a week — well then, and I tell you the truth, he could make sole taste worse than skate. That's what it can do to a normal sane human being.'

Mary regarded the shaking head fearfully. 'She's really took bad, then?'

He replied sepulchrally, 'I had hoped to die peaceful in my bed, and it will be a thankful release when it comes. But not in the ruins of the Bentinck Hotel.'

Mary shivered.

In the hall Major Smith-Barton was as usual communing with Starr on the matter of horseflesh, while a disapproving specimen of dogflesh looked on, thinking that a good run in the park would be more to the point, even on so cold a February afternoon.

'Mrs Trotter not about?' the major asked, when matters of priority had been dealt with.

'No, sir. Out all morning.'

'Hmm! Out most of yesterday, too, wasn't she?'

'Yes, sir. Good deal lately.' Each knew what the other was thinking, but neither could have brought himself to discuss Louisa's private life in fuller detail.

They turned to look at a well-dressed middle-aged man who had just come through the front door. 'Good afternoon, sir,' Starr greeted him. The major went off up to his room for more extended perusal of the racing pages.

'Morning,' the gentleman responded. He was very straight-backed and well groomed, and his tone was that of a man accustomed to being obeyed. 'I should like to see some apartments. Sitting room, bedroom, bathroom, et cetera. I gather you have such arrangements.

'Yes, sir. Only —'

'Good. If you'll kindly lead the way.'

'I'm sorry, sir,' Starr told him, 'but I can't take on any new guest without the proprietor's permission.'

'Then I'll see the proprietor.'

'Mrs Trotter's not here just now, I'm afraid, sir.'

The gentleman frowned. He was clearly not a man who liked his wishes to be thwarted in any way. He looked at his watch. 'When will she be back?'

'I ... I've no idea, sir. She didn't say.'

'Didn't say? Well, really ... Look here, there's surely no reason why I should not at least inspect some of the vacant accommodation in the meantime.'

Starr swallowed but answered resolutely, 'Not without Mrs Trotter being here. She's very particular, you see.'

At the word 'particular' the gentleman positively scowled. 'What exactly do you mean to imply by that?'

'Nothing at all, sir. Nothing personal, I mean...'

The gentleman had taken out a silver card case. He opened it and extracted a visiting card. 'In that case,' he said, 'I should be obliged to you if you would give Mrs Trotter my card and tell her that I shall not be troubling her after all. There are plenty of hotels in London.'

He turned and marched swiftly out of the door. Starr examined the card. It bore a noble name and title.

He looked down at Fred. 'What a way to run a hotel, old son,' he said miserably.

In casual conversation one morning not long after Major Smith-Barton's arrival, he and Charles Tyrrell had discovered they had some things in common, the principal being that Charlie's father, the Earl of Haslemere, had been a senior contemporary of Smith-Barton's at Eton. There was enough in this to warrant an evening together with cigars and port in Charlie's apartment. Louisa was out supervising a banquet. Despite her sudden infatuation and preference for Charlie's company, she remained practical enough not to treat all her clients in as cavalier a fashion as she had done the German Embassy.

'Very nice drop of port, this,' the major said.

'Croft's '72,' Charlie answered. 'I brought it up from home. My father's been forbidden to drink the stuff, to his fury.'

'I was given a pipe of port as a christening present by a very generous godfather,' the major recalled. 'Sad to say, I never touched a drop of it.'

'How was that?'

'When I was twenty-one it was just ready to drink. Unfortunately, my debts were just ready to be paid. I had to sell the lot to raise the booty. Oh well, probably saved me from chronic gout.'

Charlie smiled. He liked the man. He himself might end up something like this someday. He poured the major another glass.

'Thanks, old boy. You know, your father was the best fag-master I ever had at Eton. Always gave me a tip for everything I did — a halfpenny, or a sausage. Something like that. How is your father, anyway? Heard lately?'

'Not awfully good, actually. You know that bad fall I told you he had out hunting in December? Mama wrote yesterday to say it still hasn't got right, and since none of the doctors seems able to do anything new they're just off to New York to see a quack over there.'

'Sorry about that. Yes, awfully nice chap. Not like that other brute who messed with him. Duckworth, don't you know? He was a brute. If his eggs or his toast weren't just right he'd wallop my backside black and blue. I hated his guts.' The major sipped his port in a reflective silence, then added, 'Never thought I should feel sorry for that Duckworth. But I was, in the end. He joined some smart cavalry mob, treated his chaps like he treated me at school. They mutinied and Duckworth was court-martialed. Out in the Sudan, I think. It broke him. Last time I saw him he was an old man of forty-five, drinking himself to death in Boodle's. Gone to pot.' He sighed, and added, to Charlie's surprise, 'Rather like this place.'

'This place? What do you mean? You're not implying Louisa's bullying the servants?'

'Lord, no! Most charming woman. Just … well, things seem rather to be going to the dogs. You probably wouldn't notice, but Starr chatters away a bit to me. Shouldn't let him, I suppose, and shouldn't be mentioning it to you.'

'No, no. I'd sooner hear.'

'Well, he's not too happy himself.' The major chuckled. 'Perhaps that dog of his has been complaining. But I can tell you, that other cook … what's her name?'

'Mrs Wellkin?'

'That's it. Definitely thinking of making a move. Reckons she's getting far too much shoved on to her just lately.'

Charlie said thoughtfully, 'That's bad.'

'Miss the place myself if it folds up. A great pity, don't you know, after all they tell me about Mrs Trotter making such a great effort to get it going in the first place.'

'A great pity, indeed,' Charlie agreed, and determined to have a bit of a heart-to-heart with Louisa at the next opportunity.

He was not able to see her all the next day or evening, though. She had another inescapable function to attend to — a grand and long luncheon — and then a banquet involving a member of the royal family. Charles had to meet his parents for dinner at the Hotel Cecil. In those sumptuous surroundings he received some information which altered the tenor of what he had to tell Louisa, when at last he did get her to herself in her room on the morning after that.

'My dear,' he said, having perched himself on the corner of her desk and gently but forcibly pushed aside a pile of papers on which she had been trying, without much success, to concentrate. 'My dear, I have to go away.'

Her eyes widened and she half started to get up. He leaned forward and kissed her brow, at the same time pressing her back into her chair.

'Not for good, you wide-eyed pigeon,' he smiled. 'Just to the States for a while. Mama's really worried about the guv'nor. It's the least I can do to be there along with her.'

Louisa relaxed with relief. 'Oh, Charlie, I thought for a minute... 'Course you got to go. Only wish I could, too.'

He shrugged. 'Look, old sport,' he said. 'Don't fly off the old handle, or anything, but it couldn't have happened at a better time.'

'What's that supposed to mean?'

'Well, with all respect for poor old Papa, I ... I think it's about time you concentrated a bit more on the Bentinck again, rather than on its first resident.'

Louisa searched his face, but his gaze didn't falter. 'You going off me, or something?' she demanded.

He shook his head. 'Anything but. But you're going off it. I'm very much to blame. It was all your life until I —'

'I know it was, Charlie. But it wasn't enough. I've only learned to see that now.'

'You're right. But, my dear, the Bentinck and all it stands for isn't any less part of your life, just because I happened to come along. And — no, don't get cross — it … isn't quite what it was before, is it?'

'Here! Who's been talking to you, Charlie Tyrrell? What's being said behind my back?'

'Nothing,' he lied. 'I'll be coming back — you have my word on that. But if you once let you reputation slip — your *real* reputation, I mean, as the best cook in London — you'll find it very hard to get back again.'

'What's wrong with my cooking? You saying I'm slipping, then?'

'I'm saying, as kindly as I can, that I came along and built a slide under your feet. Thank God, your feet haven't gone from under you yet, but you're beginning to lose your balance, Louisa. In the few weeks — I hope — I'll be away, I'd like to think of you getting back to normal, really building this place up to the standard it deserves. When I get back, I'd like to find every apartment taken, by the right sort of people, and a waiting list as long as your arm, and the name Louisa Trotter being bandied round every club in St James's. Is that too much to ask of the girl who didn't give a fig for her beauty, but wanted to be known as the best cook and bottle-washer in London?'

Louisa jumped up and into his arms. 'Oh, Charlie! But you will come back, though? It's not the same as it was when I first said those things. You know how it's changed.'

He kissed her warmly. 'Of course I know,' he whispered. 'It's never been the same since you carried in that ice-cream swan.'

They kissed again, then stood apart.

'I hope your dad gets better,' she said. 'And it'll give Mary a chance to give your rooms a right doing.'

CHAPTER SIXTEEN

Charles's departure, more than his strictures, had the desired effect upon Louisa. Rid of the sweet distraction of his attentions, she plunged herself into every department of her work with renewed vigour and enthusiasm. Mrs Wellkin ceased all talk of thinking of leaving. Mary bustled and glowed. Merriman's step up and down the stairs seemed to falter less. Starr was kept alert at the hall desk dispensing assistance, letters, keys, advice. Even Fred's growth of spring fur seemed to have benefited from some percipient stimulus.

Only one permanent resident found himself conversely deflated at this time. That was Major Smith-Barton, DSO, who one morning some two weeks after Charles's going, presented himself apprehensively in the doorway of Louisa's parlour, where she was now working with her old brisk efficiency at the accounts. He requested a few words.

''Course, Major,' she said welcomingly. 'Come and sit down.'

He closed the door carefully and did so. He cleared his throat, made a remark about the weather, then said, 'It's, er, rather awkward, Mrs Trotter … but I've a … a favour to ask you.'

Louisa recognized the symptoms. 'Is it about money?' she asked, neither sympathetic nor hard.

'Well, yes, it is, rather. Shortage of same. That is to say, temporary shortage of same…' He looked at her hopefully, but she offered no easy way out. He was compelled to go on. 'It's been a bit difficult lately, don't you know? Trustees being a bit tiresome — that sort of thing. Won't be long, of course. Just a question of getting things sorted out.' He paused again, but she still kept silent. He concluded wearily, ''Course, I realise I can't go on staying here with my bill unpaid.'

To his sudden relief Louisa gave him her famous smile. ''Course you can, Major. It's not going to ruin us. The old place wouldn't be the same without you.'

The major felt tears at the back of his eyes. 'I say, that's most awfully civil of you, ma'am. I am most … most awfully grateful…'

'Forget it. Let's have a glass of wine to drown our sorrows.' She pressed the electric bell on her desk.

'Had any news from Charlie Tyrrell?' Major Smith-Barton asked, thankful to change the subject.

Louisa indicated a picture postcard on her desk. 'Yes. They had a terrible voyage, poor dears. Sick as cats all the way. And New York's cold as charity.'

Merriman came in.

'Bring us a bottle of wine and two glasses, will you?' she told him. 'And not that muck you gave me last night. Bottle of the Bollinger '93.'

'Yes, madam.'

Starr, brushing Fred in the dispense off the hall, saw Merriman getting the bottle and said, 'He's short of the tinkle. That's old Whiskers's trouble.'

'How can you tell that, Mr Starr?' asked Mary, who was ironing.

'Always tell. When guests get specially friendly and confidential, and then borrow a guinea off you to put on a certainty.'

'He's not paying for this wine, I can tell you that,' said Merriman, forcing the bottle into the ice in the metal bucket. 'She is. Drinking the profits.'

'But how can a gentleman not have money?' Mary wondered ingenuously.

Merriman deigned to explain, 'It's not that he hasn't got any money. It's just that he hasn't got any available. He'll never have any available. People like him never do, and never will. Money just slips through their hands, like a piece of wet soap, if you take my meaning. It wouldn't happen to a servant, as you might say a working man. Only to a gentleman.'

'Why is that, Mr Merriman?'

'It's in the nature of things, and there's nothing can be done about it.'

Carrying the bucket, bottle and glasses on a tray, Merriman creaked away. Starr gave Mary a wink.

'Don't you listen to old gloom, Mary. People like the major have their ups and downs, that's all. One day soon you'll probably find he'll be so flush he'll be taking a whole set of rooms, 'stead of just one, and buying himself a string of racehorses into the bargain. We've seen 'em, haven't we, Fred?'

As arranged, Charles Tyrrell's entire apartments were given a thorough spring-cleaning in his absence. Mary did most of the work, but Louisa felt impelled to look in often, in her extra-proprietorial capacity.

One early May morning, when the sun was shining warmly and birdsong could be heard plainly above the street noises, Mary entered Charles's sitting room, both arms draped with freshly laundered net curtains. She was surprised to see Mrs Trotter standing at the piano keyboard, pensively picking out notes with one forefinger. There was a dejected droop to her shoulders, which for weeks now had seemed so resolutely squared.

'Sorry, ma'am,' Mary said, conscious of having interrupted a reverie. 'I thought I'd get Mr Tyrrell's curtains back up again.'

'All right, Mary,' Louisa said. She seemed to come to some decision. 'Look, just put them down a minute and come and sit down here.'

She indicated the settee. Mary carefully draped the curtains over chair arms and obeyed gingerly.

'I'm going to have a baby,' Louisa told her bluntly.

The maid couldn't prevent her lips parting and her mouth opening. 'Oh, lor' ... ma'am!'

'I been round the doctor's, and I'm nine weeks gone. Oh, don't look so po-faced, girl. I'm sure even in Wales people make mistakes sometimes.'

'But ... but what are you going to do, ma'am?'

'Have it, of course!'

'But...'

'Look, I'm not having anyone doing me in messing about with dirty knitting needles, and I hope you wasn't going to suggest it. Anyway, I happen to believe if God makes a baby he has a reason, and you have to lump it. It'll be all right for a while yet. Then when it begins to show I'll go off somewhere. I'll cut out all the outside cooking that Mrs Wellkin can't manage, and you'll just have to run this place.'

'Oh, but I couldn't, ma'am. I never could.'

'You will, by the time I've finished with you. And no one's ever to know about it 'cept you and me.'

Mary stared again. 'Not even...'

'No, not even him. You won't tell no one. Swear on it!'

There was such vehemence in the way she said it that Mary, who was no Catholic, fumbled the sign of the cross over her breast and hastily promised, 'Cross my heart and hope to die ... ma'am.'

In the days following Louisa proceeded to put Mary through a strict, secret course of management and book-keeping. What the little Welsh girl lacked — which was a good deal — in education, and to a lesser degree in brightness, she made up for in willingness and utter devotion to her mistress.

'The credit's bigger than the debit,' Louisa explained again, pointing to figures in an account book, 'so you subtract the debit.'

Mary struggled mentally for some seconds then said tentatively, 'That makes eleven pounds and fivepence three-farthings.'

'Good girl. That's profit, and not bad for one day.' She produced the cash box from the middle drawer of her parlour desk. 'I keep the cash in here, locked up. Always. When there's enough, take it round to the bank in St James's Street.'

'Excuse me, ma'am. What's "enough"?'

'When it's so heavy that you need both hands to carry it. Now, next page. Tomorrow's Friday, so we pay all them bills. That lot there. Make a list of 'em, and tick 'em off as paid. As to letters, you want to answer all of 'em the same day they come. That way it's more polite. Especially people enquiring about rooms and that.'

Mary looked from the pile of bills on their spike to that very morning's mail, comprising at least two dozen envelopes, some of them bearing coats of arms. She blew out her cheeks at the prospect of such responsibility

'How will I ever tell if they're the right sort of people?' she asked. 'I mean, not being a snob like you, ma'am.'

Louisa took no offence at the term. She knew it was meant in a complimentary sense.

'There's ways of telling,' she said, picking up the first letter on the pile and ripping it open crudely with her thumb into the envelope flap. She scanned it briefly. 'A Mister Worthington-Jones,' she said. 'See that book there — *Who's Who*. You look 'em up in there first. Even if they are in, they mightn't be the right sort, and if they're not in, they might. But it's somewhere to start. Worthington-Jones. Maybe Jones, with the Worthington tacked on for luck. But it's nice paper. Hand-made and white. Never trust coloured papers. And the address is printed from a plate — engraved. Feel that. Common people wouldn't go for that.'

'I see,' Mary said, marvelling. 'But supposing I write back, thanking him for his…'

'Esteemed enquiry.'

'Yes. But when he turns up I still don't know if he's right or wrong?'

'You can always ask Starr or Merriman. They'll have a fair idea. Watch whether that dog's hair bristles. Or, if you're really in trouble, try Major Whiskers.'

'He may not be here by then, may he, ma'am.'

'He'll be here all right. I reckon, like the poor, he'll always be with us,' Louisa said.

A few more months went by. Charles wrote dutifully from America, but he had little good news to convey. His father was referred to one distinguished medical man after another and resigned himself to beginning yet another new type of treatment at the hands of each. As always, there was optimism at first, hopeful signs, then setback and final capitulation. It became clear that the strain was telling on the old man's general constitution, and that he was too frail to be brought back to England. Charles had not the heart to leave him and his mother in a strange land and return home; and as it began to be apparent that the earl's life itself was becoming endangered, his son saw it as his duty, not only out of love but as heir, to stay on.

Louisa missed him, but understood, and put all her thought and energies into running her dual business and training Mary. Then the time came when she could go on no longer. Letting it be believed that she was feeling a bit strained and so would go into the country for the long rest she had never had chance to enjoy, she slipped out of London, telling no one but Mary where she was going. It never even occurred to her to confide in her parents.

A week later she read in a newspaper of the death in the United States of the Earl of Haslemere. The widow and the new earl, the report read, would be accompanying the late earl's coffin to England and the funeral would take place in the parish church of the family estate.

Charlie wrote personally to Louisa to tell her the news, and his letter was forwarded to her by Mary. At least the knowledge that he would be travelling about a good deal, and much preoccupied, gave her the welcome excuse not to write back.

One autumn morning Major Smith-Barton looked up from *The Times* in the hall of the Bentinck, where he liked to sit and watch the comings and goings, and saw Charles stride in through the door. He wore mourning and his face showed strain.

'Charlie, my dear fellow!' the major hailed him. 'How splendid to see you again.'

Charles's face lit up with genuine pleasure as he came over to shake hands.

'My goodness, we've all missed you,' the major declared.

'Well, thank you. I've missed this place, too. My word, it seems to be fairly buzzing.'

The hall was very busy indeed, with several people at the desk being dealt with by Starr and cabmen bringing in and taking out luggage.

'Oh yes, going splendidly. Always full up with an awfully good lot of people,' the major said. 'I, er, say, Charlie, I was very sorry to see about your father.'

'Yes,' Charlie said. 'It's been pretty grim. In the end, quite frankly, it was a merciful release. But I'll ask you to excuse me just now, Major. Got rather a lot to do.'

He nodded and went away towards the stairs, where he encountered Merriman, coming down with a tray full of the debris of a meal and looking rather flustered.

'Hello, Merriman,' he greeted him. 'You well?'

'Fairish, sir … m'lord, I mean. Middling, you might say in the circumstances.'

'Well, as soon as circumstances permit, be a good fellow and bring a bottle of wine to Mrs Trotter's room, will you?'

'Mrs Trotter's, m'lord? But she's not here, you know.'

'Not here? No, I didn't.'

'Beg pardon, m'lord, I thought you'd have known somehow. Been away a few weeks now.'

'Where?'

'Holiday, sir. All the work getting her down at last, you know. Said she didn't want to risk another go like that last one, so she decided to get a good rest.'

Charles's surprise and concern changed to relief. 'Well, I'm certainly glad to hear that,' he said. 'Perhaps her letter missed me. These past weeks have been pretty hectic. Who's running things in the meantime, then?'

'Mrs Wellkin's keeping up the cookery end — though it's been cut down a lot for the time being — and Miss Philips looks after the hotel.'

'Miss Philips?'

'Mary, m'lord. A real little treasure, that girl is. If you'll excuse me, m'lord, they'll be getting impatient in Number 8 if I don't get their Madeira.'

Charles nodded dismissal and Merriman tottered off towards the dispenser. Instead of going on upstairs Charles turned and went into Louisa's parlour. Mary looked up from Louisa's desk, stared for a moment, then pushed herself to her feet by the chair arms.

'Mr ... Lord Haslemere!' she gasped. 'We wasn't expecting you back. Your ... your rooms aren't all ready yet. I mean, it'll take a couple of days to air them out properly...'

Charles smiled reassuringly. 'It's all right, Mary. I'm only passing through London. I called in to ... what's all this about Mrs Trotter, then?'

He had read nothing untoward in Merriman's impassive features, but he detected at once the aura of embarrassment about this young woman, and noted how she looked away and fumbled with her fingers.

'It ... it was all the work, m'lord ... and her nerves was getting a bit bad ... and the doctor...'

'Doctor? As bad as that?'

Mary bit her lip. The reference had slipped out. 'He said she ought to go away for a while. We ... was all glad she agreed. We've been managing very well, m'lord.'

'Where is she?' he asked casually.

Her difficulty in answering was obvious to him. 'I don't know, m'lord. I mean, not for sure. Somewhere on the coast...'

'Which coast?'

'Well ... she said she might travel about a bit.'

Charles said sharply, 'Mary — I want to know where Mrs Trotter is.'

His face was hard, and his usually smiling eyes had a strange light in them which made her frightened.

'I swore I wouldn't tell anyone,' she begged. 'She made me swear, m'lord.'

He brushed past her to the desk. Amongst the bills, invoices and other papers on its top was his own letter to Louisa telling her he would be in London for the day and calling in. The hotel address had been crossed out and beside it had been written in ink, presumably by Mary, *3 Aspen Villas, Weston-Super-Mare, Somerset.*

'All right,' Charles said kindly. 'You were doing as you were told.' He picked up the letter, pocketed it, and left the room.

A few hours later he was outside the little private lodging house in the seaside town. The wind was chilly off the sea and autumn leaves were on the pavements and in the gutters. From the path up to the door he could see her, sitting in a small glassed-in conservatory. A shawl was round her shoulders, which seemed unusually hunched, and she appeared to be staring into space. At any rate, she didn't see him approach.

The front door was held open by an iron doorstop. Another door led off it to the left into the conservatory, behind Louisa's back. Charles opened this door and stepped inside.

'Is she all right, Betty?' Louisa asked without turning.

'That,' said Charlie, 'is what I was going to ask.'

She jumped violently and twisted round. 'Oh, crikey!' she exclaimed. 'You didn't half give me a turn!'

He went and gave her a long, tender kiss, then sat down in a wicker chair beside hers.

'Sorry about your poor old dad,' she said. 'So you're Lord Haslemere now, eh?'

He ignored both remarks, but said quietly, 'So it's a girl, is it?'

She looked defiantly at him for a moment, seeming about to challenge him, but then said flatly, 'I'll kill that Mary.'

Charles produced the re-addressed envelope. 'Not her fault. I found this.'

'I see. And then I s'pose you wrung it all out of her about the ... baby?'

He shook his head. 'I worked it out for myself. It's three hours on the train down here from town. Plenty of time to think. You left the hotel just when things were getting really busy. That didn't sound like the Louisa Trotter I used to know. She wouldn't have left the place even if she was dying ... unless she had something to hide. That, and counting up how many months it's been since ... well, it didn't need a Sherlock Holmes to deduce what it was.'

'I haven't been too clever, have I?' she admitted. 'Do they all know now?'

'No one else. You don't think I would?' He took her hands in both of his and asked fondly, 'Was it a bad time?'

'Bit rough,' she nodded.

'But why didn't you tell me, Louisa?'

'Because it's none of your business, that's why,' she retorted with a return of her characteristic spirit. 'It's my mess and I got to clear it up.'

'God, you are pig-headed sometimes. None of my business? How can you say anything so idiotic?'

'For pity's sake, it's *not your fault*. Men were born to chase after women, or there wouldn't be no human race, would there? And women have to watch out, or they cop it. I broke me own rules. I knew what I was doing —' She broke off, looked fondly at him, and suddenly smiled. 'It's a nice little baby,' she said. 'Very healthy. And no trouble — like her ma.'

'You really thought you'd get away with it?' he wondered.

'I nearly did, clean and clever. Another week.'

'Then what were you going to do?'

'I've been trying to work it out. Was doing when you crep' in just now. Whatever happens, she'll be looked after proper. Never lack for nothing.'

'Except a mother and a father,' he reminded her.

'You didn't have to say that, Charlie.'

'I think I did. I want you to marry me.'

They just sat there for some long seconds, holding hands and searching one another's eyes. Then Louisa said, 'You're a real gentleman, Charlie. But you don't have to do the decent thing, not this time.'

'I love you, you silly woman.'

They heard the baby cry in another room, and a girl's voice making comforting sounds to it. Louisa jerked her head in that direction. 'Would you have asked me to marry you if it hadn't been for her?'

It was a question he couldn't answer honestly without hurting her, and one he knew he must not lie about.

'It's not a fair question,' he compromised.

Louisa recognised his dilemma and solved it for him. 'It's the greatest compliment I'm likely to be paid in my little life. I appreciate it, Charlie, I do really. But, you see, you're Lord Haslemere and I'm Louisa Trotter. Oh, I know how many Gaiety girls has married the nobility and all that. But quite honestly, I'm not cut out to be a wife — anyone's wife. Never have been.'

He was going to interrupt, but she went on.

'I mean, that baby ... it's a nice enough little baby. But I don't love it. It could be anyone's, for all I'm concerned. I don't know why. I can't help the way I am. So, you see, I wouldn't be no good as Lady Haslemere, either. Best left as Louisa Trotter. You do see, Charlie, love? It's best to be honest about things.'

He nodded. Against his inclinations, he knew she was right.

'It was a wonderful thing we had together,' she said, 'and I shan't never forget it. Never. But it's all over, Charlie. So we might as well frame it and then we'll always have it handy to look back on. Cheer us up when things is bad.'

'Perhaps you'll change your mind, Louisa. Women get depressed after having babies, don't they?'

She shook her head. 'I've not been too depressed. Not really, except the quiet of this place. Like a cemetery with seagulls. All I want is to get back to noisy old London — and my hotel.'

He sighed, but smiled and gave a shrug of surrender. 'That sounds like the old Louisa talking,' he said in a relieved tone. 'But listen — would you mind, please, if I took charge of the baby? Responsibility for it?'

'You? But how could you? I mean, what'd your ma...?'

'I can arrange everything perfectly discreetly. As a matter of fact, we'd be doing a kindness to someone else into the bargain.'

'How? Who?'

'One of the grooms and his wife on the estate have just lost their own baby. They're dreadfully upset, and they're an awfully nice, decent couple. If you'd agree, Louisa...'

Suddenly, she saw the future clear ahead again. It needed no consideration to tell her that this was the heaven-sent solution.

'Yes, Charlie. Yes, I will. Thanks for being so good to me ... for it all...'

He kissed her long and hard, then got up, raising her from her chair by her hands. 'Now take me to see her,' he said.

'Morning, Starr. Morning, Fred,' Major Smith-Barton greeted the porter and his dog a few mornings later.

'Morning, sir,' Starr responded. 'No one's speaking to Fred, though.' He indicated the animal's collar, twined with coloured ribbons. 'Got him all dolled up ready to greet Mrs Trotter coming back this morning, and what does he do but go absent without leave. Some lady friend down St James's Square, you ask me.'

'Devil with the ladies, eh, Fred?' the major asked. 'Anyway, she's back at the helm, is she?'

'Yes, sir. And she sends her compliments, and would you be good enough to see her in her room as soon as you came down.'

The major's face fell. He nodded, squared his shoulders, and went off to Louisa's door.

'Poor old Major Whiskers,' Starr confided to Fred when the door had opened and closed. He hasn't a had a bad run for no money, though.'

Louisa thanked the major for his expression of welcome and asked him to sit down. She had one of the hotel's billheads in front of her and he could see his name at the top. There was much writing on the paper, and many figures, and two more sheets were clipped underneath.

'When I came back to see your bill still unpaid I couldn't hardly believe my eyes,' Louisa said. There was no concession to his feelings in her tone of voice.

'I really am most dreadfully sorry, dear lady,' he said. 'Thought I'd best to wait till you got back and explain, don't you know?'

'Can't live on tick all your life, can you?' she said unrelentingly.

'No, no. Matter of fact, though, I'm expecting a draft any day now. Confounded things always seem to come in arrears. Tell you what, I'll pop down to the bank again this morning. Ask 'em to…'

'Come off it, Major,' Louisa said, tapping the bill. 'Any draft you get goes straight on the ponies. I believe if you had a real win you'd pay up…'

'Believe me…'

'Only it's a mug's game, and you ought to know it. Well, I do, and I'm sorry, but this hotel isn't run as a charitable organisation for the bookies. Not no more.'

The major nodded hopelessly. 'You've all been so jolly kind to me here. Rather dug in now. I … I just wish I could think of some way of … of making it up to you.'

For the first time Louisa smiled. '*I* can, Major,' she said, getting up.

That afternoon a party of new arrivals entered the hall of the Bentinck. They were an elderly country peer and his middle-aged *grande dame* of a wife. A lady's maid followed, bearing a jewel case and her mistress's personal bag. A coachman deposited some luggage in front of the desk.

'Afternoon, m'lord. Afternoon, m'lady,' greeted Starr, who was already acquainted with them from one of his previous situations. He turned and beckoned with a raised forefinger. From across the hall, where he had been standing beside the porter's chair, Major Smith-Barton, DSO, marched briskly forward and grasped the baggage.

'Hullo, Henry,' he greeted the astonished peer. 'Anthea. Splendid to see you again. Hope you're both well?'

'Y … yes. Very.'

'Jolly good. Just follow me, then.'

As they proceeded up the stairs, Louisa, who had come to the door of her parlour, heard the major asking, 'Put up here before ever?'

'No, no. Just a short visit to town. Not worth opening up the place in Belgrave Square.'

'Quite right. Couldn't do better than here. First-class place. Wonderful cooking. Hear there's a fine lot of partridges in Norfolk this season…?'

Louisa smiled. Then she smiled again to see Charlie come through the front door.

'Hello, Starr. Hello, Fred,' he said, patting the dog, who gave him a lick of familiarity. 'Celebrating Mrs Trotter's return, I see.'

'Yes, m'lord. Fred and I are highly delighted at her recovery. And so am I. Ah, Merriman, a bottle of wine in Mrs Trotter's room, if you please.'

'With pleasure, m'lord. Welcome back, m'lord.'

Louisa went into the room, and Charles followed. They remained standing. Each could sense the difficulty of the moment.

'I'm glad you've come back,' she said at length.

He went over and kissed her, gently and chastely. 'But of course I have,' he said. 'This is my home.'

ACKNOWLEDGEMENTS

This book is based on the first five episodes of the television series THE DUCHESS OF DUKE STREET, created and produced by John Hawkesworth for BBC television.

The author wishes to thank John Hawkesworth and the BBC and to acknowledge that in writing the book she has drawn largely on material from scripts by the following writers:

DAVID BUTLER

JEREMY ROWL

JACK ROSENTHAL

JOHN HAWKESWORTH

A NOTE TO THE READER

If you have enjoyed this novel enough to leave a review on **Amazon** and **Goodreads**, then we would be truly grateful.

Sapere Books

Sapere Books is an exciting new publisher of brilliant fiction and popular history.

To find out more about our latest releases and our monthly bargain books visit our website: **saperebooks.com**

www.ingramcontent.com/pod-product-compliance
Lightning Source LLC
Chambersburg PA
CBHW071131200626
46817CB00018B/2710